"Is it an insult if I tell you that there's not one thing about you that I don't find intriguing? Not your wild hair or your callused hands or the neat way you fit against my side."

"If it is," she said, her eyes wide with surprise, "I can't say I mind."

"Good to know," he responded, edging in close.

"Porter," she began, her voice husky.

"If you're going to tell me this isn't a good idea, you'd better do it quickly, because from where I'm standing it seems like the best idea I've had in years."

She laughed, a little breathless. A little nervous, but she didn't tell him to back off, and he couldn't make himself do it.

He leaned down. Just enough to taste her lips. Once and then again, his left hand splayed against the door near her head.

And then her arms were around him, her hair sliding across his forearms, and he was lost in her touch and in that kiss. The house gone. The memories gone.

All of it fading to make room for this. Whatever it was. Whatever it was going to be . . .

Books by Shirlee McCoy

The Apple Valley Series

THE HOUSE ON MAIN STREET

THE COTTAGE ON THE CORNER

THE ORCHARD AT THE EDGE OF TOWN

The Home Sweet Home Series

SWEET HAVEN

SWEET SURPRISES

BITTERSWEET

The Bradford Brothers

HOME WITH YOU

HOME AGAIN

THE MOST WONDERFUL TIME

(with Fern Michaels, Stacy Finz, and Susan Fox)

Published by Kensington Publishing Corporation

HOME AGAIN

SHIRLEE McCOY

ZEBRA BOOKS
KENSINGTON PUBLISHING CORP.

http://www.kensingtonbooks.com

ZEBRA BOOKS are published by

Kensington Publishing Corp.
119 West 40th Street
New York, NY 10018

Copyright © 2018 by Shirlee McCoy

All rights reserved. No part of this book may be reproduced in any form or by any means without the prior written consent of the Publisher, excepting brief quotes used in reviews.

To the extent that the image or images on the cover of this book depict a person or persons, such person or persons are merely models, and are not intended to portray any character or characters featured in the book.

If you purchased this book without a cover you should be aware that this book is stolen property. It was reported as "unsold and destroyed" to the Publisher and neither the Author nor the Publisher has received any payment for this "stripped book."

All Kensington titles, imprints, and distributed lines are available at special quantity discounts for bulk purchases for sales promotion, premiums, fund-raising, educational, or institutional use.

Special book excerpts or customized printings can also be created to fit specific needs. For details, write or phone the office of the Kensington Sales Manager: Attn.: Sales Department. Kensington Publishing Corp., 119 West 40th Street, New York, NY 10018. Phone: 1-800-221-2647.

Zebra and the Z logo Reg. U.S. Pat. & TM Off.
BOUQUET Reg. U.S. Pat. & TM Off.

First Printing: November 2018
ISBN-13: 978-1-4201-4524-3
ISBN-10: 1-4201-4524-X

eISBN-13: 978-1-4201-4525-0
eISBN-10: 1-4201-4525-8

10 9 8 7 6 5 4 3 2 1

Printed in the United States of America

Chapter One

Words had power.

Clementine Warren had always known that.

Words woven together in just the right way captured the imagination, bridged divides, healed hearts and, sometimes, broke them. They convicted and absolved, created chaos and calmed it.

Words opened doors to other worlds and, then, pointed the way back home.

Wherever the hell *that* was.

Once upon a time, home had been Seattle, but that had been before. This was after.

Currently, Clementine was living in someone else's house doing someone else's work. Fixing someone else's problem. Which was a lot easier than fixing the mess Sim had made. Bills. Bill collectors. Clementine had paid and explained and paid some more. Thank God, she'd been socking money away in a secret account during the entirety of her marriage. She'd planted that tiny financial seed a few months before the wedding and tended it carefully. Every time she'd given a guest lecture on Native American lore or shared Native stories with captive college audiences, she'd taken half the money she'd earned and put it in that account.

At the beginning of her marriage, she'd intended to use the money to pay for a surprise anniversary trip to Ireland—a place she and Sim had both wanted to visit. At the end of it, she'd been saving it *just in case*.

She'd told herself she might need it for a rainy day. She hadn't expected a monsoon, but she'd gotten one.

After Sim left, there'd been just enough money to pay off the loans and credit cards he'd taken out in her name.

Like Clementine, he'd had his secrets.

Unlike her, his hadn't been altruistic ones.

She'd been surprised by his betrayal, but she shouldn't have been. They'd been together for twelve years. Married for just under ten. She knew his priorities, and she knew his weaknesses.

She'd chosen to ignore both, because she'd been desperate to do what her mother said was impossible—maintain a loving, monogamous, long-term relationship. To her, that had seemed like the Promised Land—milk and honey and all things good.

Unfortunately, Sim didn't believe in monogamy. Something he'd forgotten to mention when he'd asked her to marry him. Something she hadn't bothered to ask, because monogamy, faithfulness, companionship, and permanence were the things that marriage was built on. At least, in her mind they were.

It had never occurred to her that Sim didn't see things the same way.

"Idiot," she muttered.

She wasn't sure if she was referring to herself or her ex-husband. Maybe . . . *probably* . . . both.

She tightened the last lug nut on the used tractor tire she'd bartered six skeins of hand-pulled alpaca yarn for and tossed the tire iron into a rusty toolbox she'd salvaged from the barn. If she'd had money, she would have bought a new tire and purchased tools to replace the ones that were nearly rusted through. She might have even hired a couple of people to help with the work, but—thanks to Sim—everything she'd worked for was gone. She was at square one again—empty savings account, empty checking account.

Empty heart.

That, at least, she didn't worry about. She and her empty heart would be just fine. She didn't need a man in her life to be fulfilled and happy.

She didn't *want* a man in her life.

She wanted peace and a chance to rebuild what she'd lost.

Not just money—eventually, her finances would rebound. Friendships. Professional relationships. The sweet little Sears and Roebuck house she and Sim had bought six months before they'd married and sold three years ago to finance his dream.

She longed for those things the way parched earth longed for rain.

Right now, though . . .

She had this: Pleasant Valley Organic Farm and a bunch of old farm equipment that she'd managed to duct tape into semi-working order. It had taken weeks, but she was finally ready to prep the fields for planting. The owner of the farm, Sunday Bradshaw, had been a generous landlady and a good friend. At a time when things had been going to hell in a handbasket, Sunday's kindness had seemed nearly miraculous.

Funny how things happened.

Clementine and Sim had been driving through Benevolence on their way to somewhere else. In Clementine's mind, somewhere else had been Seattle. After all, they'd already spent two years attempting to farmstead property in Idaho, because that had been Sim's dream. In Sim's mind somewhere else had been the West Coast. He'd wanted to buy a

storefront and sell Clementine's hand-pulled wool and
hand-dyed yarn. They'd been arguing about it over breakfast
in a tiny diner in an itty-bitty town, and Clementine had
grabbed a newspaper off a rack near the door just so she'd
have an excuse to end the conversation. She'd seen Sunday's
ad there. *House for rent.*

The price had been right, and Clementine had decided
that staying in a neutral location until she'd figured out
exactly what was going to happen to her marriage was the
most practical option.

So, she and Sim had ended up in the small ranch-style
house on Sunday's property. One acre of land to plant and
harvest, and acres of farm surrounding it. Bucolic location,
charming people. And, Sim . . . Still spending money like
they had an endless supply when all they really had was
Clementine's teaching income. Three online college classes
a semester barely paid the bills. Sometimes, she'd been late
with the rent. Sometimes, she'd been really late. Sunday had
never made an issue of it. She'd been kindness personified.
And, Clementine had vowed to return the favor.

This was her opportunity, but it wasn't going to be easy.

Pleasant Valley Organic Farm had been mostly-fallow
for years.

Clementine eyed the tractor, nudging the tire with the
toe of her scuffed work boot. Used, but not threadbare. She
hoped it would last until the end of planting season.

"It's going to have to," she said, climbing onto the seat,
feeling the familiar predawn chill, hearing the quiet rustle
of leaves as the wind whispered through them. It all felt
familiar and, oddly, more right than anything had in a very
long time. She'd done this hundreds of times while she was
growing up. She knew her way around farmland and fields.
She knew how to fix broken equipment. Maybe she should
have stuck to that instead of leaving her father's farm and

heading off to her mother's world of academia. If she had, she'd have avoided meeting and marrying Sim. She'd have avoided all those years of trying so hard to make something right out of something that was obviously wrong. She'd have saved herself a lot of trouble and a fair amount of frustration.

"No sense crying over spilled milk," she muttered, turning the key in the ignition. The tractor roared to life. Just like she'd expected it to. It might have been old, beaten up, and forgotten, but it had been built well.

She pulled out of the barn, the tractor's headlights illuminating dry yellow grass. A few feet ahead, the gate yawned open, daring her to enter the rocky, weed-infested field that would soon be planted with alfalfa. Once she finished bringing the farm back to life, she'd return to Seattle and the things she'd given up when she'd agreed to Sim's cockamamie scheme. A full-time professorship at the University of Washington. A nice group of friends.

Thank God, she hadn't completely cut ties with the university. For the past three years, she'd been teaching online classes, because she hadn't been nearly as excited by Sim's midlife crisis as he'd been. And, maybe, because she'd been just a little too unsure of Sim and their marriage. No matter how many pretty lies she'd told herself about how they'd weather the storm and come out stronger because of it, she'd been pretty sure their relationship was doomed long before Sim had emptied their bank account and walked away.

Whatever the case, she hadn't burned any bridges when she'd left Seattle three and a half years ago. The head of the anthropology department at the university had assured Clementine that she could return when she was ready.

She was ready now.

Past ready.

She needed something besides a couple of online classes to distract herself from the wreck her life had become.

Tinkering with farm machinery and coming up with creative solutions to monetary limitations was okay, but she wanted to lose herself in academic life the way she used to, forget her problems while she delved into the traditions and myths of people who'd come before her.

Plus, a full-time job would give her the money she needed to start over. It was the practical solution to the problem Sim had created. The one she'd allowed him to create.

A few months ago, she'd returned to Seattle to start the long process of rebuilding herself. Not her finances. Not her career. Just . . . *her*, the woman she'd been before she'd spent all those years with Sim. She'd met with the department head, agreed to begin teaching full-time in the fall, looked at apartments near campus while she crashed on a friend's couch. She'd had everything figured out—how she'd get her own place and start living life on her terms again.

And, then, she'd gotten a call from Heavenly Bradshaw, Sunday's oldest and newest daughter. Just a message left on voice mail when she'd been touring an apartment complex, but it had changed everything.

Clementine? It's me. Heavenly. Bradshaw. Matt's dead. Sunday's in the hospital. They're saying she might not make it. You're her friend. I thought you should know.

The twelve-year-old's voice had been steady and unemotional. She hadn't asked for anything. She hadn't needed to. Clementine owed Sunday a lot, and she wasn't going to repay her by allowing the farm to fall to ruin while Sunday was recovering.

If she recovered.

Currently, Sunday was in a rehab facility, hovering somewhere between coma and consciousness—not quite in this world and not quite in another. God willing, she'd improve. God willing, she'd return home. Clementine was going to make sure that if she did—*when she did*—she'd return to lush fields and beautiful apple orchards.

Or, at least, the beginning of those things.

Farming took time.

Generations.

Clementine had months before she needed to return to Seattle and her professorship.

Fortunately, she had a good foundation to build on. In its heyday, Pleasant Valley Organic Farm had been a robust working farm, the land tilled and tended. Sunday had let Clementine read a history of the farm written by her grandfather, and she'd worried aloud that she'd be the generation forced to sell land that had been in her family for over a hundred years.

Her worry had been well-founded.

Sunday's husband, Matthias, had been a fun guy. A nice guy. The kind of guy that everyone in the little town of Benevolence, Washington, loved.

He'd also been better at playing at farming than doing it.

Better at playing at work, too.

Not that Clementine had ever said that to Sunday.

She'd kept her mouth shut. Partially because she hadn't felt like she'd known Sunday long enough to say anything. Partially because, compared to Sim, Matthias was a winner.

He'd loved Sunday.

He'd loved their kids.

He'd have given a stranger the shirt off his back.

So what if he spent more time dreaming than actually working? At least he'd cared about his family.

Sim, on the other hand, hadn't cared about anybody but himself.

"So, why are you wasting your time thinking about him?" she muttered, annoyed with her inability to get Sim out of her head for good and forever.

She didn't want him back.

God knew she was better off without him.

But her mind liked to toss random memories at her, taunting her with all the things she'd known but chosen to ignore about her ex.

Regret made a poor bedfellow.

She had a lot of it.

She also had a lot of work to do.

It wasn't getting done while she dwelled on the past.

A doe crashed through the weeds in front of her, white tail high, spindly legs barely touching the ground. It stopped a dozen yards away, turning its head and looking straight into Clementine's eyes before it took off again. If she'd been a different kind of person, she might have thought the doe was an omen or a visitor from beyond the grave— the specter of an ancestor long gone. Maybe even her father returning to encourage or to chastise.

More than likely to chastise.

Elliot Warren had been a lot of things, but a sympathetic, supportive parent wasn't one of them. He'd loved all fifteen of his children, but he hadn't had time for pep talks or fatherly advice sessions. He'd been a storyteller, a word-weaver, a guest lecturer, and, by the time Clementine had been born, a professor emeritus at the University of Wyoming. He'd raised his kids on a hundred acres of land just outside the reservation where he'd been born. He'd taught them how to till and plant and harvest, how to hunt and how to survive, but he hadn't taught them a whole hell of a lot about how to protect their hearts from lying, stealing, two-timing bastards like Sim.

Fortunately, life had done what Elliot hadn't.

Clementine might have learned the hard way, but she'd learned.

The tractor bounced across the field, its dim headlights

barely illuminating the rich brown earth and tangled weeds. Plowing before dawn wasn't ideal, but she had a schedule to keep. The seasons waited for no one.

The first pass across the field was easy. The old-school tractor did its job without a bunch of modern technology. She focused on the distant horizon and the band of gold creeping above the mountains as she aimed for the edge of the plot and the stake she'd set earlier in the week. She plowed the second row and then the third, shivering as a cold breeze blew across the field. The mountains were still capped with snow, the chill of winter still in the air, and the ground was just barely thawed enough to use the old harrow on it. The tilling should have been done at the end of harvest, old growth turned over to fertilize the ground beneath, but Matthias hadn't prepped for this year's planting. She doubted he'd prepped in previous years.

Maybe he'd planned to.

Probably he had. That was Matthias. Big plans. Little action. His three brothers didn't seem to be the same way. Not that she'd seen much of them. They'd stepped in to take over the care of Sunday and Matt's kids. Or, at least, one of them had. The other two visited almost every weekend.

She avoided them whenever possible.

She didn't need complications in her already complicated life, and the Bradshaw men had the potential to be that.

The Bradshaw *boys*.

That's what people in town called them.

As if, somehow, the three had never grown up, left Benevolence, and made lives for themselves. Nearly every conversation Clementine had at the feed store, the grocery store, or the diner began with *Those Bradshaw boys* and ended with a story about the havoc the three had wreaked on the town.

Matthias had apparently been the good brother.

The other three were hellions, rebels, and troublemakers. Or so the stories went.

Clementine had taken to listening with half an ear.

In the month since she'd returned to the farm and taken up residence in the little ranch-style house on the edge of the property, she'd kept her distance from the Bradshaw kids and their uncles. Life was easier that way, and she'd decided after Sim walked out on her that easy was what she wanted.

No more emotional drama.

No more entanglement in other people's issues.

Just simple, peaceful living.

She reached the end of another row and turned the tractor again, the loud chug of the engine masking sounds of waking birds and scurrying animals. In the distance, Sunday's house loomed up against the indigo sky. No lights. Just the dark facade of it shadowed by early morning.

She turned the tractor again, her heart jumping as a small light danced through the field to her left. She let the tractor idle as she watched it skip across the dried-out husks of a never-harvested corn crop. The stalks moved, swishing as something darted between them.

Clementine cut the engine.

The morning was silent except for the dry rasp and crackle of breaking branches and twigs.

"Who's there?" she called, climbing off the tractor and heading toward the still-moving light.

It cut off. The old cornstalks stilled. Whoever it was had either decided to move more carefully or wasn't moving at all.

She waited, listening to the silence.

No birds.

No animals.

Even Elvis was quiet, the young rooster forgoing his normal sunrise greeting.

"I said, who's there?" she repeated, pushing her way toward the place where the light had disappeared.

She wasn't afraid. Out here, the most dangerous predator was human, and she had no reason to believe a stranger had wandered onto the property. It was just far enough outside town to discourage visitors, just far enough from the highway to not be found easily by troublemakers.

No. She wasn't worried that a serial killer was sneaking through the cornfield. The most likely culprit was one of Sunday's six kids, and that *did* have her concerned. The kids had been wild before their parents' accident. Being parentless had made things worse. There'd been issues at school. Issues in town. Fights. Skipped classes. Shoplifting. Minor stuff in the grand scheme of things, but in a town the size of Benevolence, they were huge. People were talking. And no matter how hard Clementine tried not to hear, the stories were there, in her head, whispering their truth every night when she tried to sleep: the Bradshaw kids were struggling, and she really should try to help their uncles get that under control.

Only, she had enough of a mess to deal with.

The farm. Her life.

She pushed further into the weeds, thorns catching her cotton pants and long-sleeved shirt and ripping the skin beneath. Up ahead, dry stalks rustled. Whoever was moving through was too short to be seen. A kid for sure. It could be any of the six except for Oya. She was too young to escape the house on her own.

"Moisey?" she called. "Heavenly?"

Still no response, so Clementine followed the shifting cornstalks, stepping out onto the old country road that separated the fields from the rocky land that abutted the

Spokane River. She could see water gleaming in the grayish dawn, a glittering silver-green snake that wound its way through the valley. Placid in some areas. Dangerous in others. Not a good place for a child to spend time alone. Especially not this time of year when snowmelt was flooding the banks and the water was moving swiftly.

"You had better not be heading for the river," she hollered, scanning the area and catching just a glimpse of a child-sized figure darting behind an old spruce that stood on the river side of the road.

"That's it!" she said, hurrying across cracked asphalt coated in layers of dirt and debris. "It's too early in the morning for hide and seek!"

"It's too early for just about anything," a man responded.

She swung around, a scream dying on her lips as she came nose to chest with one of the Bradshaw brothers.

Not Sullivan.

He lived on the farm full-time, and she would have recognized him easily. The other two were near strangers. She'd seen them a couple times, but avoiding people made it difficult to get to know them. Porter or Flynn.

He was one or the other.

The tallest one.

The one with the broadest shoulders, the darkest hair, the lightest eyes. The one who was staring at her as if he suspected her of criminal activity or nefarious schemes.

"You surprised me," she said.

"Sorry about that," he responded, but he didn't sound it. He sounded irritated. Hopefully with the errant child and not with Clementine. She didn't want or need any kind of trouble with Sunday's brothers-in-law.

"It's not the weekend," she pointed out, because in the time she'd been back on the farm, she'd never seen Porter or Flynn during the week. "Shouldn't Sullivan be the one corralling kids?"

"He would be if he were around. Since he's not, it's up to me to track the little hooligan," he replied, moving past and heading in the direction the child had gone.

She followed, because it seemed like the right thing to do.

She certainly couldn't return to plowing while one of Sunday's kids was in danger.

"Is it Maddox? Did he sneak out?" she guessed. He was the obvious choice—the kid who'd been suspended four times since his parents' accident. The one who'd nabbed a candy bar from the five and dime and stood right outside the door munching on it. The trouble-maker-of-all-trouble-makers if the town rumor mongers were correct.

"No."

"Milo?"

"No," he repeated.

"Should I keep guessing, or are you going to make it easy and tell me?"

"The quiet one."

"Twila?"

"Are there any other quiet kids in that house?" he asked, glancing over his shoulder, his eyes seeming to glow in the early morning shadows. They weren't blue or silver, but some clear, sharp shade in between.

"Heavenly can be quiet," she pointed out.

"If your definition of quiet is chasing her twin brothers around shouting death threats at the top of her lungs, then yeah. I guess she's quiet, too."

"Death threats?"

"They ruined her choir dress."

"Should I ask how?"

"You can ask anything you want," he responded, walking a circle around the spruce.

"Damn," he muttered. "She's gone."

"Twila is quiet. Not stupid. She wouldn't stand here waiting for you to find her."

"None of the kids are stupid. That's the problem. Every minute of every day, they're thinking up new trouble to get into. I don't know how Sullivan has managed for this long."

"It's only been two months."

"I've only been running the show for twenty-four hours, and I'm ready to call in the cavalry."

"Running the show?"

"Yeah. Rumer and Sullivan eloped."

"They eloped?"

She sounded like a parrot, repeating everything he said, but she couldn't stop herself. She also couldn't wrap her mind around the fact that Rumer Truehart and Sullivan Bradshaw had run off together. Shortly after the accident, Rumer had been hired as a housekeeper, nanny, and cook. She'd been the light in the darkness, the one ray of hope that the Bradshaw kids would be okay until Sunday recovered. The kids adored her. She adored them despite all their challenges and troublemaking capabilities. And now she was gone. Off getting married and leaving a sharp-eyed behemoth to take care of six traumatized children. This was not good. At all.

It also wasn't Clementine's business.

She was here to tend the land. Not the family. She needed to keep that in mind, because she knew herself too well. She was a sucker for sob stories. She got involved in things she shouldn't because she tended to care too much. But, after Sim, she'd decided to close that part of herself off. No more rushing in to save the day. She wasn't a heroine from an ancient tale. She was a woman who needed to get her crap together so she could have a secure, stable and enjoyable life.

"Yes," he said as he scanned the landscape.

"As in, they ran off and got married and didn't tell anyone they were going?" she persisted, because she still couldn't believe it. Or, maybe, she just didn't want to.

"They let me in on their plans a few days ago," he replied.

"That was good of them. Seeing as how they were leaving six kids behind."

He glanced her way, smiling just enough for her to know he had a sense of humor. "I said something similar when Sullivan called, but I can't be too upset. He's held down the fort for two months. It's my turn to step in."

"Fort? More like a juvenile detention center if the stories being passed around town are any indication."

"It might not be that bad."

"Might not be? That leaves open the possibility that it is."

"Right."

"Rumer seemed to have things under control. At least, every time I've been at the house, she did."

"She did, but Rumer isn't here. She's off marrying my brother. Only God knows what kind of hell is about to descend on the house now that she's gone." He moved through thick tumbleweed, heading toward the river.

She pushed through after him.

"It might take a while for the kids to gear up to anything close to hellish behavior."

"Sullivan and Rumer left twenty-four hours ago. I'm already outside before dawn searching for an escapee. I think it's safe to say the kids didn't need any time at all."

"You have a point," she admitted.

"Fortunately, my brother and his new wife will be back in a week or two."

"That's vague."

"They said a week. I told them to take their time and relax. They both deserve the break." He'd reached a narrow path that led to the river and stopped there, scanning the sparse foliage and boulder-dotted landscape. "Twila! You'd better stay away from that river!"

A family of quail scurried from the thick scrub to his right, but he was already jogging toward the river. Bare feet. Jeans. Short-sleeved, white T-shirt that clung to broad shoulders and a narrow waist. She noticed those things just like she noticed the first glint of morning light sparkling on the surface of the river.

A hundred yards away, an old dock stretched into the water. Beside it, a boathouse stood on spindly legs, its wood siding gray from age. Clementine had been on the dock and in the boathouse many times. Neither were sturdy enough to be called safe.

The Bradshaw kids knew that.

How many times had she heard Matthias warn them away from it? How many times had he made empty promises about fixing the dock and resealing the canoe that had been housed in the ramshackle building for longer than he'd been alive?

Too many times to count.

Matthias had been big on promises and small on follow-through, and now Twila was picking her way across rotting planks. Clementine could see her—a small, dark shape moving toward the far end of the dock and the deeper waters of the river.

"Shit," Matthias's brother muttered, sprinting toward the dock.

"I'll second that," she responded, following.

They both reached the dock, and he stepped on the old wood.

Clementine pulled him back.

"I'll go," she said, walking onto the dock.

He grabbed the back of her jacket. "My niece. My risk."

"Your niece weighs next to nothing. You weigh what? Two hundred?"

"Good guess," he responded, his gaze suddenly on her. His eyes really were an interesting shade of silvery blue. Rimmed with black or navy, they seemed oddly light against his tan skin and dark lashes.

"I'm good at making predictions, too. And, I predict that 200 pounds is too much for this structure." She tugged her jacket free and stepped onto the wobbly planks.

He followed, and the entire structure shifted.

"Shi . . . oot," her companion muttered.

"I told you, I'd go," she responded. "This thing is not going to hold your weight. If it goes down, Twila will go down with it."

"If you both just leave, there won't be a problem," Twila called. She'd reached the end of the dock and was sitting with her legs dangling over the edge, her long dark hair falling nearly to the splintering wood.

"You know that's not going to happen, kid," her uncle responded, stepping off the dock. "So, how about you make it easy on all of us and come on back?"

"Sitting here is easy for me, Uncle Porter. Going home is easy for you. How about we both do those things?" Twila responded with just a hint of irritation in her voice.

Porter.

That was his name.

Clementine filed it away and focused on Twila. She'd

known the family long enough to understand that Twila was generally the peacemaker, the obedient one, the child least likely to be rude to adults. Her response to her uncle bordered on that. There had to be a reason. Maybe she was angry that Sullivan and Rumer had left. Maybe Porter had done something to offend her. Maybe she was just getting tired of being the *good* kid.

"You sound angry, doll," Clementine said, easing across the rotted wood, slowly making her way to Twila's side.

"I'm not a doll and I'm not angry. I'm just sitting here. Trying to mind my own business. Just like Heavenly always tells me to do."

"Have you and your sister been fighting?"

"We always fight."

"More than usual?"

"No."

"You're sure? Because it's a little early in the morning to be outside. I figure you must have a reason for that."

"You're outside," Twila responded, staring out across the river, her hands folded neatly in her lap, her fuzzy pink pajamas clean and neat despite her trip across the field. She'd shoved her feet into winter boots, the white trim glowing in the dim morning light.

"I have a lot of work to do," Clementine replied.

"You can get back to it if you want."

"I'd rather sit with you."

"Why?" Twila finally met her eyes. She'd always been the solemn and quiet one of the group. Reserved. Polite. Neat. Never in trouble in school or at home. Still, Sunday had worried about her as much as she'd worried about her rowdy twins and rebellious tween. *She holds too much inside. She worries too much about being perfect. Of all my kids, she's the one that I know the least. Lord knows how*

*much I've tried to change that, but Twila is a treasure box
without a key. At least, not a key I've ever been able to find.*

Sunday's words were hanging in the air, tripping across
the flowing river, and Clementine wanted to do right by her
and by the little girl she loved so much.

"Because you look lonely," she finally said, and Twila
sighed.

"Just because a person is alone doesn't mean she's
lonely."

"Is that your way of telling me to go away?" Clementine
asked.

"You said you had work to do. That sounds much more
important than sitting beside me on this dock."

"Nothing is more important than you."

Twila stiffened. "That's what Mommy always says."

"Because it's true. So, tell me why you're out here."

"It's quiet, and I need to think."

"About?"

"Uncle Porter," she whispered.

Clementine resisted the urge to look over her shoulder
to see if Twila's uncle had heard. The river was flowing, but
this area of the Spokane was placid. Even in early spring.
The morning was just quiet enough, the breeze moving in
just the right direction to carry their words to his ears.

"What about him?"

"Heavenly said he's an assassin. That's why he's got
muscles and a gun."

"He has a gun?"

"Yes," Twila hissed, glancing at her uncle, maybe checking to be certain he hadn't moved closer. "I've even seen it."

"You have?" This time, Clementine couldn't resist. She
looked, and Porter was exactly where she'd left him—
standing with his hands tucked in his jean pockets, his

stance relaxed but watchful. There was something about the curve of his lips, the hint of amusement in his eyes, that let her know she'd been right—he *could* hear every word.

"He had it under his jacket when he got here." Twila paused, her legs swinging back and forth with just enough force to make the dock sway.

"Maybe you should stop that, hun," Clementine suggested, setting her hand on Twila's scrawny leg to still the motion. "This dock isn't in very good shape, and the river is frigid this time of year."

"Do you think he is one?" Twila asked, ignoring Clementine's comment as she glanced back again. The fear in her eyes was unmistakable. She wasn't worried about the dock collapsing. She wasn't worried about falling in the ice-cold river. She probably wasn't even worried about getting in trouble for leaving the house without permission. She was worried about her uncle and about the possibility that he was exactly what her sister had claimed.

"Of course he isn't," Clementine assured her.

"Then why does he have a gun?"

"Because I work for a private security company, kiddo," Porter responded. "I protect people from assassins and criminals."

"You weren't supposed to hear that! Heavenly said she'd have my head if I told you that I knew." Twila swung around so quickly, she nearly tumbled off the dock.

"Whoa!" Clementine managed to grab the back of her pajamas and yank her away from danger, but she was done. *Done.* There was no way on God's green earth she was spending another second on that dock. "Come on. Let's go."

"I'm not ready."

"You're going to have to be," she said.

"Mommy always says to follow our hearts. My heart

led me here, and I'm staying until I'm done," Twila said stubbornly.

"Would your mother allow you to be on this dock? Ever? Even if your heart led you to it?" Clementine countered. Thank God, she had some history with the Bradshaw kids. She'd babysat for them on plenty of occasions before Sim left her. She'd established enough of a relationship with each of them to know which buttons to push to get them to cooperate.

"Mommy isn't here, so I don't know if she would," Twila replied.

"You know that she wouldn't," Clementine corrected, taking Twila's hand and turning away from the river. "Because this isn't a safe place, and it would break her heart if anything happened to you."

"It's a very safe place. I come out here all the time," Twila said, but she didn't resist as Clementine led her back to the shore.

"All the time?" Porter asked calmly, but the sun was peeking above the mountains, golden light seeping across the horizon, and Clementine could see the tightness of his jaw and the sharp edge to his gaze. Any amusement he'd felt at being called an assassin was gone. Probably replaced by terror at the thought of Twila spending lots of unsupervised time on the dock.

"Yes."

"Sullivan and Rumer know about this?" he asked, his voice still calm and carefully modulated.

"I might not have asked them. After school, I come here to study because the twins and Moisey are so loud. It's hard to concentrate." Twila stepped off the dock ahead of Clementine, trying to skirt past her uncle. Probably hoping to avoid further questions.

He stepped in front of her, crouching so they were eye to eye. "Don't ever do that again, okay? Don't ever come here to study or to think or to just sit on the dock without asking first."

"Why not? I used to come here with Daddy all the time. He showed me what boards weren't too rotted to walk on."

"You came here with him. Not alone. If you want to come again, tell me. I'll bring you down, and I'll make sure the dock is safe before I do it," he said, brushing a loose strand of hair from her cheek.

Something inside Clementine shifted as she watched.

That icy cold place in her heart, the one that had been there since the day she'd realized Sim had left and taken everything of value with him, melted. Just a little. Just enough for her to wonder how someone who looked as tough as Porter could be so gentle.

Twila seemed to wonder the same. She eyed him for a moment, and then said, "You're really not an assassin?"

"No, I'm not," he assured her.

"You're one of the good guys?"

"I try to be." He straightened. "You said you come down here all the time."

"I won't anymore."

"Good, but I'd like to know how you managed to get out of the house without Rumer seeing you."

"I climbed out my window."

For a split second, Clementine could see the fear in Porter's eyes. It was there and gone so quickly, she'd have missed it if she hadn't been looking.

"You're on the second floor of the house."

"I have the fire escape ladder, Uncle Porter. It is perfectly safe."

"Is it?" he murmured, running his hand over his short-cropped hair.

"Yes. Daddy showed us how to use it. We practiced a lot. We even had fire drills. Just in case there was ever a fire. We're all supposed to meet near the tree swing. Did you know that?"

"No. I didn't." He cleared his throat. "From now on, you can only use the ladder if there's a fire," he said. "Okay?"

Twila frowned, but shrugged. "You should probably tell Heavenly that, too."

"Your sister climbs out the window?" His eyes narrowed, and he glanced toward the house. Obviously trying to figure out exactly how he could keep kids from escaping it.

"Sometimes. But don't tell her I told. She'll be angry."

"Right. We wouldn't want that. Come on. Let's go home." He put his hand on her shoulder, steering her back to the path that led away from the river.

Clementine should have taken that as her cue to return to the tractor and her work. She didn't want to get involved in the family's drama. She had enough drama of her own.

For some reason, though, she followed them along the path and across the road, past the field she'd been plowing and into the yard at the back of the Bradshaws' house. A large oak stood in the center of it, an old swing hanging listlessly from a thick branch. Sunday used to sit there on warm summer days, watching as her kids raced around the yard, playing and laughing. She'd been there at other times, too. Clementine had seen her late at night, when the house was dark and the world was quiet, sitting alone, a small flashlight trained on the page of a book she was reading. No e-reader for Sunday. She'd liked to hold her books, to carry them around in oversized purses or tucked into the pocket of her jackets. She'd been a sweet, funny, hardworking lady, and she'd deserved better than what she'd gotten.

Porter and Twila walked up the porch stairs. He opened the back door. "Inside and into bed. No snacks. No books. What you did was dangerous, and if you repeat it again, I'll take away your library card for a month."

"My library card?" she asked, her hands on her hips, her dark eyes blazing. "Mommy would never do that."

"She might if she knew you were climbing out the window and going down to the river at night," he responded.

"She won't know, because she isn't here. If she were," she replied, her voice breaking, "I would never do that."

"Twila—" he began, but she darted into the house, closing the door with a quick, hard snap.

"Well," he muttered, still facing the closed door. "That went well."

"If your definition of well is upsetting a ten-year-old, then I guess it did," Clementine replied. She meant it as a joke, but Porter didn't take it that way.

He swung around, standing in the yellow glow of the exterior light, his jaw shadowed with a beard, the muscles in his shoulders and arms bunched with tension. "This isn't my thing, Clementine. I don't do kids."

"You're standing on the back porch of a house filled with them. Obviously, you do."

"Let me rephrase that: I don't do well with kids. I don't have them, don't want them, would rather avoid them at all cost."

"You sound like my ex." The words slipped out, shouting bitterness as loudly as the gold and pink streaks on the horizon shouted dawn.

"From your tone, I'd say that's not a good thing."

"I shouldn't have said that." She turned, heading back to the abandoned tractor and hoping Porter wouldn't follow.

Of course, he did.

The story of her life on repeat these past few years: Hope. Pray. Believe. Be disappointed.

"You didn't answer my question," Porter said, stepping into place beside her, his long stride shortened to match hers.

"You didn't ask one."

"I thought you'd get the implication, but since you didn't: Is being compared to your ex as bad a thing as it sounds?"

"Yes, but I'm sure you're nothing like him."

"What's he like?"

"He's not worth talking about."

"You brought him up."

"I shouldn't have."

"So you said."

"There are six kids in that house who are a lot livelier than this conversation. Maybe you should go check on them?"

"Are you giving me the brush-off?"

"Yes."

He laughed, the sound like a well-told story. Deep. Rich. Full. Satisfying.

She could feel her lips twitching in response, her muscles relaxing. "I'm glad my honesty amused you. I've got a lot of work to do, so I'd better get to it. See you around, Porter."

"Work is what I wanted to talk to you about," he replied.

"The farm you mean?"

"Yes."

"You picked an odd time for the conversation," she responded.

"It's an odd time for just about anything. Not quite daylight and definitely not dark." He gestured to the horizon, ripe with dawn but not yet completely light. "It's the time I have, though. The baby wakes up at seven. On the dot."

"Babies are notorious for putting a wrench in the works and changing schedules unexpectedly. It would probably be best if you weren't out here if Oya wakes up."

"You know a lot about babies?" he asked hopefully.

"Probably about as much as you know about farming," she responded, heading toward the field again. If he wanted to follow, so be it. "I have siblings, though. They have kids. I've heard stories of toddlers raiding cookie jars at midnight and fingernail polishing the walls in the wee hours of the morning."

"I woke Heavenly before I left the house. She's sleeping in the room with Oya and Moisey until I return. Plus, Rosie Whipple is stepping in as a nanny until Sullivan and Rumer return."

Rosie Whipple?

Clementine had never heard of her. Not that she spent much time meeting people in town. Especially since she'd returned. "A friend of yours?" she asked, assuming the new live-in must be familiar to the family. Porter might not know anything about kids, but if he worked for a private security firm, he knew a lot about danger and about keeping people safe. She doubted he'd let just anyone work around the kids.

"Rosie is a friend of Rumer's grandmother. She used to own a day care in Spokane. Now she's retired."

"Not if she's helping around the Bradshaw house," she responded, and he smiled.

"Yeah. It isn't much of a retirement, but she was bored and needed extra cash for a trip she's got planned in the summer. Between the two of us, the kids are never unattended. They're just very good at escaping when they want to."

"I didn't mean to imply that they weren't being supervised carefully enough."

"Sure you did," he said easily. "Now, about the work you've been doing around here. We really appreciate it. I wanted to thank you."

"Sullivan thanks me all the time," she said truthfully, moving a little more quickly, because she wanted to end the conversation and get back to work. The sun was rising rapidly, pink and gold and purple lightening the gray-blue sky. Even with the chill of winter still in the air, the sun would be hot by late morning.

"You deserve more than thanks. Flynn owns a ranch in Texas. He's got a decent idea of what the going rate for a farmhand is, but you're more of a farm manager–farmhand– farm owner all rolled into one."

"I don't want to be paid."

Not because she didn't need the money.

God knew she did.

But because the Bradshaw kids needed it more.

"You're a professor, right?"

"I don't recall telling you that, but yes."

"And you could be working at the University of Washington this semester."

"Look, Porter, I'm not sure where you're headed with this, but I'm not comfortable with the fact that you know what I do and where I work."

"It's common knowledge, Clementine."

"Whose knowledge?"

"The sheriff's. The people in town."

She'd concede that was probably the case. She'd lived in the ranch house for two years before the fiasco with Sim.

"I'm picking up classes on campus in the fall. Full-time. Right now, I'm teaching online classes. I travel to Seattle once a week to meet with students. But I don't see what that has to do with the farm." She climbed onto the tractor, ready to start the engine and finish the row.

He was standing right beside her, though, his hand resting on the tire. His knuckles were nicked and scarred, his forearm tan.

"With your education and experience, you could be doing a lot of things that would bring you a healthy salary," he said.

"I haven't built my life on costly things." Though she'd sure as heck like to have a little extra money for things like tires and tools. "Besides, Sunday helped me out when I needed it. I'm repaying the kindness."

"Sunday? Not Matthias?" he asked.

"He was a good guy. Everyone thought so, but he was . . ." She couldn't say what she was thinking—that he'd been too busy not working to worry about things like renting out the ranch house for income or caring about the farm Sunday had inherited from her parents.

"What?" he prodded.

"He was a good guy, but he didn't have the kind of business sense Sunday had. She decided to rent the ranch house to bring in extra income. My ex and I needed a place to stay. She offered us the house for a lot less than she could have gotten for it. She never made me feel like that was a favor. She was . . . is just a really nice lady. I want her to come home to a farm she can be proud of. That's what I'm going to give her. No charge. Thanks for thinking about it, though." She started the tractor, planning to finish the row, but her eyes were drawn to the house she'd once shared with Sim.

Their last home together.

Her last marriage-saving compromise.

Sometimes she thought she could have tried harder.

Then, she reminded herself that she'd given up a great job to pursue Sim's dreams. She could have kicked him to the curb the day he'd announced that he'd taken ten-thousand-dollars of their hard-earned money and bought a craggy piece of land on the western edge of Idaho. He'd planned to run an alpaca farm, but he hadn't bothered checking with Clementine before he'd made the purchase. There'd been no perc test for a septic system. No permits for building, either. Sim, of course, had not bothered to consider any of those things before he'd plunked down the money.

After a couple of years fighting bureaucracy, trying to get someone somewhere to agree to let them spend thousands of dollars to run lines to the public water system, she'd told him it was time to call it quits. She'd wanted a home. She'd wanted to go home. To Seattle.

They'd settled on living at Pleasant Valley Organic Farm while they saved enough money to purchase a home. She'd been hoping for a fresh start. Instead, she'd gotten betrayal.

Which, in every good story, was the beginning of something wonderful.

She just hadn't gotten to the wonderful yet.

And, now, she was staring at a house that she'd left dark, because she learned to be frugal, to not waste resources.

The lights were on, the living room curtains open. She'd left them closed. Since only she and the Bradshaws had keys, the house should be exactly the way she'd left it.

Except, she and the Bradshaws weren't the only ones with keys. Sim had one. He'd taken it with him when he'd left.

"Is everything okay?" Porter asked, still standing close to the tractor.

"Rat bastard," she growled, turning off the engine and sprinting toward the house.

Porter said something, but she was too busy running to answer.

There was a sporty red car in the driveway, parked next to her beat-up Pontiac. It had Sim written all over it— ostentatious and impractical.

She pounded up the porch stairs, turned the doorknob. It was unlocked. Just like she'd expected. Sim never locked doors, turned off lights, stayed faithful.

The door swung open, and she stepped in, the aroma of freshly brewed coffee filling the air and boiling her blood. She was already seeing red when he stepped into view— tall, thin, wire-rim glasses perched on his nose. Brown eyes. Salt and pepper goatee.

"Darling!" he crowed, as if it hadn't been nearly a year since they'd seen each other and six months since their divorce was finalized. "I've missed you."

He moved toward her, arms opened wide enough to embrace a woman three times her size. Absolutely expecting her to step right into them. What she wanted to do was slam her fist into his soft stomach.

"That's probably not a good idea," Porter said as he crowded into the foyer behind her.

At first, she thought she'd spoken aloud.

Then, Sim stopped cold and she realized Porter had been speaking to him. His arms dropped to his sides and his eyes narrowed, his thin lips pressing so tightly together, they were barely visible.

She'd once thought him handsome and sexy.

She'd obviously been blinded by her desire to do what neither of her parents ever had—settle down, build a nuclear family, have the kind of committed relationship that lasted a lifetime.

Sim's gaze jumped from Clementine to Porter and back again.

"Who's he?" he asked, some of his cheerful facade slipping away.

"Who are you?" Porter responded, dropping a hand on Clementine's shoulder. She could have stepped away, but she couldn't say she minded the look of surprise on Sim's face. The slight hint of discomfort in his eyes.

"I'm her husband," he said, his gaze resting on Porter's hand, his lips puckering the way they always did when he was unhappy.

"Ex," Clementine corrected. "If you came to deliver the key, you could have mailed it. That would have made me a lot happier."

"Honey, don't be that way," he said, finally meeting her eyes again. He smiled the smile that had charmed her socks off when he'd been a first-year professor substituting in a class she'd been taking . They'd started dating at the end of the semester. The rest was history. Bad history. History she wasn't going to repeat.

"Get out," she responded, all the questions she'd wanted to ask, all the accusations she'd wanted to lob his way, all the recrimination and words she'd held inside for all these months dying as she turned away.

She bumped into Porter as she made her escape. Quickly, because her face was hot and her eyes were hotter, and if she didn't watch herself, she might start crying from the sheer amount of rage that was coursing through her blood.

Cold morning air cooled her cheeks, the sun glinting off golden grass and the distant river. She had a field to plow and work to do and a life to build that didn't include Sim.

Everything else might be in shambles, but at least she

was free of the albatross that had hung around her neck for nearly ten years.

"Thank God for that," she said as she ignored Sim's frantic plea to just *give him a minute* and strode down the porch stairs, across the yard, and back to the work he'd interrupted.

Chapter Two

So, this was the ex. The one that no man would ever want to be compared to. Clementine's tone had made that clear. Looking at the guy made it even clearer. Entitled came to mind. Oily. Sniveling.

Unwanted, unnecessary, and out-of-there.

Porter eyed the guy, not bothering to introduce himself. There was no need. One of them was going to leave. It wasn't going to be him.

He stepped to the side and gestured toward the door.

"I'm pretty sure she told you to go," he said.

"Who are you?" the guy asked for the second time, his brown eyes set a little too closely together, his hair a little too styled, his goatee a little too well-groomed.

Everything about him was a little too much for Porter.

Or maybe it was just the fact that he'd arrived on Clementine's doorstep unannounced, walked into her house without permission, and was pretending he belonged there that was troubling. On the heels of a very bad twenty-four hours, Porter wasn't in the mood to be diplomatic or reasonable. He was in the mood to kick Clementine's ex to the curb.

But the guy had come for a reason, and Porter was just curious enough to want to find out what it was.

"Porter Bradshaw. My sister-in-law was your landlady."

"I'm Simeon Galloway. Sunday and I have always gotten along well. I'm sure she wouldn't be as eager to send me on my way as Clementine seems to be." He offered a practiced, polished smile that set Porter's teeth on edge.

"Since Clementine is the one living here, Clementine's opinion is what matters."

"My wife—"

"*Ex*-wife," Porter corrected.

"She's a little upset, but she'll come around. She always does."

"She asked you to leave, and now I'm telling you to go. It probably isn't the best idea to keep arguing with me about that."

"Tell you what," Simeon said, the smarmy smile still glued to his face. "How about we go to the farmhouse? Have a cup of coffee with Sunday, and see what she has to say?"

"Sunday is in a rehab facility recovering from a car accident."

"Then how about we discuss it with Matthias? He's always been a reasonable guy," he said, completely ignoring what Porter had said about Sunday.

"My brother was killed in the accident that injured Sunday," Porter said bluntly, the truth still hard to speak, and much much worse to live.

"Matthias is . . . dead?"

"Yes. He passed away a couple of months ago," Porter said, a hard knot of grief filling his chest just like it always did.

Grief.

Guilt.

Regret.

He should have been around more.

He should have made more of an effort to understand

Matt's dreams and goals, and maybe, he should have helped him achieve them. He'd visited six months before the accident, bringing a gift to the newest member of the family and staying for exactly two days. Just like he always did.

Forty-eight hours wasn't a lot of time, but it was enough to notice how run-down the farm had looked, how tired Sunday seemed. He'd wanted to ask his brother what was going on, but Matthias had been his normal cheerful self, outlining all his dreams for the land and the house and the kids he and Sunday were raising. It had all sounded great, because Porter had wanted it to. The truth was, he hadn't wanted to get involved.

He liked his life neat and clean and free from drama.

He pursued emotional and financial independence the way other people pursued love, because those things allowed him to have the uncomplicated lifestyle he craved. Matthias's life had been messy. In every way a life could be. All a person had had to do was walk in the front door of the farmhouse to know that.

"I'm sorry to hear that," Simeon said, his voice tinged with just enough sympathy to be believable. "I liked your brother. He was a good guy."

"He was. Now, how about you give me your keys and head out?"

"Keys?"

"To the house?"

"Right. Sure." He dug into his pocket, pulled out a key fob, and dropped it into Porter's hand. "There you are. Keys to the front and back doors."

"Great. Have a safe trip back to wherever you came from."

Sim laughed. "I came from Thailand. I'm not going back anytime soon."

"Good luck finding somewhere to stay."

"I thought I'd be staying here, but Clementine didn't exactly give me the warm reception I was hoping for."

"You're divorced. What kind of reception did you think you'd get?"

"We were friends before we got married. I figured we'd be friends after. We're both reasonable people, after all. Or, at least one of us is. Clementine can be a little emotional. As you saw." He straightened his tie, then shoved his hands into the pockets of his slacks.

"She didn't seem emotional. She seemed determined to get you to understand that she didn't want you here."

"I think you misread the situation, Porter," he began.

"Good-bye, Simeon." Porter cut him off, gesturing to the door again, because he hadn't misread anything. He'd spent most of his childhood listening to his father talk about how senseless his mother was, how stupid, how incapable. He recognized the arrogance behind Simeon's words, the superiority.

The guy was a jackass.

Probably worse.

Porter would have been happy to inform him of that, but Simeon was already walking out the door, the air around him reeking of cologne and nicotine, his hands still in his pockets, his demeanor relaxed and unfazed. His shoulders were tense, though, his muscles taut.

He was angry.

More than likely, he was used to getting his way.

"Tell Clementine I'll give her a call," he said as he climbed into a sporty red car.

Porter didn't respond.

He watched as Simeon sped away. His mood had been dark when he'd realized Twila had left the house. It was darker now.

This was *not* how he liked to spend his time.

He liked things organized, planned, and controlled.

This farm in this town in this area of Washington didn't allow for any of those things. At least, it hadn't in the short amount of time Porter had been back. If he were smart, he'd pack all six kids up and cart them back to LA. He'd hire a nanny, a housekeeper, and a cook, and he'd go back to work and forget Benevolence, Washington, and all the bad memories he had of it.

Of course, the idea was impractical.

His two-bedroom apartment wasn't big enough. Even if it had been, he doubted his neighbors would appreciate the noise and chaos six kids brought.

He also doubted the kids would adjust easily or well.

All six of them had been in tenuous and difficult situations before they'd joined the family. They needed stability and consistency. Now more than ever. It would be unfair to drag them away from what they knew because he hated the town he'd grown up in.

Or, at least, hated what it represented.

The town itself wasn't bad. Nice people doing nice things. Nice buildings on nice streets. Nice schools. Nice teachers. Nice everything.

Except for the house on the corner of Main and Evergreen. Built by a railroad magnate to impress his East Coast bride, it was as close to a mansion as Benevolence had. Of course, Porter's father had purchased it when he'd decided to return to his hometown. He'd been a hero—a guy who'd left, made good, and returned. A software developer who'd earned millions, he'd been determined to make sure everyone in Benevolence knew how successful he was.

The house had been part of that.

The beautiful wife and cute kids.

The family that had been as much a possession as the house and everything in it.

Porter scowled.

Walking down memory lane wasn't improving his mood.

He'd dated a psychologist once who'd told him he had a few unresolved issues related to his childhood.

He had a hell of a lot more than a few.

He could acknowledge that as easily as he could acknowledge his piss-poor mood. He didn't want kids, didn't spend time with kids, knew nothing about kids. And yet, somehow, he was supposed to play Mr. Mom for the next one or two weeks.

Sullivan hadn't given him an exact return date.

He and Rumer were tying the knot and then spending some time in Sullivan's Portland apartment. Alone. They deserved it, and Porter wasn't going to begrudge them their break.

But . . .

He and kids didn't mix.

At all.

Speaking of kids, they'd be up and moving by now.

He wanted to make it very clear to every single one of them that leaving the house without permission was a felony offense punishable by lockdown—no phones, no television, no computers or electronic devices. Just the four walls of their rooms and plenty of time to contemplate their crimes.

He walked into the field Clementine was plowing, surprised to see a half dozen neat rows cut into the dark soil. She worked hard, and she worked fast. Sullivan had been saying that for weeks. The proof was everywhere—trees pruned, garden soil turned, yards mown. And now this—a field being plowed for eventual planting.

She glanced his way, offering a quick wave. She looked like she belonged there—driving the tractor, her braided hair falling to the middle of her back, loose curls escaping to curve around her ears and across her cheek. If he'd had to guess her occupation, he'd have said she was a home-steader or a farmer. He wouldn't have guessed a professor and lecturer. She'd also been listed as a storyteller on her university profile page. He *could* see that—Clementine weaving words and spinning tales.

What he couldn't see was how she'd ended up married to Simeon. They didn't seem to fit. The polished preppy pro-fessor and the earth-mother farmer.

Not that it was any of his business.

He walked through an old gate and headed up the path that led to the farmhouse. He could see its yellow siding glowing gold with dawn. The yard was quiet. Just like he'd expected it to be. Everything still and peaceful. He walked to the side of the house, eyeing the window Twila had escaped from. She'd closed it and pulled the ladder inside.

First things first—get the ladder before some other kid decided to use it. After that, he'd gather everyone around the kitchen table and explain how things were going to be.

Then, he'd make them breakfast. Eggs, bacon, and oat-meal. Just like his mom had done before she'd gotten sick.

That sounded right, and having a plan was better than not.

He jogged up the stairs to the back door, stepping aside as it swung open.

He expected to see Rosie, carrying a cup of coffee and enjoying her last few minutes of peace before the house erupted into chaos.

Instead, Heavenly scurried out, closing the door softly behind her, using her key to lock it. Everything quiet and surreptitious.

"Going somewhere?" he asked.

She jumped a foot, swinging around to face him, her

eyes lined with coal-black makeup that didn't belong on anyone let alone a girl her age.

"What are you doing out here?" she asked, tugging her skirt down to cover an extra micro-inch of flesh. It was still too short. So was her shirt. He could clearly see the pale skin at her waist. If she'd been his daughter, he'd have pulled her coat closed, buttoned it up to her chin, and told her to march back inside and put on something that covered more than it revealed.

"I asked first."

She scowled. Of course. "I have choir practice."

"At seven in the morning on a Saturday?"

She hesitated. "Okay. So, I'm hanging with friends at the diner."

"I don't recall giving you permission to do that."

"Uncle Sullivan said it was okay."

"I guess he'll confirm that when I call?"

"It might have been Rumer. She could have been the one who told me."

"Heavenly, how about we don't do this?"

"Do what?" she asked, but the fight had already seeped out of her. That was an improvement. The first month after the accident, she'd been carrying a thousand-pound chip on her narrow shoulders. The newest member of the Bradshaw family and the oldest, she'd still been adjusting to life on the farm when Matthias had died. She didn't like being told what to do. She didn't like having to help with the younger kids. Mostly, he thought, she didn't like not being in control of her life.

"Pretend you're not trying to sneak away."

"I'm not pretending anything. I told you where I'm going."

"Told me. Right. Only you're thirteen, and you don't get to decide where you're going and inform me after the fact."

"Twelve," she corrected.

"Like I said: you don't get to decide."

"Sunday always said I was wise beyond my years and capable of making good decisions." She settled her hands on her narrow hips, and the skirt rode up her scrawny legs again. The kid needed to eat. She also needed to wear more clothes.

"I'm guessing she said that because you often made bad ones, and she wanted to encourage you to do better."

Her cheeks went bright pink, and she frowned. "I'm meeting kids from the youth group. They have a stupid prayer meeting every Saturday morning. Matt and Sunday always let me go."

"If it's stupid why do you want to?"

"Because I don't feel like hanging around with a bunch of little kids all day," she replied. That, at least, sounded like the truth.

"So you're telling me that a bunch of teenagers willingly wake up early on Saturday morning to go pray at the diner?"

"We eat, too. And the meeting is at eleven, but it's going to take me a while to walk there. If I get there early enough, I can wash the windows and sweep the sidewalk for extra cash. I do the same at the five and dime. It's on the same street."

He knew the diner.

He knew the five and dime.

He'd done just about every odd job he could when he was a kid, trying to earn money to make his escape from his father's house.

"You're not planning to run away, are you?" he asked, the gruffness in his voice making Heavenly stiffen.

"Why would I do that?"

"I don't know, but if that's why you want to earn money, forget it."

"I need money for clothes, damnit!" she nearly yelled. "And for coffee when I'm at the prayer meeting. If I'd wanted to run away from this hellhole, I'd be gone already."

She ran inside and slammed the door, the sound reverberating through his head.

"Looks like that went about as well as your conversation with Twila," Clementine called out, her voice as surprising as the kernel of worry that had settled in his stomach, the niggling concern that he was about to fail Heavenly and prove to her that adults really were as stupid and uncaring as she suspected.

"Apparently, I'm really good at pissing off young girls." He turned and watched as Clementine crossed the yard, her old work boots scuffed and dirty, her khaki pants loose fitting. She'd taken off her jacket and rolled up the cuffs of her oversized cotton shirt. She wasn't traditionally pretty. She wasn't beautiful, either, her cheekbones and chin too sharp, her eyes too large. She was taller than average. Curvy beneath her flowing clothes.

Comfortable in her own skin.

Creamy smooth, flawless skin.

He couldn't help noticing that. Or the way that all the disparate parts that were Clementine came together to make a stunning figure.

"Heavenly is always pissed off," she said, stopping at the bottom of the stairs. "If that's any comfort to you."

"It's not."

She laughed. "You're going to survive this, Porter."

"And you know this because . . . ?"

"My dad raised fifteen kids. Mostly on his own. He lived to be eighty-six. He'd probably have reached a hundred if he hadn't smoked like a chimney and drank like a fish."

"Were you the youngest?"

"And my mother's only. I spent three weeks every summer

traveling the world with her, and the rest of the year living with my father. Which proved to be a good thing when Dad died, and I moved in with Mom. Things might have been awkward if we hadn't ever spent time together."

"Sounds like an interesting story," he said, wanting to ask questions. Lots of them, because he'd known a lot of people during his thirty-two years of life, but he'd never known a college professor who could also plow a field, prune an orchard, and bring a farm back to life.

"Some people might think so. My father was a shaman and a storyteller. Full-blooded Native American. He married his first wife when he was seventeen. They had four kids. She left when he decided to bring home the baby of his mistress."

"I take it the baby was also his?"

"Of course. His wife wasn't too keen on raising another woman's child, so she left. The mistress moved in, and Dad had three more kids with her. He repeated that pattern several times."

"How did your mom feel about that?"

"Mom had her own string of lovers, and she knew Dad was a collector of all things. Words. Stories. Herbs. Women. Kids. She didn't care. He was thirty years her senior, and she was nearing forty when they met. She was attracted to his brilliant mind and his unique way of viewing the world. Or so she says. Neither of them were expecting to add to their families, but here I am."

"Life is full of surprises," he said, glancing at the farmhouse filled with kids who should never have become his responsibility. Matthias had been the youngest brother. He'd lived in the safest place. He should have survived long enough to see his kids grow up, graduate college, have kids of their own.

"Yes," she agreed. "It is. Do you want me to talk to Heavenly for you?"

"No, but if you want to take her clothes shopping, I wouldn't be opposed."

"Clothes shopping?"

"She says she needs to buy some, and I'm about as good at shopping for girls' clothes as I am at keeping kids from escaping."

"That's why she was out here? Because she wanted to go clothes shopping?"

"She was out here because she was going to walk to town for a youth group prayer meeting. At least that's the story she's telling."

"There's one at the diner every Saturday morning. I see the group every time I go there," she said, confirming at least part of Heavenly's story. "Six or seven kids all sitting at tables talking and laughing loudly enough to annoy the hell out of anyone who goes there for a quiet breakfast." She smiled to take the sting out of the words.

"Is that why you go there? For a quiet breakfast."

She snorted. "Every one of my breakfasts is quiet, so that's not something I'm going to leave the house searching for. I go to trade alpaca yarn for Ms. Robinson's fresh eggs and homemade jam. I could live off that stuff. And coffee. I need that, too."

"I can make a pot, if you want some."

"I need to get back to work. I just came over because I wanted to ask you if you . . ." Her voice trailed off and her cheeks went a pale shade of pink.

"What?"

"Got the keys from Sim," she continued. "But I suddenly realized that wasn't your job. I should have gotten them before I ran out."

"I got them." He dug them out of his pocket and held them up. "And you didn't run. You had work to do."

"Right." She grinned. "That's what I told myself as I was sprinting away. But I do have to work. It shouldn't take longer than a couple of hours. I'll bring Heavenly to the diner after I finish the field. When she's done there, I'll bring her to the little boutique on Carlisle. She should be able to find something to wear."

"You don't have to do that," he said, but he sure as hell would appreciate it if she did. He couldn't imagine walking into a boutique with a teenage girl, trying to help her choose appropriate clothes.

Just thinking about it made him break into a cold sweat.

"I owe you for getting rid of Sim," Clementine said, bending to pull a vine-like weed from the bottom stair rail. "Now, we'll be even."

"I'm pretty certain you could have handled Sim on your own."

"Sure I could have, but it was nice not to have to. I'll be back at ten. Can you tell Heavenly to be ready?"

"Sure."

"See you around, Porter." She strode away, her long braid bouncing against the middle of her back, her pant legs swishing through ankle-high grass. He should have turned and gone back inside. Instead, he stayed where he was. Just watching the way she moved, strong and graceful and at ease, and thinking about how different she was from other women he knew. No polish or paint. No colored hair or high heels. No artifice or facade. Just herself.

Which was nice.

Probably better than that, but he wasn't going to put another word to it.

* * *

Porter was watching her go.

Which was fine with Clementine.

She'd never been nervous about being the center of attention. She traveled all over the country as a guest lecturer and storyteller, and she was almost never nervous before a gig.

According to her father, true storytellers didn't have to be nervous. What they did was organic, natural, and comfortable. Their stories weren't just part of them. They *were* them. Woven into nerve and sinew and bone, sunken deep into DNA. A person didn't become a storyteller. He was born one.

Clementine had scoffed at the idea, of course.

Unlike her father, she'd always had both feet planted on solid ground. She loved the ancient stories the same way she loved the ebb and flow of all spoken word.

But that didn't mean she believed in myth, legend, or lore.

She climbed back onto the tractor, the sun brighter now, the little rancher glowing, the field brown and gold and ebony earth. This she knew. This she could do. Line up the tractor with the stake she'd planted the previous day, keep her focus on that as she drove. No need for fancy gizmos or brand-new technology. All she needed were her eyes and her hands. One row. Turn. Another row. Dry weeds uprooted, dark soil revealed, insects and worms scurrying and sliding through the fertile ground. It smelled like spring and like life, like hope and happiness.

It smelled like home, but she couldn't allow herself to think too much about that, because she'd already decided that home was going to be Seattle, with its gray skies and wet weather.

Her mother, Lillian, still lived in the pretty home she'd bought in the seventies, close to the university where she taught anthropology three days a week. At sixty-three, she still enjoyed a robust social life. During school breaks, she traveled the world with her live-in boyfriend, Gallagher Mendelson. They'd been together for five years.

A record of which Lillian was both proud and appalled by.

Clementine wasn't expecting it to last, but she liked Gallagher. She liked Seattle. She liked gray skies and cool rainy days. She liked seeing her mother once a week and driving to Pike Place to buy fresh herbs and artisan cheeses.

She wasn't sure if that was enough to build a new life on, but she'd give it a shot, because she wasn't going to sit around feeling sorry for herself.

And she sure as hell wasn't going to let Sim walk back into her life. She couldn't believe he'd been in the house, couldn't believe he'd actually opened his arms and expected her to walk right into them.

"Jackass," she whispered, finishing the last row and turning off the tractor. She shifted in the seat, surveying the field. It looked like it should—rich soil ready for planting. The beauty of it was almost enough to take away the sting of Sim's unexpected visit.

Almost.

She glanced at her watch as she climbed off the tractor. It was nearly ten, and if she was going to pick Heavenly up at the house, she'd have to hurry. She jogged to the rancher and unlocked the door, bracing herself for the stale smell of coffee, cologne, and cigarettes. It was a scent she knew well, as familiar as winter chill or summer heat. It was one of the first things she'd noticed about Sim, and one of the first things she'd liked.

Now, it beat out skunk on her list of top ten smells she hated. She wrinkled her nose and walked to the window above the sink, cracking it open to let in some cool fresh air. She dumped the coffeepot, filling it with soap and water before she ran into her bedroom and changed into yoga pants and a fitted T-shirt. She pulled a wool vest over the long-sleeved shirt, grabbed two skeins of alpaca yarn from the basket near the spinning wheel, shoved her feet into running shoes, and grabbed her purse from the hook near the door.

She flicked off the lights, closed the curtains, told herself she wasn't afraid of coming home and seeing Sim again, because he wasn't coming. And, if he did, she'd take the pot of stinky, soap-filled water and dump it on his head.

She didn't want him around. He had no right to be around. Period.

End of story.

And, unless he had her half of the money he'd taken from their joint savings account, she had nothing to say to him. Not now. Not ever.

She climbed into the old Pontiac she and Sim had purchased when they'd moved east from Seattle. It was a heavier car than Sim's sporty Porsche and could easily pull a small hauling trailer. She'd almost been excited when they'd signed the paperwork to sell their house and left for the land Sim had described as beautiful. He'd told her about deep streams and thick forests and twenty-five acres of cleared field. She'd been pissed, but she'd been willing to go along with things. They'd been married seven years by that point, and she'd begun to realize that the opposites who'd attracted all those years ago were drifting apart.

He liked to watch sports on the weekends.

She liked to hike.

He hated indoor pets.

She wanted a dog.

He liked his meals at a certain time every day. She enjoyed spontaneity. She saved money. He spent it. He liked bars.

She liked theaters. She wanted a couple of kids. He wanted freedom.

The list of their differences had been longer than the list of guests they'd invited to their wedding.

They'd drifted so far apart, she hadn't thought they'd ever be able to bridge the divide. She'd been willing to try, though. Her parents might have had countercultural ideals, but they'd both believed in fulfilling obligations and promises.

They'd taught her to do the same.

Otherwise, she'd have probably walked away the day Sim showed her photos of the property he'd purchased and asked her to take a leave of absence from her professorship to help him build his dream.

She started the Pontiac and headed to the farmhouse.

It had been quiet there earlier. Now it was bustling with activity, an older heavyset woman standing in the shade of two giant birch trees, hanging wet linen from a clothesline.

A playpen was a few feet away, little Oya standing up and looking over its side, her chubby cheeks and rosebud mouth hidden by vinyl, just her clear blue eyes and fine white hair visible.

"Hello there!" the woman called cheerfully. "You must be Clementine. Porter said you were coming. He and Heavenly will be out in a minute." She swiped her right hand across a frilly apron and offered a handshake. "I'm Rosie Whipple. I'm helping out with child care until Sullivan and Rumer return."

"It looks like you're helping with a little more than that," Clementine responded, grabbing a pillowcase from the basket at Rosie's feet and hanging it quickly.

"Doing laundry is part of child care. So, is cooking and cleaning. Kids are messy creatures."

"I'll take your word for that."

"You don't have any?"

"No. I did have a lot of brothers and sisters."

"Younger?"

"No. I'm the youngest."

"In that case, it's not the same thing," she said as Clementine grabbed a fitted sheet and hung it next to the pillowcase. "I see you've done this before."

"A couple of times," Clementine agreed.

"Raised in the country?"

"Yes."

"Hereabouts?"

"Wyoming. Right outside the Wind River reservation."

"I know it. Can't say I ever spent much time there. Me and Harold used to travel, though. Always by road and always in his RV. He loved that beastly house on wheels. Me? I preferred home."

"When did he pass away?" she asked, hanging a fitted sheet and then a baby blanket.

"Who?"

"Harold?"

"He didn't pass away, hun. He left me twelve years ago. I'd probably forgive him for it, if he hadn't left me for Alabama Winslow."

"I'm sorry, Rosie. That must have been difficult," she responded. Thanks to Sim, she knew just *how* difficult.

"Alabama is a man."

"A man?" she repeated.

"Yeah."

"I doubt that makes it easier."

"Eh. I wasn't too bothered by it. Leaving is leaving, right? Fortunately, I've always known how to take care of myself, and I've never needed a man to help me get through life. I sure as heck didn't miss cleaning up the messes Harold was always leaving around. Dishes in the sink. Socks on the floor." She shuddered.

"So, you weren't heartbroken?"

Rosie snorted. "Nah. It wasn't even a little emotional. We'd been married for twenty-two years. The marriage had run its course. We both knew it. We were just habits to each other. I'd be able to forgive and forget, if Alabama didn't have better legs than me. Damn his scrawny hide." She laughed. "I joke about the situation, but I suspected Harold was gay long before he figured it out, and I wasn't surprised when he sat me down and told me. I wasn't angry or upset, either. I figured he had a right to his happiness."

"That's big of you."

"What good does it do to be small? The way I see it, we only get to walk on this earth once. We might as well do it the best way we can."

"You're right about that. So"—she took another sheet from the basket—"where are Harold and Alabama now? Traveling the country in Harold's RV?"

"Four months out of the year, they are. When they're not doing that, they live next door. We have summer barbeques and grand holiday parties together."

"That sounds like fun."

"It sure as he . . . ck beats boring, right?" She smiled again, her gaze dropping to Oya. "I need to watch my mouth around the little one. She's starting to talk. She said Mama yesterday. Clear as day. It's a shame her mother wasn't around to hear it."

"Hopefully, Sunday will be home soon."

"Wouldn't that be great? In the meantime, the other kids and I are trying to record it. Next time they visit their mom, they can play it."

"That's a great idea."

"I have them occasionally." She lifted Oya from the playpen and pulled a cell phone out from the apron pocket. "Looks like it's time to wrangle Moisey into her dance gear.

She's not so keen on going to class today. She says ballet is boring."

"Maybe she should stay home then?"

"Porter thinks it's best if she goes. I agree. Stability of routine is important for kids. Especially when they've been through trauma." She turned toward the house, her tight curls bouncing merrily. "I'll prod Heavenly into moving while I'm inside. That girl is slow as molasses in the winter. Thanks for helping with the hanging." She hurried away, tickling Oya as she went.

The baby giggled, the sound like the beat of a butterfly's wings. Delicate and light.

Sunday was missing all this. The wash on the line, the giggle of her baby, the drama of teenagers. She was missing milestones and birthdays, and she didn't know it.

While her kids grew and changed, she lay in a bed in a rehab facility, barely aware of her surroundings.

"I'll go visit her today," Clementine vowed, lifting the basket and carrying it to the porch. "Even if it's hard. Even if I don't want to do it. Even if it breaks my heart a little."

"Even if what breaks your heart a little?" Porter asked, and she realized he was stretched out on the porch swing, knees bent, feet flat on the worn seat, hands behind his head.

Sexy, relaxed, confident.

Dangerous.

"Visiting Sunday," she replied, turning away, pretending to look at the field, the horizon, the sheets fluttering in the soft breeze.

"The kids and I were there yesterday. We'll head over again tomorrow after church."

"You're taking the kids to church?"

"Moisey begged me."

"Moisey?"

"She thinks if she can get a piece of wood from the cross

at the front of the church, she can stick it under Sunday's mattress and that will wake her up."

"Where did she get that idea?"

"Where does Moisey get any of her ideas?" he responded, the old chains creaking as he shifted.

She glanced his way, of course, telling herself the noise had drawn her attention. "She gets a lot of them?"

"Since her mother was hospitalized, yes. Whether or not she had a lot of them before that, I don't know. Unfortunately, I didn't spend a lot of time with her before the accident." He stood and stretched, running tights hugging muscular thighs and calves, a blue compression top clinging to his abdomen and shoulders. He had a narrow waist and a flat stomach, and she thought she could see a six-pack through the thin material of his shirt.

"I'm planning on going for a run while Heavenly is doing her thing," he said, and she met his eyes.

"I was planning the same."

"There's a great trail behind the church. We can go there after we drop her off."

"We?"

"I want to meet the youth leaders, and I want to make sure Heavenly knows that I'm going to be sticking my nose in her business a lot. She's a pretty kid, and she's vulnerable. I'm going to make sure no one takes advantage of that."

"If you're going, then I'll stay here and do some more work in the fields," she said quickly, trying to extract herself from the situation. It was one thing to take a teenager to a clothing boutique. It was another to go running with a guy who looked like he'd stepped off the pages of a fitness magazine.

"Why?" he asked as the door opened and Heavenly stepped out.

"Why what?" she asked, her lips stained purple-red, her eyes thickly lined. It looked like she'd applied her makeup with a trowel, and Clementine wanted to grab a wet rag and wipe her face clean.

"Clementine and I are planning to go for a run while you're hanging out with your friends."

"They're not my friends. They're the youth group from church," she corrected, hiking a faux leather purse up on her skinny shoulder. She wore skinny jeans that were an inch too short, black pumps that looked a size too big, and a white eyelet shirt that sagged low on her chest. Her coat looked like it had fit her two years ago, the hem falling to her thighs, the sleeves hitting her at mid-forearm.

Clementine didn't know much about teen fashion, but she didn't think this was it.

"What size are you, Heavenly?" she asked, and the young girl stiffened.

"Why?"

"Because I have a sweaterdress back at my place that I was making for my niece's birthday. I thought her favorite color was blue. Apparently, it's green."

"I don't need your charity, Clementine," Heavenly said haughtily, her chin up, her eyes flashing.

"What charity? I want you to try it on, because you and my niece are almost the same size. If it fits you, I'll use the same pattern to make the green dress."

"What's her name?" Heavenly asked, obviously doubting Clementine's story. Her doubt was justified. Clementine had made the sweaterdress, but she'd planned to barter it for some canning jars at the local flea market the next weekend.

"Apple Blossom. She's fourteen, but she's not much bigger than you." That, at least, was true. She did have a niece named

Apple Blossom. She and her family lived in Anchorage, Alaska.

"I'll try it on, I guess, but we need to hurry. I hate walking in after everyone else is already there. They stare, and it's embarrassing."

"It won't take long," Clementine promised, opening the back door so that Heavenly could slide into the Pontiac.

Porter was climbing into the passenger seat, and every hope she'd had that he'd forget about their run fled as he closed the door.

Chapter Three

The dress fit perfectly, the waist snug, the A-line skirt falling an inch above Heavenly's knees. Even better, Clementine had insisted that the teen remove her makeup before pulling the dress on over her head. She'd also dug a pair of fleece-lined, knee-high boots from her closet. They were big, but more functional than the black pumps. Now Heavenly looked like the young woman she was becoming rather than the wounded foster kid she'd once been.

Clementine watched her walk across the crowded diner and take a seat at a table filled with chatting kids, and she felt just a little bit of pride at what she'd accomplished.

That should have been a warning.

Pride always led to downfall.

She'd had that pounded into her head by her father when she was a kid. Humility, he'd always said, was the key to success, and pride was the surest way to fail. *Keep it real and right and as close to truth as you can make it, and never brag about even your greatest accomplishment. That is the way to succeed, but more importantly, it's the path to fulfillment.*

She quoted his words in lectures sometimes, when she told the stories he'd passed down to her.

So, yeah, she was feeling a little bit proud, and she should have been expecting trouble, but she wasn't. She was too busy watching Heavenly take a seat at the youth group's table, lift a menu and hold it up so that her face was hidden.

"She's embarrassed that we walked her in." Clementine stated the obvious.

"She'll get over it. Come on. Let's go introduce ourselves." Porter grabbed her hand and tugged her to the table.

Which would have been okay except that she had no desire to meet the kids or the youth group leaders, and she sure as hell didn't want to stand in the middle of the Saturday morning brunch crowd. She'd come back to Benevolence to repay a favor. She'd planned to keep to herself while she did that, because she knew exactly how people felt about her. The fact that she'd been part of the biggest drama to ever happen in Benevolence had sealed their opinions, and there wasn't much she could do to change that.

Even if there had been, she wouldn't have tried.

She would be in Benevolence for a few months, and she had no desire to explain her part in what had happened, no reason to justify what she'd done. She didn't want to go into details about the young couple who had been living with her and Sim, the baby who had been born and then abandoned. She didn't want to defend her decision to a group of people who'd already tried and convicted her in their minds.

A year ago, she'd explained the facts to the sheriff.

Just the facts.

No weaving words to make things better. Just an account of things as she'd experienced them. The sheriff had decided not to press charges, even though she'd withheld information that could have led him to the young mother sooner.

She'd had her reasons.

Phoebe Tanner had been young and scared. She'd made

a mistake. Had the mistake resulted in baby Miracle's death, Clementine would have felt obligated to go to the police. But the baby had been found and taken to the hospital. She'd gotten treatment for a heart defect. She'd been thriving in the care of Willow Lamont, and Clementine hadn't felt that going to the police would make things any better.

She'd explained all that to the sheriff, but she'd had no desire to explain it to the rest of the town. She sure as hell hadn't intended to give interviews to the local or national press. Leaving town had been the best and, really, only option.

Of course, she'd thought she'd be leaving with Sim.

She'd planned on returning to the house and telling him that they had to pack up and go back to their old lives. Only she'd returned to an empty house, an empty bank account, and the sickening knowledge that she'd been duped by the guy she'd spent ten years trying to love. Funny how hard she'd worked at something that should have been as natural as breathing.

Maybe that kind of love existed. Maybe it was fulfilling and right and comfortable and exciting. But for Clementine, love had only ever been work, and she'd been exhausted by the time she'd found the empty accounts and the empty house.

It had been a bad day.

The four years of days preceding it had also been bad.

Clementine had vowed that the next days and years and decades were going to be better.

And yet, here she was, standing in a diner in the town that held her partially responsible for the drama that had unfolded there over a year ago. She couldn't really blame them for that. She was a college professor, well educated, perfectly capable of going to the police about something as serious as an abandoned baby. The fact that she hadn't put her right up there with Charles Manson and Ted Bundy in the town's list of evil people.

She could feel the judgmental gaze of every person there. Usually when she traded yarn, she walked into the owner's little office, handed over the beautiful skeins of hand-dyed alpaca, and walked out with the eggs and jam. People noticed, but they didn't dare comment. They just stared as she moved through, watching suspiciously, as if they worried that she'd pull a gun and rob the place.

Today, of course, was different.

She was with two people who were part of the second biggest story that had ever happened in Benevolence. Matthias's death had rocked the little town to its foundation. Clementine hadn't had to be there to know that the entire community had been shaken. People died of old age here. They weren't killed by drunk drivers when they were on their way home from their anniversary dinners.

Two months after Matt's body had been pulled from his crushed vehicle, the town was still buzzing with frenetic energy, desperate to make something good out of something horrible.

She doubted anyone living there thought she could be part of that good thing. As a matter of fact, she figured three-quarters of the community would be very happy to run her out of town. They questioned her motives, doubted her sincerity, wondered—loudly enough for her to hear—whether she was going to stir up more trouble, but they weren't going to chase her away.

She'd promised to help Sunday.

She was going to do it.

But that didn't mean she had to offer more fodder for the

gossips, and it didn't mean she had to stand in the middle of a hostile crowd.

"Well, look who we have here!" a man said, his cheerful voice cutting through tense silence. "Clementine Warren! I've been hoping I'd get a chance to speak with you."

She didn't have to turn around to know who the voice belonged to. She turned anyway, because her father had taught her to never have her back to a predator. As far as she was concerned, Randall Custard was that.

A puffed-up peacock of a man with perfectly tailored clothes and a too wide smile, Randall was the owner, editor, and chief reporter for the *Benevolence Times*. He'd spent his life snooping out stories in a town that really didn't have any.

The abandoned baby left beside the town's iconic chocolate shop had been the story of a lifetime, and he'd been determined to obtain exclusive interviews with everyone who'd been even slightly involved.

Clementine had been nose deep in it, but the story hadn't been hers to tell. It had been Phoebe's. They'd met at a farmers' market near Spokane. Phoebe and her husband, Elias, had been selling herbs. Clementine had been selling hand-pulled yarn, and she'd felt just sorry enough for the young couple to strike up a conversation.

The next thing she'd known, she'd had two kids living in the rancher. Neither had a clue about how the world worked. They'd been raised in a religious cult, sheltered from life, and somehow, they'd broken away and were trying to live on their own terms.

Even after baby Miracle was born and it had become obvious that Phoebe and Elias hadn't seen eye to eye on what to do with the sickly little girl, Clementine had respected the fact that two eighteen-year-old kids were willing to go it alone rather than subscribe to the fanatical ideals of their parents.

And then she'd woken up one morning and the baby was gone, the town was buzzing. Life as she'd been trying to create it had been shaken and tossed and turned on its head.

"I'm not giving any interviews," she said to Randall, walking past him and heading for the door, the bag of yarn thumping against her thigh.

"Who said I wanted an interview?"

"Don't you?"

"Well . . . yes, but that's not the only reason I wanted to talk."

"No?" She stepped outside, inhaling a calming breath, exhaling her tension.

Her yogi mother would be proud.

"Of course not." He followed her outside, sunlight gleaming on his handlebar mustache.

That was new.

Had he applied glitter to it?

She shifted her gaze, because it wasn't polite to stare. Even at abominations like Randall's mustache. "Okay. I'll bite. What do you want to discuss?"

"I'm sure you've heard that the town is having a fund-raiser for the Bradshaw family."

"No. I haven't," she said.

"Well, then it's a good thing we ran into each other."

"We didn't run into each other, Randall. You approached me. Obviously with an agenda." She unlocked her car, tossed the yarn bag into the backseat, and shoved her keys in her vest pocket. "Since I'm going for a run and don't have a lot of time, how about you tell me what that is."

"The community is obviously very concerned about the

Bradshaw kids. With Sunday in the hospital and probably not going to recover—"

"She'll recover," she said, even though she had no idea if it was true.

Words had power. She might not believe things could be brought into being by speaking them, but she wasn't going to let Randall's negative words go unchallenged.

"We're all hoping for that, but I visited the rehab center a couple of days ago, and the nurses I spoke to says it doesn't look promising."

"The day doesn't ever look promising before the sun rises," she replied.

"You understand what I'm saying, Clementine."

"I understand that I'm still standing here instead of running. What do you need, Randall?"

"Okay. I'll be brief. The town council voted to host a black-tie dinner and silent auction. All the proceeds will be put into an account that will be used to keep Pleasant Valley Organic Farm running until the kids are old enough to decide what they want to do with it."

"That's very generous. I'm sure the family will appreciate it."

"We don't need appreciation. We need a venue. One that is spectacular enough to garner public attention. Not just here but in neighboring towns."

"And?"

"We've been discussing it, and it's been decided that the Lee Harris house will be the perfect location."

"I have no idea where that is or what it has to do with me."

"It's that huge house on Maine and Evergreen. Wrought iron fence, overgrown yard, boarded up windows?"

She'd seen it mostly because it was impossible to miss.

The Gothic mansion was as out of place in Benevolence as she was.

"I still don't know what that has to do with me."

"It belongs to the Bradshaws."

"Sunday owns that house?" She knew she sounded surprised. She felt surprised. The place was ostentatious in the extreme. Something Sunday had never been. She'd inherited the farm from her parents, and she'd kept the house cozy, comfortable, and inviting. Even the land had a comforting feel. The way the fields and orchards were laid out, the lazy river winding through the golden landscape. The generations who'd lived there and worked the land hadn't been doing it for wealth and comfort. They'd done it for love. All a person had to do was stand on the farmhouse porch and look out over the fallow fields to know that.

"Not Sunday. The Bradshaw brothers," he corrected. "They grew up there."

"They did?"

"Yes. Their father was born here. His father was the town drunk. His mother wasn't around. From what I've heard, Porter's dad was raised in a trailer on a tiny piece of land right outside town. He went to school but never hung out with the other kids. Never made friends. Disappeared right after he graduated high school. Twelve years later, he made a fortune in software development. He bought that house and moved back. When he died, he left it to his sons. I guess none of them want it, because they haven't occupied the property since he died."

"It's an interesting story." A very interesting one. One that intrigued her. Made her want to ask questions and learn more. She was a collector of stories. Just like her father.

But she wasn't going to collect this one. She was here

for a couple of months. Not to gather myth and lore, but to bring Sunday's land back to life.

"I still don't know what this has to do with me."

"We need the Bradshaws' permission to use the property."

"If you think I can help you get that, you're mistaken."

"You live on the farm."

"So?"

"You're helping bring it back to life. They owe you."

"No. They don't."

"They do. And that gives you an in none of us have."

"I'm not doing it, Randall."

"If Sunday doesn't recover, what are those kids going to do?"

"Their uncles will be here for them."

"Here? Or somewhere else? From what I've heard, one of them lives in Portland. One is in LA. The other one is down in Texas. *Texas!*"

"Texas is not the pit of hell."

"It's thousands of miles from home, Clementine. The first stable, loving home any of those kids have ever had. What's going to happen to them if they're ripped away from that?" he asked, and for the first time since she'd known him, he looked sincere. Even with his glittery mustache.

Even with his smarmy, puffed-up chest.

He looked like he cared, like he really was concerned about the kids and their future, and she couldn't ignore that any more than she could ignore her promise to Sunday.

Damnit!

"With an account set up to keep the farm running and no financial burden associated with that, it's possible the Bradshaws will agree that letting the kids continue to live there is in their best interest." He pressed his advantage, and she caved, because she cared about Sunday and her wild bunch of kids.

"What are you hoping I can do?"

"Just mention it. Casually. In passing. Like it's not a big deal. See what the boys have to say and report back to me."

"They aren't boys," she pointed out. "And I'm not comfortable being a spy for the enemy camp."

"We're not enemies."

"Figure of speech, Randall. I'm not going to gather information on the sly. If I ask, I'm going to be overt about it."

"Whatever floats your boat, doll." He grinned. "Now, while I have you here, I'd also like to discuss—"

"No."

"You don't even know what I was going to say."

"You want to interview me."

"I want to take you to dinner. Now that we're both single, there's nothing holding us back from exploring the more passionate sides of our natures."

"Ready for our run?" Porter called, striding toward them, his body looking all kinds of masculine in his running gear.

Not that she was noticing that, or the way his eyes glowed like molten silver.

God, he was handsome.

And she was a fool, because she *was* noticing, her heart doing a wild little tap dance of happiness as he smiled. "Sorry for taking so long," he said. "The youth group leaders had a lot to say about Heavenly."

"Good things, I hope."

"She's got the voice of an angel and the heart of a warrior. That's a direct quote." His gaze shifted to Randall, and his smile slipped away. "Randall Custard, right?"

"I'm surprised you remember. We didn't run with the same crowds in school."

"I didn't run with any crowds," Porter responded, his voice clipped and hard. "But the school was small, and you're difficult to forget."

"Thanks."

"It wasn't a compliment. Heavenly will be done in an hour, so if we're going to get some exercise, now's probably the time."

"Right," Clementine said, as eager as he apparently was to end the conversation with Randall. "See you around, Randall."

"We were right in the middle of a conversation," he protested, jogging along beside her as she followed Porter onto the sidewalk.

"We were at the end of it."

"What about dinner?"

"No. Thanks."

"Lunch?"

"I have a busy schedule."

"I can stop by your place tomorrow. We can have a picnic near the river."

"I'm not interested," she said bluntly.

"I own the newspaper." He tossed the words out like they would change things. "And five properties in town."

"And I'm still not interested," she responded.

"You're afraid of having a rebound relationship, right?" he asked, his mustache twinkling as he struggled to breathe and talk and jog.

"I don't want a relationship. Not with you. Not with anyone."

"We don't have to have a relationship to have fun," he panted.

"She said no, Randall," Porter said quietly, tossing the words over his shoulder as he jogged up Main Street. He was a few steps ahead, his pace slow, easy. Almost lazy.

But there was nothing lazy about his tone.

Randall noticed. His steps faltered, his cocky attitude slipping. "If you're interested, Porter, all you have to do is say so, and I'll back off."

"Back off anyway," Porter responded.

"Now, hold on a minute—"

Porter swung around. "Women don't like to be stalked, Randall, and I don't like stalkers."

"What's that supposed to mean?"

"It means you're pissing me off," Clementine cut in. She didn't need Porter to fight battles for her. Especially ones being waged by a guy with a glittered mustache.

"Because I asked you out? Most women around here would be thrilled."

"Then how about you go and make their days?" she suggested.

He shrugged. "Whatever, doll. Your loss." He turned back toward the diner.

Thank God.

She was not in the mood.

At all.

"Still want to go for a run?" Porter asked, his expression unreadable. Whatever he thought about Randall and his invitation, he wasn't letting it show.

"Are the mountains ready for spring thaw?" she responded, taking off before he answered.

She halfway hoped he'd head in the opposite direction, turn left when she went right, go off on his own and take his muscular body and silvery eyes with him.

But, of course, he didn't.

He fell into place beside her, matching his longer stride to hers. It was an easy run, their feet pounding on cement and grass as they passed the dry cleaners, the tackle shop, and then the chocolate shop where baby Miracle had been found.

It was crowded. Like always. She could see customers through the shop windows, see a red-haired woman behind the counter, holding a baby.

Clementine's foot hit a crack in the sidewalk, and she flew forward, would have taken a header off the curb, if Porter hadn't grabbed her arm.

"Careful," he said.

"Sorry," she replied, glancing at the store again. They'd passed the windows and doors, and she couldn't see anything except the brick facade. That was probably for the best. She knew Phoebe's daughter had been adopted by Willow Lamont. She knew that Willow had moved to town and taken over Chocolate Haven. She knew they had been living in the apartment above the store.

She didn't need to know any more than that.

She sure as hell didn't need anyone in town thinking she was trying to get a glimpse of the baby.

"You're tense," Porter commented.

"And?"

"That makes running more difficult."

"Running is always difficult."

"You don't really think that," he responded.

"Why do you say that?"

"You've got an even stride and a natural rhythm. Running is something you do a lot. Which means it's not difficult. Even on the tough days."

"Lately, every day is tough."

"Because you're tense," he repeated. "You need to loosen up. Let your muscles relax into the rhythm of the run."

"That is a lot easier said than done," she muttered.

"It wouldn't be if you'd stop thinking about things you can't change." They'd reached the end of the commercial

area of Main Street, brownstone buildings giving way to
large lots and old houses.

"Who says I'm doing that?"

"Aren't you?"

"Yes," she replied, and he smiled.

"So, maybe you should stop."

"If only it were that easy."

"It's as easy as you make it," he replied, picking up his
pace as they reached a quiet crossroad and ran past a wrought
iron fence.

She glanced at the tangled yard beyond it, the huge house
almost hidden by overgrown bushes and trees. Realized
where they were as they raced by a cracked driveway and
turned the corner onto Evergreen.

"The Lee Harris house," she said, letting the name settle
on her tongue. It tasted bitter and hard, and she wasn't surprised when Porter didn't respond.

"You and your brothers own it," she continued.

"Who told you that?"

"Randall. Is he wrong?"

"No."

"Is this a subject not up for discussion?"

"Why would you want to discuss it?" he asked as they
reached the end of the fenced lot.

"The town council wants to have a silent auction here.
To benefit your nieces and nephews. That's what Randall
was talking to me about."

"No."

"Okay."

"You're not going to ask why not?"

"I figure you have your reasons."

He was silent again, running up a hill that led to the high
school. There was a park nearby with a running trail that
wound through trees and out onto a country road.

She'd been there before and knew it would lead them on a five-mile circuit back to the diner. She was fine with that. Just like she was fine with Porter's silence.

He had a right to his secrets, and she had no right to ask him to share them.

She was curious, though.

About his family and the huge house they'd lived in.

About the reason why the windows had been boarded up, the yard left untended. About his father—a man who'd come from nothing and made himself something. About the story of Porter's life, and how he'd gone from being small-town royalty to working private security far away from the town he'd grown up in.

Curiosity was a dangerous thing.

It made people ask questions, dig for answers, open jars that were meant to stay closed.

"If Pandora didn't teach us that, we'll never learn it," she muttered as Porter led the way into the park.

"Pandora?" he asked, his voice so calm and even, she'd have thought he was standing still if she hadn't been running beside him.

"According to Greek mythology, she was the first woman on earth. She had every gift imaginable but still couldn't stop herself from opening a jar and releasing heartache into the world."

"I'm familiar with the story. I was wondering why you were mentioning her."

"Ah, well, that's another thing altogether," she replied, her lungs burning as she struggled to keep pace with Porter.

"Does your silence mean you don't want to explain?"

"It means my legs aren't as long as yours, and I'm not nearly as fast," she panted.

He chuckled, slowing to a jog as they reached the old country road. "Better?"

"Sure," she lied, and he laughed again.

"Sorry. The past was nipping at my heels, and I was trying to get away from it."

"Bad memories, huh?"

"Enough to fill Pandora's jar," he replied.

"And destroy the peace and happiness of all the people in the world?"

"Just the people in my little corner of it," he responded.

"And that's why you won't let the town council use the house?"

"The place is a mess, Clementine. Getting it ready for an event like that would take time and money. I don't have any of the first, and I'm not willing to give any of the second to the cause."

"If I wanted to get involved, I'd mention that the town would probably be willing to spend the time and money needed to get the place ready."

"But you don't want to get involved, so you're not going to mention it?" he asked wryly.

"I definitely don't want to get involved," she agreed, her cheeks stinging from the chilly air, her heart pounding with the effort of the run.

She didn't want to get involved. She *wouldn't* get involved. She'd keep her curiosity in check, keep the jar closed, because she had a feeling opening it would be dangerous to her plans, to her heart, to her ability to go back to Seattle with a clear mind and clear vision.

And that was something she wouldn't allow.

She'd changed her life for someone once.

She wasn't going to make that mistake again.

Ever.

No matter how tempting the thought might be.

* * *

It took four hours to get all the kids settled down for the night.

Four hours, six minutes, and twenty-nine seconds, if Porter wanted to be exact.

He did.

Because Flynn needed to know what he'd missed out on. Every excruciating detail of it.

"From what I've gathered during the weekends I've spent there," Flynn said, his voice staticky and distant, the phone connection tenuous, "that's not too bad. As a matter of fact, it might be a record of kid-wrangling quickness."

"That's easy for you to say. You're camping under the stars with nothing but the coyotes and cattle to interrupt your thoughts."

"The ranch doesn't run itself, Porter. We had ten cows drop calves yesterday. You know I'd be there otherwise."

"I know neither of us would be here if we didn't feel obligated to Matt's kids," he responded, lowering his voice even though he was out in the middle of the damn orchard in the middle of the damn night. "We're going to have to talk about options, Flynn. If Sunday doesn't improve, we've got to make decisions about how to move forward."

"We agreed after the funeral that the kids should stay on the farm."

"At what cost? Your ranch? My career? We sure as hell can't expect Sullivan to give up everything he's worked for while we live our lives like we always have." He sounded angry. He felt angry.

It was seeing the house, looking at the overgrown yard and the boarded-up windows and the rusting fence. Remembering things he'd rather forget. Like his father's rages. His mother's tears. Her illness, and the feeling he'd always had that she'd died from a broken heart.

"What's going on, Porter?" Flynn asked, cutting to the chase and trying to get straight to the truth of the matter.

"The town council wants to host a silent auction to benefit the kids."

"And that bothers you because . . . ?"

"They're interested in using the house."

"I still don't see the problem."

"*Our* house."

"The one in town?"

"Yes."

"Now I see the problem," Flynn responded, and Porter could picture him pacing his campsite, dusty boots leaving tracks in the dry earth. Cowboy hat in his free hand. Frown-line between his brows. He looked more like their father than any of them, but had their mother's personality. Thoughtful. Slow to speak. Diplomatic.

"I ran by the place today. It's a train wreck. Clementine thinks the town will be willing to step in and clean it out, but I think the job is going to take a little more than a few extra hands."

"I don't know, Porter. A few extra hands can accomplish a lot," Flynn responded. "Why do they want to host the auction there?"

"I haven't bothered asking."

"Maybe you should. If there's a good reason, it might be worth it to get the help cleaning the place out."

"I didn't know cleaning it out was on our agenda."

"We've been talking about selling the property for years. This might be the right time to do it," Flynn said.

"I hope you're kidding."

"Why would I be?"

"Because we have enough to deal with. We don't need to add anything else to the mix."

"If Sunday doesn't improve, we're going to need money for her long-term care. The insurance payout will help, but it's not going to be enough for twenty or thirty years' worth of medical intervention."

"The proceeds from selling the house won't be, either," Porter pointed out.

"It'll be something. Which is a hell of a lot better than the nothing we're currently getting from that place."

He had a point.

Which only added to Porter's pissed-off mood.

He took a deep breath, shoved aside the rage, because he wasn't ever going to be his father's son. He'd decided that the day he'd walked into the kitchen and seen the bruises on his mother's arms. He'd been seven. Just old enough to understand that he was seeing the reason why she wore long pants and long-sleeved shirts all summer long, but still too young to question her when she'd told him she'd bumped into the doorknob.

Doorknobs didn't leave fingerprints.

And good men didn't let their rage hurt the people around them. He kept a lid on his.

"So you want me to talk to the town council?" Porter asked, keeping his voice calm and the words neutral. "See what they have to say about the silent auction?"

"If you'd rather not, I can. Either way, it needs to be done."

"I'll handle it," he said, because he was there, and they were talking about family. And, always, *always* family was the most important thing.

"Thanks, Porter. I'll be there next weekend."

"Unless the cows drop more calves?" he joked.

"Even if they do. See you then."

"Right." He disconnected and slipped the phone into his pocket. The moon had risen an hour ago, low in the sky and nearly full. Thanks to the work Clementine had done, he could see it through the orchard canopy. She'd trimmed back the trees, pulled up weeds and undergrowth, and revealed straight rows, carefully planted decades ago. Soon, leaves would sprout on the barren branches. Flowers would bud and bloom. In the fall, there'd be glossy apples peeking out from between green leaves.

And, God willing, Sunday would be better.

He frowned, moving through the orchard and into the field beyond. The tractor was a hundred yards away, abandoned in the middle of the half-plowed acreage, a toolbox sitting beside it.

He opened the lid, eyeing the mismatched, rusted contents.

"Not very pretty, are they?" Clementine called from the fence line.

"What are you doing out here?" he asked, closing the lid and watching as she walked toward him. Glided toward him?

He supposed it was a trick of the moonlight and the flowy light-colored sweater she wore, but she seemed to float above the rich, dark soil.

"I was working on the tractor. Then I heard you talking to your brother and decided I had some pressing business to attend far away from your conversation."

"In other words, you were trying not to eavesdrop?"

"Exactly." She opened the toolbox and took out a screwdriver. "Now, I'm going to get back to work."

"You do realize it's after midnight, right?"

"I couldn't sleep, and the tractor was riding rough this afternoon. I figured this was as good a time as any to take a look."

She pulled a flashlight from the pocket of her sweater

and trained it on the tractor's engine. "I think I know what the problem is. It's just a matter of fixing it."

"Here. Let me." He slipped the light from her hand, training it on the engine as she worked.

"You know," she said, poking at something with the screwdriver, "sound travels far on nights like this. When the air is dry and cool with winter, whispers can carry on the breath of a night breeze and land in the ear of a sleeping man."

"Is that your way of telling me you heard my conversation?" he asked, amused by the wording. Intrigued by her.

Surprised by both.

"How'd you guess?" She grinned, the beam of the flashlight illuminating her smooth skin and dark hair, softening the angle of her jaw and her cheekbones, turning her interesting features into something so beautiful his breath caught and his heart stopped.

She was a woman dressed in flannel pajamas, knee-high waders, and a calf-length white sweater, for God's sake. No makeup. No fancy hairstyle. Just curls caught up in a twist near her nape and dark lashes long enough to cast shadows on her cheeks.

"Just that intuitive, I guess," he responded, and maybe she heard something in his voice, a hint of the sudden hot desire pulsing through his blood.

She straightened, pulling her sweater closed around green and red flannel.

"This probably *isn't* the right time to be doing this," she said, setting the screwdriver in the toolbox.

"Are we still talking about fixing the tractor?" he asked, dropping the beam of light so it was aimed at the ground.

"What else is there?"

"Two people standing in the moonlight," he said. "Trying to fix themselves."

"That's an odd thing to say, Porter." She laughed, the sound hollow and humorless.

"Maybe, but it's also the truth, right? You're trying to fix whatever broke inside you when your marriage ended. I'm trying to make amends for a past I had no control over."

"Nothing broke when my marriage ended," she responded, her voice even and controlled, every word carefully enunciated.

"Not even your heart?"

She snorted. "God! No! My heart wasn't nearly as involved as it probably should have been."

"That's an odd thing to say, Clementine."

She smiled. "Touché. Come on. It's cold out here. If we're going to chat, we may as well do it on the way to my place. Unless you think one of the kids is going to make a grand escape while you're away. If you do, feel free to head back inside."

"I've alarmed all the doors and windows. If one of them tries to leave, I'll know it."

"You're kidding."

"Not even close," he said, pulling his phone out and typing in the code for the security system.

"See this?" He held it so she could see the green lights indicating alarm systems in every window and door of the house. "It's fairly simplistic but effective. The alarm is tripped when the circuit is broken. If that happens, my phone will buzz, one of these green lights will be red, and—"

"One of the kids will be in trouble."

"Lockdown for a week. No electronics. No television. No hanging with friends."

"You explained the rules to all of them?"

"In detail. Several times. I needed to make sure they

understand. There's not much worse than being punished for breaking a rule you didn't know existed."

"Did that happen often when you were a kid?" she asked as she led the way across the field. She'd left an exterior light on at the rancher, and he could see it glowing through the darkness, guiding the way back.

"When I was a kid, we got punished for breathing too loudly," he said, keeping his tone light and his body relaxed.

He didn't talk about his past.

Not to his brothers or friends or, even, his lovers.

"I'm sorry, Porter. No kid should grow up that way."

"That's why my brothers and I are determined to make this situation as easy as we can for the kids."

"But it's getting old, right? And tiring? You've made lives for yourselves and are having to put them on hold while you figure out what's best for six kids you barely know?"

"If you heard my conversation, you know that I think it's time to start planning for a future that . . ." *doesn't have Sunday in it.*

It's what he wanted to say.

What he planned to say.

He couldn't get the words out.

Saying them out loud would feel too much like quitting on his sister-in-law and his nieces and nephews. Too much like giving up hope.

Clementine nodded, unlocking her front door and opening it. "Words have a lot of power, Porter, and I'm glad you didn't speak those."

"Eventually, they'll have to be said," he responded, his voice gritty with emotions he wasn't used to feeling. He lived his life the way he wanted, made his money playing protector to people who could afford his services.

He made friends.

He dated.

He enjoyed life.

But he kept his relationships light and his commitments lighter.

He knew how easy it was to hurt someone, and he didn't ever want to be responsible for the kind of pain his father had caused.

"Maybe they'll have to be said." She touched his cheek, her fingers cool and rough from the work she'd been doing. "Maybe not. Let's wait and see what time does."

"Are you always this philosophical?"

"No one spends fifteen years with a man like my father without learning to talk like a philosopher." She stepped into the house. "I guess I've put off the inevitable long enough. Time to face my demons."

"Are they that bad?"

"Only when my house smells like cigarettes and cheap cologne," she responded, her eyes tired, her face pale.

"It still smells like that?"

"It did when I came in from the field. It was probably my imagination, though."

"Want me to come in? Go through the house with you and make sure it's empty?"

"It's empty," she said, offering a tired smile. "And it's late. Go home and get some sleep. Church tomorrow should be . . . fun."

"You say that like I should be afraid."

"Not afraid. Just . . . prepared. Is Rosie going with you?"

"I hope to God she is," he muttered, imagining himself dragging six kids through the doors of God's house. All of them dressed like paupers and screaming at the top of their lungs.

"Do you want an extra pair of hands?"

"Are you offering?"

"Only if there are no other options."

"You're not big on church?"

"I'm not big on being in the same building as a bunch of people who think I'm on par spiritually with serial killers." She smiled. "But, if you find out Rosie won't be there, give me a call. I'll sacrifice myself for the sake of your sanity."

She closed the door before he could ask questions.

Which was fine.

He already knew the story.

He'd done a background check when he'd found out she was living on the farm, made some phone calls, talked to the local sheriff. He knew about the baby found outside the local chocolate shop and about Clementine's role in the story. She'd harbored the young couple who'd given birth to and then abandoned the newborn. According to the sheriff, Clementine hadn't known what the couple intended. After the baby had been found, she hadn't had the heart to turn in the teenage mother. She hadn't been charged with a crime, but her willingness to keep silent had probably turned a lot of people against her.

He waited until the lock clicked and the bolt slid home, and then he did a circuit of the house, making sure the windows were closed and locked, the curtains and shades shut. Her ex had seemed innocuous enough, but that meant just about nothing. He'd seen men who'd looked like Mr. Rogers pull guns.

The exterior was unremarkable. No sign of forced entry. No footprints near the windows, broken branches in the shrubbery near the back deck, no cut screens or jimmied locks. Nothing to indicate that Simeon had tried to gain entry to the house.

Still, Porter felt uneasy.

The house had been built in the sixties, and the windows and the doors were old, the locks easy to pop. If he'd wanted to, he could have made entry in thirty seconds flat.

He didn't think Simeon was quite that skilled, but he'd call in a favor and get a friend in the LAPD to run a background check.

Just to be sure.

Because playing it safe with people who mattered was what he did best. And, after the day from hell he'd had, it was good to be reminded of that.

Chapter Four

She was losing her mind.

There was no other explanation for the fact that she'd smelled cigarettes and cologne every time she walked into the house for the past week.

Clementine scowled, tossing her keys onto the kitchen table and opening the window above the sink. Cold, damp air wafted in, carrying a hint of winter snow and spring rain.

To anyone else it wouldn't have meant much.

To her, it heralded the beginning of planting season.

She'd spent countless hours in the fields tilling and prepping the soil. She'd fixed the tractor so many times, her hands ached from the effort of torquing screws and turning wrenches. She'd worked a week of twenty-hour days, doing the job of five people alone.

God, she was tired.

That had to be the reason her brain was playing tricks on her. And it had to be doing that, because there was no way Sim was still hanging around Benevolence.

Was there?

She frowned, staring out at the cobalt sky, her heart

thumping uncomfortably in her chest. She needed to eat something. That might help, but she hadn't had the time or the inclination to go to the store.

She grabbed the coffeepot, frowning at the grounds sitting in the bottom of it. She usually rinsed it out before she left the house in the morning.

"You really are losing it, Clem," she muttered, digging through the cupboards, trying to find the last of the coffee.

She'd had enough for one more pot.

Hadn't she?

Someone knocked on the door, and she jumped, reaching for a knife before she thought it through, heading into the living room, her heart still doing that crazy *thud-thud-thud*.

"Who is it?" she growled, looking through the peephole, expecting to see Sim or some boogeyman waiting to pounce.

"Porter," was the response. She could clearly see that it was. He'd stepped into the porch light, hands shoved into the pockets of his coat, a shadow of a beard on his chin.

"Hold on." She slid the bolt, unlocked the door, and opened it.

"Is everything okay?" she asked, because aside from waving at him across the field or watching as he pulled down the driveway with one kid or another in the old red van, she hadn't seen him since the previous Saturday.

"Maybe I should be the one asking that question." He took the knife from her hand and set it on the coffee table. "What's wrong?"

"Nothing a cup of coffee and some food won't fix," she lied, because she wasn't going to admit that she kept smelling Sim's signature scent in the house.

"You've been working too hard, and if I hadn't had six little hellions to deal with, I'd have been over here a couple

of days ago telling you to stop." He opened the coat closet
and pulled out her wool duster coat. "Let's go."

"Where?"

"For food and coffee."

"I'm too tired to move."

"You don't have to." He draped the coat around her
shoulders, pulling the heavy fall of her hair out from the
collar. His hands seemed to linger for a moment longer
than necessary, his fingers sliding through the thick strands,
then brushing staticky pieces from her cheek.

"Sim never helped me with my coat," she somehow
managed to say. Out loud.

Damnit all.

Because she didn't want to talk about Sim and his failures.
She didn't want to think about her willingness to accept less
than what she'd longed for.

She didn't want to meander down memory lane while
Porter stared into her eyes.

"Forget I said that," she said hurriedly.

But, of course, the words wouldn't just go away. They
stayed. Floating in the air. Lingering like the scent of nicotine or the feeling of a thousand regrets.

"We've already established Sim is an ass," Porter responded
gruffly. "Wait here. I'll get my SUV and drive it over."

He walked outside before she could tell him not to
bother.

It would have been easy enough to follow him onto the
porch, tell him that she really didn't think going somewhere
with him was a good idea. Because, sure, she was tired, but
she also knew better than to tempt herself with chocolate,
good wine, or sappy love stories.

She couldn't resist any of them.

And, it seemed she couldn't resist dreaming either.

About all those silly things she'd thought she'd have with Sim. Companionship, love, forever. She couldn't resist thinking about having her own sappy love story. One where the guy treated her like an equal but still helped her with her coat.

She could spend all day in the fields, all evening planting, all the hours that were left pulling or spinning fleece. Her mind never once went to love stories or forevers unless Porter was around.

He was a vice she couldn't afford, a habit she didn't intend to foster. She knew better than to tempt herself.

But, there she was—standing in her coat, waiting for him to return.

She carried the knife into the kitchen, closed the window and made another quick search of the cupboards, looking for the coffee she was sure she still had.

She was searching the pantry when the doorbell rang.

"Come in!" she shouted.

Seconds later, Porter entered the kitchen, looking just as wonderful as he had five minutes prior.

God!

She really needed to stop noticing.

"Looking for something?" he asked, the scent of pine needles and winter fires drifting on the air as he approached. Two of her favorite aromas, because there was nothing quite as wonderful as sitting under the stars, a bonfire going and a book in hand, firelight playing over the pages.

"Just coffee. I was sure I had some left," she responded, pretending she hadn't noticed how good he looked, how wonderful he smelled, or how happy she felt to see him.

She shouldn't be happy.

She should be indifferent. That's where safety lay.

Hadn't she just reminded herself how important it was

to *not* allow herself to be tempted by things she couldn't resist?

Of course, she had!

So, indifference needed to be her reaction.

"Did you check the trash?"

"Why would I keep it there?"

"Not keep it, Clementine. Toss away the empty package. If you finished off what was left, that's what you'd have done."

"Right. I hadn't thought about that." Because she'd been certain she hadn't emptied the bag. She opened the trash can lid, and there it was. The empty package.

"I guess I did use the last of it," she said, trying desperately to remember doing it.

"We can pick up more while we're out."

"About that." She turned to face him, realized he'd moved close. Really close. So close she could have stepped an inch closer and been in his arms.

"What?"

"Us going out. Together. It's probably not a good idea."

"Why not?"

"Well, because . . ." She wracked her brain and couldn't think of a thing.

"Look, if you're worried about what people are going to think, don't."

"I'm not worried about that."

"Then what are you worried about?"

"Just . . . forgetting that I'm only here for a little while and that you're only here to help with your nieces and nephews."

"Why do we need to remember? Can't we just enjoy a nice dinner, a quiet walk? No screaming kids or breaking tractors? No meetings at the school or panicked trips to urgent care?"

"Urgent care? Is someone sick?"

"Moisey sliced her finger on a tin can. No stitches necessary. Just a few dabs of glue and a pretty pink bandage. Three hours and many tears later, and she's settled into the easy chair, watching movies with the rest of the gang. Rosie has her sister, Peg, over for the night, and they thought it would be good for me to get out for a while. Apparently, hovering over the kids and questioning every move they make isn't going to keep them safe."

"So you've been banished," she said, and he smiled sheepishly.

"I wasn't going to put that name to it, but . . . yeah."

"Rosie and Peg are right, you know," she said, grabbing her purse and hitching it over her shoulder, because she needed to avoid temptation, but she couldn't make herself refuse his request. "It's impossible to keep bad things from happening."

"True, but we can lower the risk by taking precautions."

"What kind of precautions were you planning to take? Because from what I've seen of the farmhouse, it's pretty kid safe. Sunday was big on making sure of that."

"My plan," he said as they stepped outside, "was to cover the kids in Kevlar and bubble wrap and forbid them from leaving the house. Unfortunately, that would require home-schooling, and I'm not sure any of us would survive it."

"Kevlar and bubble wrap?" She laughed, the cold air and deep blue sky filling her with the kind of pleasure she hadn't felt in a long time.

Or, maybe, it was the company that was doing that.

Careful, her mind whispered.

Her fickle heart cheered enthusiastically.

"Hey, I'm not saying I would have followed through on the plan. I was just thinking out loud while I was unsticking Milo's hands. He superglued them together while he was building a model. Rosie called for reinforcements right around the time I mentioned Kevlar. Since Peg lives in town, it didn't take her long to arrive. Next thing I knew, I was being shipped out for some fresh air and thinking time."

"Is that what they said?" she asked, still laughing, her heart thudding happily while her mind screamed that she had better watch what she was doing, because Porter was a likeable guy. And likeable was a whole hell of a lot more dangerous than sexy.

Of course, he was sexy, too. Damn him. Handsome. Smart.

And, leaning toward her, those silvery eyes the color of moonlight on a frozen lake.

"You should laugh more often, Clementine," he murmured, his lips brushing hers. Gently. Sweetly. Asking not one thing of her. Just giving. A benediction. A whisper of things that might be.

She didn't speak when he pulled away.

She *couldn't*, because all the words she'd collected over the years, all the stories, the myths and legends and lore, none of them were as right as the silence that filled the space between.

He opened the door of a dark SUV, helped her into the passenger seat, and kissed her one more time. Just as gently. Just as sweetly.

"What was that for?" she asked.

"You," he said as he closed the door.

Just that.

You.

As if one simple word could explain everything.

Kissing her had probably been a mistake.

Probably?

Definitely. Absolutely. For sure.

It *had* been, but Porter couldn't make himself regret it. Not as he drove to the diner. Not as they walked through the nearly empty restaurant, took their seats, ordered food, and ate it. Not for one minute of the time they spent together.

And now . . .

Now, as they walked along Main Street, passing dark, silent shops and empty parking lots, all he could do was think about repeating it.

Again and again and again.

It was her smile. The easy way her lips curved when she was amused. Her unrestrained laughter. Her unself-conscious pleasure in the starry sky and the chilly spring breeze.

Or maybe it was the curly mass of hair that fell loose almost to her waist. The unconscious sway of her hips as she moved.

She was beautiful, and she didn't know it, and maybe that was it most of all. The thing that made him want to take her in his arms and prove just how desirable she was.

"This is a pretty little town," she said as they walked past Chocolate Haven, its picture windows displaying beautiful white boxes wrapped in colorful ribbons. "I didn't notice when I was here before."

"You were probably distracted," he suggested, and she shrugged.

"Maybe. Sim and I were trying to get his business up and running. That required a lot of time and energy."

"*His* business?" he asked, but he already knew the answer. His friend had run the criminal background check on Simeon Galloway. The guy had no criminal record, but his name was affiliated with half a dozen defunct businesses and a bankruptcy that had happened three years before he'd married Clementine.

"*Our* business. We were planning to open an online shop that sold high-quality homespun wool and fleece yarn. He got the idea from watching me spin wool. It's a hobby I picked up when I was a kid."

"That's an interesting hobby." And unusual, but then, everything about Clementine was atypical. Her clothes. Her hair. Her knowledge of farm equipment and planting seasons.

She was a beautiful package of eclectic skills.

Skills that, in Porter's opinion, Sim had tried using to his advantage.

"Not if you grow up like I did," she said. "Anyway, spinning the wool was the easy part of the business. I had to find wool and fleece suppliers until we were able to purchase property to raise our own sheep and alpaca. That's not as easy as it seems. We wanted organic, and there are only a few places that offer that."

"You mean Sim wanted organic?"

"Well, yes, but I agreed it was a good idea. People love to know they're getting healthy, wholesome products. Even if it's product they're wearing."

"So you spent a lot of time tracking down organic alpaca fleece and sheep wool, spinning it into yarn, and readying it for sale."

"Not just spinning. The product is raw, straight from the animal. I washed and carded it to prep it for spinning. It's a long and involved process."

"And Sim did what? Spent time on the property in Idaho?"

She stopped, her eyes blazing in the darkness. "The purchase of that land isn't common knowledge, Porter. How did you know about it?"

"I like to know who I'm dealing with."

"*Dealing with?* Is that what you call what we're doing?"

she asked, a hint of something that sounded like hurt in her voice.

"I call what we're doing getting to know each other," he responded. "I call keeping an eye on your ex dealing with him."

"Why would you be keeping an eye on Sim?" she demanded.

"Because he's a jackass, and I don't trust him," he responded honestly.

"You met him once."

"Once was plenty."

She smiled. "I wish I'd thought that the day he subbed for my Anthropology of Ancient Worlds class," she said. "It would have saved me a hell of a lot of time and aggravation."

"How long were you two married?"

"You don't already know?"

"Actually, I do, but I didn't want to ruin a perfectly good date by pissing you off more than I already have."

"Is that what this is?" she asked, walking again, her hands shoved into her pockets. "A date?"

"Is that what you want it to be?"

"What I want, Porter, is for my life to go back to the way it was before I married Sim. I want to teach at the college and go home to a simple little house on a tiny little lot, and I want to be happy with what I have instead of always wanting more. Simplicity is the beginning of freedom. My dad used to say that all the time. I finally understand what he meant."

"Funny," he said, dropping his arm around her shoulders, because she looked cold and tired and too lonely for his liking, "my mother used to say something similar. Christmas morning would come, and we'd each have one present under the tree. Picture books that she'd made herself because she couldn't stand the thought of us getting nothing. Which is what my father would have preferred. We'd sneak downstairs, and she'd be sitting in the rocking chair staring at the tree, looking sad as hell, but she'd always smile when she saw us, hand us our presents and say, *They're just simple things, boys, but simple things are the best kinds*."

"Porter," Clementine began, but he shook his head.

"Don't feel sorry for me, Clementine."

"I don't."

"Liar."

"I feel sorry for the boy you were. I don't feel sorry for the man you've become. You turned out a lot better than Sim, and his parents would have given him the moon if he'd asked."

"How about yours?"

"My dad taught me a million skills, but the only present he ever gave me was a beaded deerskin dress and a pair of beaded moccasins made and worn by my great-great-great grandmother. She was the first storyteller in the family. I'll probably be the last. Unless one of my nieces or nephews shows up on my doorstep asking to learn the ancient tales." She smiled, but there was an edge of sadness in her voice. "Anyway, I used to keep the dress and moccasins in a box on the top shelf of my closet. One day, I wore them to a lecture on Native lore. The guy who was presenting pulled me aside after class and asked if I knew how much they were worth."

"Did you?"

"I didn't care. They were priceless to me, but apparently there's a lot of intrinsic value in Native artifacts. Fifty-thousand dollars' worth back then. They're worth a few thousand more now."

"You still keep them in your closet?"

"No!" She laughed. "They're in a safe deposit box. Along

with my engagement ring. Which is also worth a small fortune. It belonged to Sim's grandmother. A three-carat mine-cut diamond surrounded by sapphires and pearls."

"Sounds . . . fancy." And not exactly the kind of engagement ring he would have given a woman like Clementine. An opal was more her style. Or turquoise. Tiger's eye. A stone that was earthy and warm. Set in a platinum band engraved with the symbol for eternity.

"It is. I wore it maybe three times. Then I bought a fake diamond ring and put the real engagement ring in the safe deposit box."

"You're sure it's still there?" he asked, because he couldn't imagine a guy like Sim not selling a valuable piece of jewelry.

"Why wouldn't it be?"

"Sim likes to spend money. Even when it's not his. I imagine if he thought he could sell your things, he'd do it without a second thought. Especially since he still probably views the engagement ring as his property."

"It's not. According to my divorce lawyer." She twirled a piece of hair around her finger. "But you're right. Sim probably does think the ring is his. Fortunately, he doesn't have access to the box."

"You're sure?"

"About as sure as anyone can be about anything."

"Who's listed as co-lessor?"

"Just my mother. Why?"

"Is she able to access it without you being present?"

"My mother would never steal from me, if that's what you're implying."

"I'm not implying anything. I'm asking, because people are prone to get away with what they can. If Sim could convince someone who looked like you or your mom to play along, all he'd have to do was get a fake ID, get a copy of the key, and send her in to retrieve the items you've stored."

"He wouldn't do that," she said, but he didn't think she believed it.

"What bank are they stored in?"

"Benevolence Federal. I moved them there after I rented the house."

"Does Sim know that?"

"Probably. Now, how about we change the subject? Talking about Sim is ruining my mood."

"We weren't talking about him," he said, shifting the conversation because she wanted him to. "We were talking about simple things, and about how happy they can make us. Those books my mother made? They are still my favorite gifts."

"Did you keep them?"

"The last time I saw them, they were in a box in the attic, hidden away so that my dad wouldn't destroy them like he destroyed everything else I owned."

She didn't say anything.

No questions. No exclamation of sadness. Nothing.

But her arm slid around his waist and she tucked herself in close, soft curves pressed against his side, her hair floating in the cold breeze, tickling his neck and chin.

And, God!

It was just about as perfect as anything had ever been.

He hadn't ever wanted this kind of closeness. He hadn't ever needed it, but he sure as hell enjoyed it. He wasn't sure what that said about him or about Clementine or about what they were together. All he knew was that he'd have walked this path a million times if it meant having her beside him.

They reached the corner of Evergreen and Main, the old wrought iron fence gleaming dully in the streetlight, the house jutting up from behind overgrown hedges. Someone had left a ladder lying in the yard, a riding mower beside it.

Preparation was already underway.

He wasn't sure how to feel about that.

He'd called the mayor two days ago, asked enough questions to understand exactly how important opening the house to the public was going to be. A successful silent auction meant a secure future for Sunday and her kids. The town council wanted to attract bidders from all over the region, men and women who were interested in seeing the legendary opulence of the Lee Harris house and who had pocketbooks deep enough to bid high on a wide variety of items.

A cruise for two offered by Martin and Sheila Crandell.

A year's supply of fudge from Chocolate Haven.

A trip to wine country and a stay in a bed and breakfast.

A hunting excursion. Deep-sea fishing. Day spas and trips to Silver City. The mayor had listed one item after another. Big ticket items and smaller ones. Everything donated by someone in the community.

That had surprised Porter, because it had never occurred to him that anyone in town cared. Sure, they'd attended Matt's funeral and they'd given lip service to grief, but when push came to shove, they were the same people who'd turned their backs on the abuse and neglect he and his brothers had suffered.

In his mind that made them culpable.

But maybe it only really made them human.

After all, Daniel Bradshaw had ruled his home with an iron fist. He'd kept the world out and his family in. He'd never broken bones or bruised faces. He'd never raised his voice in public. He'd put on a good show of being a great husband and father, and Porter couldn't blame people for believing it.

Hell, he'd have believed it if he hadn't lived the truth.

He and his brothers had never said a word to anyone about their father. When they were young, they'd kept his secrets because they were afraid. As they got older, they kept them because they didn't believe anyone in the community cared enough to help.

It was possible they'd been wrong.

It was possible that if they'd given neighbors and community members a chance, things would have changed. Maybe Daniel would have gone to jail and the boys would have been sent to foster homes. Maybe the old house would have been sold and the town would have whispered about the scandal forever after.

Maybe a dozen things would have happened, but he and his brothers had kept their secrets. The town had been ignorant or pretended to be. Daniel had lived and died as a bitter, hateful human being.

And all of that had brought Porter here. Back to the town he'd despised and to the house he'd have been happy to burn to the ground.

"It looks like someone's been working on the place," Clementine said, stopping near the fence and staring into the yard. She looked like she belonged to the house, her long wool coat nipping in at the waist and brushing the top of black leather boots, her face austere and aristocratic. All she needed was a corset, a hooped skirt, and a parasol.

"What?" she said, brushing her hand over her hair and frowning. "Haven't you ever seen curly hair in the wild?"

"In the wild?"

"Free-form? Unconfined? Springing in every conceivable direction?"

He laughed, tugging one of the strands and watching as it sprang back. "I like free-form and unconfined."

"You wouldn't be saying that if you were sleeping next

to it. Sim used to . . ." Apparently, she'd realized what she was saying. "Never mind."

"Why?"

"I wouldn't want to bore you with the details."

"The details sounded pretty interesting to me," he responded, setting his hands on her waist and studying her face. With her hair down, she looked young and sweet and soft.

Hell, she didn't just look soft.

She was soft.

Everything about her. Eyes. Hair. Body.

His gaze dropped to her lips, his hand tightening a fraction as he remembered just how velvety they were. Just how warm and inviting.

"This is not a good idea, Porter," she said, her hands resting on his shoulders, tentative and light, as if she weren't sure whether to push him away or pull him closer.

"I'm pretty sure you've said that before."

"And I meant it as much then as I do now." She sounded scared and vulnerable, nervous and unsure.

Not at all like the woman who could fix tractors, plow fields, and knit dresses out of homespun yarn.

He let his hands drop and took a step away.

"I called the mayor a couple of days ago," he said, watching as her muscles relaxed. "My brothers and I agreed to let the town council use the house for the silent auction. It's planned for the end of the month, so there's a lot of work to do."

"That's fantastic, Porter! It's going be a wild success. I mean, who wouldn't want to visit a place like this?" She turned toward the house again. "Have you been inside?"

"Not yet. I've been a little busy picking suspended kids up at school, changing diapers, keeping teenagers from mauling brothers."

"And bringing crying little girls to urgent care?"

"That, too."

"Well, we're here now. No suspended kids, angry teens, dirty diapers, or cut fingers. Want to check it out?"

He planned to say no.

As far as he was concerned never was too soon to step inside the mansion.

But Clementine looked eager and excited, her eyes gleaming with enthusiasm, and he found himself nodding instead of shaking his head. "Sure."

"You have the key?"

"The mayor put a lockbox on the front door. I have the combination."

"Perfect. Come on." She grabbed his hand, and he could feel the calluses on her fingertips and palms from years of planting fields and spinning wool. He could imagine sitting beside her as she worked, watching as she pulled the fibers into long strands.

Damn. He had it bad.

Whatever *it* was. He didn't know, and he couldn't seem to make himself care.

"How about we make a deal?" he responded, stopping as they reached the cracked driveway and the listing gate.

"What kind of deal?"

"I bring you in the house, and you show me how to spin wool."

She laughed, the sound fading as she met his eyes and realized he was serious. "You're not kidding."

"Why would I be?"

"Because watching someone spin wool is like watching a slug climb a cornstalk. Painfully boring and tedious."

"Is that how you feel about it? Or how Sim feels?"

"I don't give a damn what Sim feels about anything,"

she said, stalking up the driveway, her hair floating in a cloud of curls as she moved.

"But he *was* the one who told you that, right?"

"Does he have to be part of every conversation?"

"Your refusal to answer is answer enough."

"Fine. Yes. He said that. And I can't say he's wrong."

"I can."

"Based on what? Have you ever watched someone spin fibers?"

"No, but I've met Sim. As far as I'm concerned, every word out of his mouth is suspect. So, are you going to show me?"

"Why do you want me to?"

"Because"—he lifted her hand, ran his thumb over the calluses—"I want to know where these came from."

"They came from decades of work, Porter. But I'll show you how to spin if it'll make you happy." She yanked her hand away and walked to the front door.

"You think that was an insult," he commented as he opened the lockbox and retrieved a set of skeleton keys.

He didn't want to go inside.

Everything in him was screaming that he shouldn't.

There were too many memories there, the walls and floor steeped in decades of hatred and fear.

"Wasn't it?" Clementine asked, and he focused his attention on her because that was easier than remembering the past.

"Is it an insult if I tell you that there's not one thing about you that I don't find intriguing? Not your wild hair or your callused hands or the neat way you fit against my side."

"If it is," she said, her eyes wide with surprise, "I can't say I mind."

"Good to know," he responded, edging in close, his

blood hot with the kind of longing that didn't leave room for anything else.

"Porter," she began, her voice husky, her pulse thumping wildly in the hollow of her throat.

"If you're going to tell me this isn't a good idea, you'd better do it quickly, because from where I'm standing it seems like the best idea I've had in years."

She laughed, a little breathless. A little nervous, but she didn't tell him to back off, and he couldn't make himself do it.

He leaned down. Just enough to taste her lips. Once and then again, his left hand splayed against the door near her head, his right hand still clutching the keys.

And then her arms were around him, her hair sliding across his forearms, and he was lost in her touch and in that kiss. The house gone. The memories gone.

All of it fading to make room for this. Whatever it was. Whatever it was going to be. He didn't know, couldn't put a name to it, but right then, standing in the shadow of the house he hated, it was all that mattered.

Chapter Five

Something dropped on the porch floor near her feet, the quiet clank of metal breaking into the foggy haze of desire that had chased every rational thought from Clementine's head.

She ignored it.

Or would have if Porter hadn't pulled back, let cold air seep between them.

"Damn," he whispered, his eyes hot, his fingers still tangled in her hair.

"Where did you come from, Clementine? Because it sure as hell isn't any world I've ever lived in."

He reached down, grabbing the keys he'd dropped.

"And, in case you're wondering," he added, "that wasn't an insult either."

He unlocked the door, pushed it open, and she was still standing silently, all her words gone. Just like they'd been when he'd kissed her before.

"I called to have the electricity turned on," he continued as he stepped inside. "Let's see if the lights are working."

He flicked a switch, illuminating a spacious foyer. She could see it clearly from her position *frozen solid on the front porch*.

"Hey," he said, taking her hand and pulling her across the threshold, "aren't I the one who's supposed to be afraid?"

"It's archaic to think that only men can be commitment phobic," she responded stiffly.

He frowned. "Afraid of the house, Clementine. Not of you or us or whatever you think I was talking about."

Right.

Of course.

The house.

The one he'd grown up in.

The one he'd left and never returned to. Until now.

"Are you?" she asked, her cheeks hot, her lips still tingling from his kiss, but her mind finally functioning again. "Afraid of being here, I mean?"

"I'm embarrassed to admit I thought I would be." He glanced around, the frown still creasing his brow.

"Fear is nothing to be embarrassed by."

"Maybe not, but I was special forces in the military. I faced a lot of dangerous situations and a lot of really terrible people, so being afraid to come home? That's not a comfortable feeling for me."

"Home isn't a place, Porter. It's a feeling. One you have when you're at exactly the right place with exactly the right people."

"Then I guess this isn't home."

"It was once. For someone," she responded, eyeing the stained wallpaper and marble floor, the mahogany banister and curved staircase. "And it will be again, but it might need a little . . . love to get there."

"Love, huh?" He touched the railing as he moved through the space, his fingers trailing through thick layers of dust. "I think it'll take a lot more than that to make this a home. My father bought it because it was a showpiece. He wasn't concerned about warmth or functionality."

"What about your mother? Did she like living here?" she asked, her voice echoing through the cavernous hallway.

The place felt like a museum.

Or a mausoleum.

It sure as heck didn't feel comfortable, happy, or welcoming.

"That's a good question," he responded, opening pocket doors at the end of the hall and stepping into what had probably once been a ballroom. A grand piano stood in one corner, ivory keys peeking out from beneath a torn black cover.

"You never talked about it?" she asked, her heart heavy as she followed him from one huge, nearly empty room to another. If there'd ever been happiness here, the walls hadn't soaked it up. All she felt was sadness, heartache, and regret.

"By the time I was old enough to think about things like that, my mom was dying of cancer. We talked about that and about the fact that she didn't want to leave me and my brothers. We talked about how much she loved us, but we never talked about this house. Or my father." He added the last as if it didn't matter, but she knew it did. She knew that every dusty floor and dark corner was a reminder of the man who'd wanted a showplace more than he'd wanted a home.

They walked through a 1980s kitchen and a huge dining room, stepped through a small parlor and, then, back into the foyer.

"It's just like I remember," Porter said as he headed upstairs. There should be photos on the walls, vases in the built-in niches. Beautiful textiles tossed over comfortable chairs. Meaningful things filling the space.

"This was my room," Porter said, opening one of several doors and stepping inside. There were no overhead lights, no lamps, no moonlight filtering in through the boarded-up windows. It was pitch-black, the space cold and dead feeling.

"Maybe we should come back in the morning," she said, grabbing his arm and tugging him back into the hall. "With the windows boarded up, it's too dark to see anything."

"There's a light in the attic," he responded. "We'll go up there and look around. Then we'll leave. Unless you'd rather go now?"

"I don't mind staying," she lied.

"Good, because you've made me curious. I want to see if the box of books is still there."

"Great. Glad I asked you about that," she muttered, and he laughed.

"It's not that bad, is it?"

"Not compared to a crypt at the cemetery," she replied.

"I'd take a crypt over this place if my father were still around."

"That's one of the saddest things I've ever heard," she said, following him up another flight of stairs. The higher they climbed, the darker it got. She wasn't sure if they were in the attic or just another level of the home.

"My childhood wasn't a happy one. That's for damn sure. Wait here. This place is packed with stuff, and I don't want you to fall."

"And it's okay if you do?" she questioned, but she did as he'd asked, standing still and listening as he moved through the darkness.

She heard the quiet rattle of a chain. Light spilled from a bulb hanging from a ceiling beam, and she realized they *were* in an attic. One stuffed to the rim with things.

"Wow," she said, trying and failing to take it all in. Couches. Love seats. Chairs. Most covered by white sheets. Framed pictures leaning against walls. Lamps. Bed frames. A crib.

"Yeah. It's a lot. None of us wanted to deal with it after our father died, so we carried it up here to keep it safe from renters and left it."

"Is this original to the house?" she asked, pulling a sheet off a Victorian settee. Crushed blue velvet and scrolled wood made it look like a period piece, but she was no expert.

"It could be. I think my mother said the place was furnished when Dad bought it. Which might explain why we were never allowed to sit on the chairs or sofas." He pulled a huge mirror away from the wall. "I hid the box in the floor between the joists. Let's see if it's still there."

She moved closer, watching as he removed a loose board and lifted something from the cavern beneath it.

A shoe box?

She'd expected something bigger.

"Is that it?" she asked, and he nodded, turning the box so she could see the stack of three-by-five cards it contained. Someone had punched holes in the edges of the cards and woven colorful threads through them.

"She made the books out of card stock. I guess she was hoping they would last." He lifted one, smiling a little as he turned the pages. "I don't think she expected any of us to keep them."

He passed her the book, and she studied the first page. A cover sketched with colored pencils. No title. No words. Just a drawing of four cars with smiling faces, puttering along a road, heading somewhere together.

Each page showed the cars on that same road, happy white puffs of exhaust floating from their tailpipes. Mountains in the background. Then the ocean. City skyscrapers. Bridges. Valleys. The cars traveled the globe, the details of each page extraordinary and vivid, words unnecessary, because the cars told the story. Expressions changing with the turn of every page. Joy. Fear. Excitement. Nervousness. Triumph.

"Your mother was very talented," she said, handing him the book and accepting another one. This time, it was the story of a mother cat and her kittens searching for a home. They went to a dilapidated barn, rain falling through the holes in the roof and landing on their scruffy heads. From there, they traveled to an inhospitable church where a lady with a beet-red face and purple curls chased them with a broom. They tried the garbage dump and a fancy house and the culvert beside a road. And, finally, just when the mother cat seemed to have given up hope, found the perfect spot under the porch at a poor man's farmhouse. He fed them scraps of food and they chased away the rats, and on the last page, they were in the house, cuddled together on the hearth in front of a crackling fire.

Home.

The word was etched into the fireplace mantel. The first and only one she'd seen in either book. She could feel the longing in it, and her eyes burned, her throat tightened. She wanted to reach through the pages and into the past, pull Porter and his brothers and their mother out of the mausoleum of a house and into her childhood home. The one filled with the scent of fry bread and incense. The one with mats on the floor for sleeping and roosters prancing outside the windows. The one where food and water and love were the only things necessary for survival.

"Don't cry," Porter said quietly, taking the book from her hand and placing it in the box.

"I'm not crying," she said, sniffing back tears. "Much."

He smiled gently, cupping her jaw and kissing her forehead. There was nothing of the passion and heat she'd felt on the porch. This kiss was warm comfort and friendship, and she didn't think she'd ever felt one just like it. Not from any boyfriend she'd ever had. Certainly not from Sim.

She sniffed again, because thinking about that made her realize how pitiful her search for love had been. Even when she'd thought she'd found it, she'd really only been settling for the holey barn or the inhospitable church or the garbage dump.

"I shouldn't have brought you here. This place sucks the joy out of everyone," Porter said.

"It's not the place. It's that story and what I saw in it. The mother so desperate to find a safe place for her babies. Seeing those drawings was like seeing pieces of your mother's soul."

"She would have left," he said, taking her hand and turning off the light. "If she'd lived."

"Do you really think that?"

"Yes. I found stashes of money after she died. A plastic-wrapped wad of it hidden in a container of flour. A purse filled with coins at the bottom of the dirty clothes hamper. She was a stay-at-home mom, and my dad was a tightwad, but she'd managed to squirrel away nearly a thousand dollars."

"Did you use it to leave town?"

"I brought it to a battered woman's shelter in Spokane. It took me all day to hitchhike there, but if it helped one woman escape her abuser, it was worth it. Come on. Let's get out of here." He turned off the light and tugged her back through the crowded space, the shoe box under his arm.

She could have said something.

She probably should have.

Her childhood had been filled with words spoken by profoundly gifted people. She'd spent summers with her mother, listening to some of the most well-respected philosophers in the country discuss the meaning of life and the pursuit of joy. She'd spent the remainder of the year with her father, soaking in ancient stories and modern lore and advice on how to make her way through the world. He'd brought her to visit tribe elders and faith healers. She'd visited churches and synagogues. She'd heard the best orators and the most passionate spiritual leaders, and she'd tucked bits and pieces of every lecture, meeting, and visit in her heart.

But none of that had prepared her for Porter, for his mother's books, for the oppressive feeling of loss that seemed to emanate from the walls of the home he'd grown up in.

"It will be good to fill this place again," she said as they reached the stairs. "It needs noise and laughter and a little happiness."

"Or to be burned to the ground," Porter added.

"I hope that was a joke," she said, meeting his beautiful eyes. His face was scruffy, his eyes shadowed, the week of caring for his brother's kids obviously taking its toll.

He managed a smile, though. A real one that gleamed in his eyes and softened his face. "I don't have gasoline and a match, if that's what you're worried about."

"I'm worried about making this right," she responded, running her hand over the smooth banister. "Because everything about it is wrong. A house like this should be a happy place. Not a boarded-up relic of what used to be."

"A happy place, huh?"

"You can't imagine that?"

"I can imagine a lot of things," he replied, his gaze dropping to her lips. "Most of them have nothing to do with this place."

"Maybe it's time to change that," she managed to say, her mouth dry, a lot of imaginings filling her head. All of them having nothing to do with the house and everything to do with the man walking down the stairs beside her.

"Maybe, but right now, I'm going to let the town council do its thing and expend my energy and effort on the kids. They deserve and need that a hell of a lot more than this house does."

Clementine and Porter had reached the second landing, and she could see the door to his room and the deep blackness beyond. She could picture lights and fabrics and colors and kids. A vision of what could be.

Her vision. One she had no right to.

This wasn't her house, her past, her life.

She was just passing through on her way to somewhere else.

"Are they going to open the whole place to the public?" she asked.

"From what I understand, yes. They're hiring caterers and a string quartet. The mayor is getting the piano tuned, and he's hiring a concert pianist to play it. The town council even hired a planner to organize the event. From what I've heard, she's planning fairy lights and lit footpaths through the garden, if she can get it cleared. The wisteria and lilac should be blooming by then."

"That sounds magical."

"A hundred dollars a ticket for entry, and it's going to be a black-tie affair. If that's your idea of magical, then I guess it will be."

"I meant the lights and the garden paths, but the event sounds wonderful, too. Will you and your brothers attend?"

"I can't speak for them, but I'll only be there if the right person is with me," he said, and she thought he might ask her to join him. Thought that, just maybe, her trip to somewhere else might take a detour into his arms.

They were on the second landing, and he was studying her face, reading something there that she thought only he could see. Because, she'd never had a man look at her like that—as if the answer to every question he'd ever asked was in her eyes.

The front door flew open, banging against the wall with a crash that shook the foundation of the house and broke the spell that held them there—staring into each other's eyes and faces.

"Get down!" Porter commanded.

And then she was on the floor, not sure how she'd gotten there. Cheek against cool wood. His weight pressing her into the floor, dust tickling her nose and throat.

"What—?" she tried to say.

"Shhhhh," he whispered in her ear.

She nodded, trying to let him know she understood.

It was a mistake. A big one. Her hair dragged across the floor and dust motes danced in the air, coating her lips and her skin. Filling her nose.

She was not going to sneeze.

She wasn't!

She did.

Loudly and with passion.

Which disturbed more dust and made her sneeze again.

And again.

And again.

Feet pounded on the stairs.

Lights flashed, someone screamed, all hell broke loose.

And she was still lying there, doing nothing but sneezing like a damn fool.

If Porter had been carrying his firearm, Randall Custard might be dead. That thought joined a dozen others that were pounding through his mind, the staccato beat of them nearly drowning out the sound of Clementine's sneezes.

He stood, pulling her up with him, his focus on Randall

and the camera flash. One. Two. Three photos in quick succession as the reporter hurried across the landing, his suit-clad body vibrating with excitement.

"Take one more picture, Randall, and I'll toss you and that damn camera into the river," Porter growled, his heart still racing, his blood still pumping adrenaline through his system.

He didn't know who he'd been expecting when the door flew open.

Not his father. That was for sure.

But not Randall, either.

He'd expected trouble, because that's all that had ever visited the house. If he'd been carrying his gun, he'd have probably pulled it, pointed it, maybe even fired it. He didn't know, was glad he hadn't had a chance to find out. Randall was a nuisance, but he sure as hell didn't deserve to die for it.

"You wouldn't dare!" Randall responded, unaware of just how close he'd come to dying.

"Want to test the theory?" Porter growled, lifting the shoe box he'd dropped and tucking it under his arm.

"What I want is to know what you're doing in here," Randall responded, twisting the end of a mustache that made him look like the gatekeeper from *The Wizard of Oz*.

"I was going to ask you the same question," Porter responded, his gaze shifting to a woman who was jogging up the stairs. Maybe midtwenties and just a hair over five foot, she looked like she'd been planning on a nice evening out. Fitted dress that hugged her skinny frame, high heels that would have made any kind of quick escape impossible, and a hat perched precariously on top of her bleached hair.

"What the heck?" she yelled, her gaze darting from Randall to Porter and back again. "Randall, you told me this was going to be the story of the century. You promised

I could write it. You said it would be on the front page of every newspaper in the country by morning!"

"It is. You can. It will be, honey pie."

"Honey pie?" she spat, her eyes narrowing. "Let me tell you something, Randall. I may look like an airheaded floozy, but I'm not one. Everyone in town knows the Bradshaws own this place. Since that," she said, jabbing her finger toward Porter, "is one of the Bradshaws, we obviously didn't stop a break-in. We didn't save millions of dollars' worth of antiques, and the only thing I'm going to be writing is my resignation. You want a coffee girl and gal Friday? Maybe you should pay more than five bucks an hour."

She kicked off her shoes, turned on her heels, and headed back down the stairs.

"Now, wait a minute, Harley," Randall called. "We still have a great story. We caught one of the Bradshaws stealing from his brothers."

"Give me a freaking break," the woman said, tearing the hat from her head and tossing it in his direction. The hair flew with it, landing with a skittering slide at his feet. "That is the stupidest thing I've ever heard. I'm leaving. You can keep the wig. I hate it."

"I offered to pay for you to get your hair bleached," he called as she stomped down the rest of the stairs.

"Take your money and shove it where the sun don't shine," she replied, walking outside and slamming the door.

"I don't think she's happy with her potential for upward mobility in the job," Clementine said between sneezes. "Maybe you should think about that the next time you hire someone, Randall."

"Your observational skills are keen. I've got a job available in investigative reporting if you're interested," Randall responded, lifting the camera and pointing it in her direction.

"Don't," Porter warned.

"What? Women love to see their faces in the news."

"I'd rather see mine on a wanted flyer at the post office," Clementine managed to gasp between sneezes.

Her eyes were watering. Her nose was red.

And somehow she still made Porter smile.

"Is that supposed to be a joke?" Randall asked.

"Just a statement of fact," she replied. "Now, if you'll excuse me, I think I'd better get out of here before I sneeze my head off. Literally." She jogged downstairs, and Porter followed.

"What's in the box?" Randall asked as they reached the front door and stepped outside. "Money that your dad had hidden away? I've heard he was quite the miser. Didn't like to spend any of his hard-earned cash. Didn't trust banks. People say he has hundreds of thousands of dollars hidden in the walls of this house."

"People are stupid," Porter said, and Clementine laughed, the sound harsh and raspy.

Randall didn't seem amused.

"There's a little truth to most stories, Porter, and if you've got money you're trying to steal from your brothers, I'm going to have to call the police."

"Call them," he said, because he wasn't going to stand on the front porch of his father's house arguing. He also wasn't going to tell Randall what was in the box. The contents were no one's business but his own.

"Fine. I will." Randall took out his phone and hurried across the yard, his face a pale oval in the darkness, his mustache shimmering in the streetlight.

"It's glitter," Clementine wheezed, the words ending on a harsh cough.

"What?" he asked, worried about the wheeze, the cough, the tightness in her voice.

"He glitters his mustache. I noticed it the other day. Who does that?" She coughed. Sneezed. Coughed again.

"Clementine. Are you okay?" he asked.

"Dandy," she said, the words raspy, her voice tighter.

"Later we'll have to talk about your definition of that word. Right now, we're going to the hospital."

"Don't be silly. I'm allergic to dust mites. They're probably all over that house," she said. "I'll be fine. I just need my inhaler." She dug in her purse, frowned. "I guess I left it at home."

"Do you actually have one?" he asked, his stomach churning with the same sickening feeling he had every time he walked into Sunday's rehab room. Worry. Fear. Helplessness. The desperate need to *do* something.

"Yes. At least, I did. I haven't had to use it in months."

"We'll get one at the hospital." He took her arm, urged her down the porch stairs, his heart beating with a different kind of fear than what he'd felt when Randall burst into the house.

"I don't need to go to the hospital."

"I hate to agree with a thief," Randall said, striding toward them. "But Porter is right. You do."

"He's not a thief," she argued, the words barely audible, her lips a dusky shade of blue.

"We need an ambulance," Porter said, urging her out of her coat, tossing the dust-covered wool onto the ground, hoping to remove some of the allergens that were closing her airways.

"I already called for one," Randall responded, an unlikely ally in the fight to get Clementine to the hospital.

"I don't need an ambulance," she responded, a hint of doubt in her voice.

That worried Porter as much as her gasping breath and blue-tinged lips.

"What's going on?" Randall's former employee called, stepping out from behind an overgrown bush, a cigarette in her hand. "Is she okay?"

"You've got an EpiPen, Harley, right? For your bee allergy?" Randall asked.

"Geez, yeah," she responded, dropping her cigarette and running toward them.

"Is she anaphylactic? Are you?" she asked, touching Clementine's forehead.

"Not that I know of," Clementine croaked, her voice nearly gone, her eyes swollen, her breath wheezy, raspy, and way too quick.

She was struggling, her eyes glassy, her face pallid, slipping away while they all stood around watching.

"Get out the pen," Porter barked.

"Okay. Okay." Harley pulled a box out of her purse.

"Have you ever used one before?" Porter asked, his hand on Clementine's back. He could feel the quick, tight rise and fall of her shoulders as she struggled to breathe.

"Only on an orange at the doctor's office," Harley said, the sound of sirens nearly drowning out her words.

"Maybe it isn't a good idea," Randall murmured. "If you do it wrong, you could be sued. The ambulance will be here any minute and—"

"Shut up, Randall," Harley said, the EpiPen out of the box and held tight in her trembling hand. "I just need to take off the cap."

"One of my nieces uses an EpiPen. I can do it," Clementine said, the words strangled and soft, her movements swift as she grabbed the device and flipped open one end. She slammed it into her thigh, holding it there as she continued to gasp for breath.

"Five, six, seven, eight," Harley counted out loud.

"This isn't a dance, Harley," Randall snapped.

"Nine, ten. Done," she finished.

Clementine nodded, pulling the pen away and trying to smile.

"That should do it," she gasped, and then she crumbled, her hair puddling onto overgrown grass as she fell.

Porter caught her, the shoe box falling as he lowered her the rest of the way to the ground.

Her eyes were closed, her lips blue.

She was still and silent and less animated than Porter had ever imagined she could be.

"Is she breathing?" Randall asked, lifting the camera as if he thought he'd take a picture.

"Yes, but you won't be if you snap a photo," Porter responded, resting his hand on Clementine's sternum. She *was* breathing. Shallowly, air whistling through her constricted airways.

"Should we try rescue breathing?" Harley asked, kneeling beside him, her finger probing Clementine's neck, searching for her carotid artery.

"Not if the air isn't going to get through," he responded, worried that the EpiPen hadn't worked, that she'd stop breathing, that the ambulance would arrive too late.

"There's the ambulance," Randall cried, pointing to the corner of the street and the vehicle that was speeding toward them. "I'll wave them in."

He sprinted toward the road.

Porter stayed where he was. Hand still on Clementine, his body humming with adrenaline and fear and worry. Everything inside him, everything he was, willing her to keep breathing.

God, if only wanting something were enough to make it happen! Matt would be alive. Sunday would be healed. The kids would be back in the sweet embrace of their nuclear family. And he'd be in LA. Doing his job. With no idea that Clementine existed.

He frowned, his hand resting just over her heart. He could feel it thumping frantically, skittering in her chest like a wild colt. Her muscles were taut. Shoulders. Pectorals. Neck. He'd have tried to knead the tension from them, but he was afraid if he lifted his hand, her heart would stop, her breathing would cease, and she'd be gone.

"Are you trying to clear my chakra?" she gasped, her eyes still closed.

"Your what?" he asked, not because he hadn't heard her. Because he wanted to keep her talking. If she was talking, she was breathing. If she was breathing, she was alive.

And alive was a hell of a lot better than the alternative.

"My chakra, because if you are, don't bother. My mother attempts it every time we're together, and it hasn't worked yet. All I really need is to get the rest of the dust mites out of my lungs." She hadn't opened her eyes, but he thought her breathing was easing, the effort to inhale and exhale less labored.

"Your mother tries to clear your chakra?"

"She's a yogi. Very into energy healing and a little disappointed that I haven't followed in her footsteps. Not that she'd ever admit it." She coughed, and he could feel it rattling deep in her chest.

"I'd like to meet your mother."

"Why? You need your chakra cleared?" she asked, her muscles relaxing. He could feel that the same way he could feel her breath deepening, her frantic heartbeat slowing. Everything in her softening.

"I want to understand a little more about where you come from," he responded.

"You don't have to meet my mom to understand that. I

come from the heart. That's almost always my motivating force," she replied.

"And when it isn't?"

"Probably a place of loyalty. It's my Achilles heel. As evidenced by my ten-year marriage to Sim." She sighed. "Oh well. At least I can say I always have good intentions. Although, we all know where those lead."

"It's been more wittily than charitably said that hell is paved with good intentions; they have their place in heaven, too," he quoted.

"Robert Southey?"

"That's right."

"Should I assume that you're into English poetry?"

"I was into a girl in high school who was. I memorized enough to impress her for two semesters of high school English, but she went to the prom with Ryan Miller."

She smiled. Just like he'd hoped she would.

He could have said more.

He could have told her that he hadn't attended senior prom, that he hadn't even wanted to. By the time his peers were dressing in their tuxes and sneaking alcohol into the prom venue, he'd already graduated and was in boot camp in Florida.

Yeah. He could have said a lot. Maybe he would have. To keep her talking and alert. But the EMTs were running toward her, telling him to back off so they could work, putting an oxygen mask on her face, and lifting her onto a gurney.

She said something.

He wasn't sure what.

Too much noise, too much activity. One minute she was lying on the ground with three medics tending to her. The next, she was being carried away, her dark hair spilling over the side of the gurney and trailing through the dead leaves that littered the yard.

He waited until the ambulance pulled away, and then grabbed the shoe box, sprinted back to the diner, jumped into his SUV, and headed for the hospital.

Chapter Six

Clementine was dancing. Whirling through the house, her long skirt sweeping across dark wood floors, photos and paintings and textiles going in and out of focus as she moved to the rhythm of a slow minuet. Candlelight or firelight or fairy lights shimmered in the corners of the room.

She didn't know which.

She didn't care.

Because she was there, twirling through color and texture and life. Laughing as she stared into silvery blue eyes, leaned into a broad chest and strong arms. Breathless. Dizzy. Excited. Because he was there. She was. Pressed close to one another. That was all that mattered.

He was all that mattered.

The one-in-a-million love. The kind that wasn't supposed to happen but when it did, always lasted.

Always.

Because it was meant to be.

Like dandelions in bright green lawns.

Like crickets at the end of summer.

Like sunrise and sunset and oceans' ebb and flow.

Like mother cats and their babies curled up in front of crackling fires.

"Is she dead?" someone whispered. A boy from the sound of it.

She looked around, trying to find him.

But the minuet had ended, and she was alone, standing in Porter's pitch-black room.

"Don't be an idiot. Do you think we'd be allowed in here if she were?" someone else hissed.

"Don't call me an idiot!" the boy shouted.

"Shhhhhh," a little girl said. "I can't wake her up if you're yelling."

"You're not going to wake her up. She's dead. Just like Dad. They only let us come to the hospital to see her because you were crying so much. After we go, they're going to pack her in a coffin and bury her in the ground."

"Shut up, dweeb!"

"Shhhhh!" the little girl said again. "I need to concentrate."

Cool palms pressed against Clementine's cheeks. Warm breath fanned her face. She smelled bubble gum and grape soda and tried desperately to open her eyes, but she was trapped somewhere between dreams and consciousness and she couldn't break free.

"This is when it's going to happen," the little girl intoned. "I'm going to will my energy into her. Every last bit of it. Just like in that book I got from the library where the boy is dying and his friend puts hands on him and gives him her energy, and he lives. Only I'm not going to die like she did. I'm going to live in the shadow land of dreams and find Mom there and bring her back home."

She took a deep breath, and Clementine could swear she felt something. Not just the inhalation of breath. The expulsion of power, drifting through cool palms and warm skin, sliding through sluggish blood, drifting languidly to her heart in quick, bright pulses of energy.

Her eyes flew open.

She was in a bed.

In a hospital.

Bright light above her blocked by Moisey Bradshaw's face.

The little girl's eyes were squeezed shut, her hands still resting on Clementine's face. Behind her the other Bradshaw children huddled together, standing tensely at the foot of the bed, their gazes focused on their sister.

"Don't miss me too much when I'm gone," Moisey murmured, her afro glittering with dozens of firefly clips. "And don't let them bury me even though it might look like I'm dead, because I'll only be wandering through dreams."

"I don't think your mother would want you to do that, sweetie," Clementine said. "The dreamworld can be a dangerous place for mortals."

Moisey's eyes opened, and for a split second Clementine thought she could see straight into the little girl's fiery soul.

"I did it," Moisey breathed, her hands smoothing Clementine's hair, patting her cheeks, tugging a blanket up under her chin.

"I did it!" she repeated, turning to her siblings, her arms stretched wide in joyful celebration, a bright pink bandage wrapped around her right index finger.

"No, you didn't," Heavenly said bluntly, Oya balanced on her scrawny hip. She glanced at Clementine. "Did she?"

"Well," she hesitated, not wanting to crush Moisey's spirit or destroy her dreams, but not wanting to say something that wasn't absolutely the truth. Sure, she'd thought she'd felt something—little zips of energy that could have been anything or nothing—but she'd also been on the verge of waking up before Moisey touched her.

"I *did*!" Moisey broke in excitedly. "And now I'm going to do the same with Mom!"

She darted for the door, but Clementine managed to snag her sweater and yank her back to the bed.

"Not so fast, hun. You can't wander around without an adult." She stood carefully, still holding onto Moisey, testing her legs, because she remembered the dusty floor, the struggle for breath, her muscles giving out.

Porter.

Quoting poetry and saying he wanted to meet her mother.

Which should have been an easy thing to brush off or ignore or even agree to, but Clementine had had to go and get philosophical about things.

I come from the heart?!

She'd sounded like her mother. On steroids. After spending three months in a naturalist commune.

She scowled, pulling the cannula from her nose and grabbing her purse from a table beside the bed. She remembered part of the ambulance ride to the hospital. She remembered being given another shot of epinephrine. She remembered hearing something about twenty-four-hour observation.

But she didn't remember falling asleep.

She sure as heck didn't remember agreeing to have all six of the Bradshaw kids dropped off in her room. Heavenly, Oya, Milo, Maddox, Twila, and Moisey. They were all there, eyeing her as suspiciously as she was eyeing them.

She'd been their babysitter plenty of times before the whole baby Miracle thing. She knew how often and how easily they could find trouble.

She also knew how big their hearts were, how deeply they loved, and how lost they must be without their mother.

She opened her arms and four of the six walked into them.

Heavenly, of course, stayed back.

She was the newest member of the family, the oldest,

and the most reluctant to let her feelings show. She was also
the most likely to keep the others in line. Despite her desire
to come off as tough, gruff, and rebellious, she had a strong
desire to be part of a family.

"I'm a little afraid to ask how you all got here," Clementine said, kissing each of the kids on the top of the head
before stepping away.

"Rosie and her sister brought us," Twila offered. "Uncle
Porter said they could."

"Because Moisey was crying and sobbing and yelling
because she eavesdropped on a phone call and heard that
you were in an accident," Milo said, his white-blond bangs
falling across his forehead. The twins were identical.
Except for their scars. Old cigarette burns and cuts that
she'd never asked about.

Maybe she should have.

She could have built a stronger bond with the kids, but
even when she'd babysat them regularly, she'd been reluctant to do so.

She'd told herself it was because she wasn't the motherly
type. She didn't coddle injuries and hover protectively. She
liked to teach things. Like how to plow a field or build a
chicken coop or clean, card, and spin wool.

But there'd been more to her reluctance than that.

Years ago, she'd wanted kids of her own.

Not fifteen like her father had had, and not one like her
mother. Two or three. Maybe four. She and Sim had discussed
it when they were dating, and he'd seemed as eager as she'd
been to be a parent.

They'd married the day after she'd graduated with her
BA. While Sim taught anthropology classes and fiddled in
the business world, she'd worked as a teaching assistant and
earned her doctorate.

She'd mentioned having a baby after she received a full

professorship, but the timing had never been right. At least, according to Sim it hadn't. First, because she was in school, then because she was teaching.

The year she'd turned twenty-nine, she'd hung up her dream of being a mom. Not because her biological clock was running out, but because she couldn't stomach the idea of bringing an unwanted child into the world.

And Sim?

He didn't want kids.

He'd given lip service to wanting them to keep her happy.

He'd sit across the dinner table, sipping wine and giving his opinion of baby names. Hell, he'd even bought a baseball bat and mitt for the son he'd said he was looking forward to having.

But the truth was he wanted to be the one and only, the center of her attention, the person she worked for, catered to, supported and encouraged.

A baby would have changed that.

Sim was smart enough to know it.

It had taken her a while, but eventually, she'd figured it out. Once she had, did she leave the lying bastard?

No! Of course she hadn't.

She'd put aside the dream, tossed out the baby name books, gifted all the quilts and booties and baby sweaters she'd made to the local hospital, and then she'd kept as far away from kids and babies as she possibly could, because being around them reminded her that she was giving up a lot to have forever with Sim.

"Moisey is an eavesdropper, an eavesdropper, an eavesdropper," Maddox chanted, dancing around like he'd had six pounds of sugar for dinner.

"I am not!" Moisey shouted. "I overheard, because Rosie talks loud. She has hearing aids, you know! Because she can't even hear herself barely at all!"

"Rosie isn't the only one who's loud," Heavenly said, hiking Oya a little higher on her hip. "Your voice could break glass."

"That's not very nice," Twila said, putting her arm around Moisey's shoulders. "Not everyone can have a beautiful singing voice like yours."

"I wasn't talking about her singing. When she speaks, it's like nails scraping chalkboard."

"That's enough, Heavenly," Clementine warned. "Your sister is right. You're not being very nice."

"Why should I be? We had to come out here because she was crying, and now we're going to be stuck here forever. I have two tests tomorrow, and I need to study."

"If you didn't want to come," Clementine said, "you could have stayed home. You're old enough. Or you could have brought your schoolbooks with you. One of your siblings could have entertained Oya while you studied."

Heavenly scowled, but she didn't argue.

Which was good, because Clementine's head ached and her throat burned, and all she really wanted to do was go home, chug six glasses of water, and sleep.

"Tell you what, how about we all calm down, go find Rosie and her sister, and get home?" she suggested, keeping her voice calm and her expression neutral, because that was the best way to deal with Sunday's kids.

"They're down in the cafeteria. Getting coffee and a snack because of Peg's blood sugar. She needs to eat or she faints. We were supposed to not talk while they were gone," Twila said, biting at a cuticle and looking worried. "They said if we were good, we could get a treat. Do you think we were good, Clementine?" she asked.

"You were better than good. You were perfect."

"She's always perfect," Moisey said, patting Twila's shoulder. "She's the best of the best. Mom always said that."

"Sunday said we were all the best of the best," Heavenly said with a tiny smile. "She lied a lot, but she was still pretty cool."

"I wish we could visit her instead of going home," Moisey said. "I have the power to bring her back right here in my hands. I can feel it. I bet it came upon me when I cut my finger today. Blood seeped out and power seeped in."

She held out her hands and stared at them.

"If an entire medical team doesn't have the power to bring Sunday back, neither do you," Heavenly said, the gentleness of her tone surprising Clementine.

"Why not? Remember in church? The pastor talked *forever* about laying hands on people and healing them. And it wasn't just Jesus who was doing it. Anyone who had faith as big as a pumpkin seed—"

"As small as a mustard seed," Twila corrected.

"Right. Thanks. Anyone with faith that small could tell a mountain to run, and it would just get up and go," Moisey continued. "And if someone wanted to heal someone else, he only had to believe he could and it would happen. Back in those days, lame people were running and jumping up all over the place. Blind people were seeing puffs of smoke on cloudy days. Deaf people were hearing pins drop in hay fields. And dead men . . . Dead men were rising up and living again!" She pressed her hand to her chest, enraptured by the tale.

And it hit Clementine like a bolt of lightning. Moisey was a storyteller. Born to bring ancient tales back to life. She'd soak up everything she was told, memorize the details, and repeat them for the sheer pleasure of feeling the words in her mouth, tasting their truths on her tongue.

Just like Clementine and her father and all the generations who'd come before him.

If she were planning to stay longer than it took to get the

fields planted, Clementine would teach Moisey some of the ancient tales. But she wasn't. She had a life to go back to. A life she'd given up for too long because of Sim.

"Only special people can do what the pastor was describing," Heavenly explained. "Adults. Not kids. But if it makes you feel better to think you can do it, go ahead. Just don't ask about visiting Sunday tonight, okay? I really do have two tests, and I need to study."

"It's not about me feeling better. It's about Mom coming home. I need her there, Heavenly. Because my heart is broken into a million pieces, and she's the only one who can put it back together."

"We have to put our own hearts back together, Moisey. That's just the way it is." She shifted her grip on the baby, so she could take Moisey's hand. "Come on. Let's do what Clementine said and find the sisters, okay?"

They walked into the hall: Moisey, Heavenly, and Oya. Twila. Maddox and Milo. They were a disparate group of kids—different ethnicities and backgrounds, different circumstances that had brought them into the family—that had become a family because of Matt and Sunday.

Now Matt was gone.

Sunday was out of reach.

And the kids were trying to find their way back home.

Clementine followed them into the corridor, her legs rubbery, her heart beating a little too fast.

She told herself it was because of the epinephrine she'd been given, but she thought it might have as much to do with Moisey and her broken heart.

Children should never be left to piece themselves back together.

"I was thinking," she said as they reached a bank of elevators, "it would be nice if we did a project together."

"What kind of project?" Milo asked, punching the call button once, twice, and again before Clementine caught his hand and tugged him back.

"One that will teach you a little patience," she said, and he scowled.

"Maddox and I don't want to learn how to knit baby hats for the hospital. Do we, Maddox?"

"No," his twin agreed. "We don't."

"Who said that's what we were going to do?" Clementine asked, because knitting hats was the last project she'd pick for the Bradshaw kids. They needed to saw wood and pound nails and build something that would last.

"They're supposed to be doing it as community service," Twila said. "They can't return to school until they make five hats each."

"You were suspended again?" Clementine asked, wondering how many more chances the twins would have before they were expelled.

"Only because Dallas Winter said Moisey stuck her finger in a light socket and that's why her hair is so curly." Milo punched the button again.

"He said that, and you were the one who got suspended?" That was it! She was going up to the school the next day. She might not be their mother, their aunt, or even their kin, but she wasn't going to let the boys get suspended for someone else's bullying.

"No. I got suspended for punching him in his lying mouth."

"Milo, you know that hitting doesn't solve problems," she said.

"Maybe not, but it shuts people up fast," he responded, flipping nearly-white hair out of his eyes and glaring at her.

"Your mother would be really sad to hear that you think

that's okay," she reminded him, and he looked away, his lips pressed tightly together, his chin wobbling.

He was trying not to cry, and she didn't have the heart to keep pushing him until he did.

"What about you, Maddox? Did you punch Dallas, too?"

"I don't believe in physical violence," he said.

"So, you're just knitting hats in solidarity with your brother?"

"No. I got suspended for stealing five dollars from Dallas's backpack."

"Stealing? You actually took property from someone else and thought that was okay?"

"I didn't think it was okay. I thought that Moisey didn't need to cry anymore, and I thought buying her something at the five and dime would cheer her up."

"He bought me a pink pencil with smiley faces," she offered.

"And that cost five dollars?"

"It cost twenty-five cents."

"What did you do with the rest of the money? Spend it on candy? Buy something for your mother?"

"I put it back in Dallas's bag when I got to school the next day. That's how I got caught. Mr. Williams saw me zipping the bag back up, and then he found the change, and I pretty much had to tell him the whole story."

"Maddox," she said with a sigh. Just that. His name. Because she had no idea what else to say.

How could she be angry at a nine-year-old for wanting to cheer up his sister? How could she judge him for taking twenty-five cents from the kid who'd hurt Moisey's feelings?

"Rosie said she'd teach the boys to knit the hats, but she's not very good at knitting," Twila said. "Everyone was getting frustrated, and Uncle Porter said that enough was enough. He was going to the store, and he was going to buy the hats, and if the school didn't like it they could kick every one of us out."

"Only he said every *damn* one of us," Moisey whispered.

"I don't think he'd appreciate you repeating that."

"I'm not. I'm just telling you that's what he said."

"I don't want to get kicked out of school," Twila said, her eyes shimmering with tears. "I like my teachers and my friends. Besides, being home without Mom around is boring."

"You aren't going to get kicked out of school. As a matter of fact, from this day forward, no one is getting kicked out ever again," Clementine said, digging through her purse until she found the pack of tissues she kept there. She handed them to Twila as the elevator doors slid open.

She ushered all the kids in, counting heads twice before she let the doors close. "Starting now, we're all going to live by the golden rule."

"What golden rule?" Milo asked suspiciously.

"Do unto others as you would have them do unto you. In other words, if you want kindness, give it. And that doesn't mean punching people in the mouth."

"I didn't want to punch Dallas," Milo said. "But Maddox and I are the men of the family now. We have to take care of business."

"First," she said, "you are not the men of the family. Your uncles are. Second, taking care of business doesn't ever involve putting your hands on someone in anger or revenge. If you wanted Dallas punished, all you had to do was talk to your teacher. Or you could have gone to your uncle or Rosie or . . ."

Don't say it, her brain screamed.

"Me," she finished as the doors opened again.

She might have said more. Maybe backtracked. Reminded the kids that she wasn't family and that going to her should be a last resort, but she stepped off the elevator and Porter was there, his hair ruffled, his eyes shadowed, his lips curved in a welcoming smile.

And she lost every word that had been in her head.

She lost every thought.

"Hey," he said, "I was just heading up to see how you were doing. I thought they were keeping you overnight."

"I think they mentioned that. I decided I'd rather go home."

"Then I guess you won't need these." He held up a canvas grocery bag that was filled with clothes. "I had Harley grab some of your things. I figured she'd probably have a better idea of what you'd need than I would. I hope you don't mind me letting her into the house."

"No. Of course not," she said, taking the bag, her cheeks hot with something that could have been embarrassment or pleasure. Maybe it was a mixture of both.

She wasn't used to being taken care of.

Even before she and Sim had split, she'd taken care of herself. If she was sick and needed medicine, she went to the store for it. If she had a flat, she changed it. If she ran out of gas on the side of a busy road, she'd walk to the nearest gas station herself. She cooked. She cleaned. She carried groceries in without ever asking for help, because she hadn't needed help.

But, sometimes, help was nice.

She'd watch her friends with their partners, juggling jobs and families and chores. They asked for help when they needed it. They gave help without complaint. And the ones who were most successful didn't keep tabs. They did things because they wanted to, because they could, because being part of a couple was harder and more challenging and more wonderful than being alone.

"Are you okay?" Porter asked, and she nodded, taking the bag from his hand.

"I'll have to thank Harley when I see her next."

"Actually, I wanted to talk to you about that."

"What?"

"Harley. I drove her to your place to get the stuff. When we finished there, I offered to drop her off at her house. She gave me an address that's a little outside town. It's basically a shack. As far as I could see, the place has no running water or electricity. When I asked her about it, she said the property belonged to her grandmother, and it's a temporary situation."

"How temporary?"

"She was pretty closemouthed about it, so I called Randall. He said she's been living there since her parents kicked her out of the house." He glanced at the kids. "Four years ago. She had a baby and gave her up for adoption, got into some debt trying to pay doctor's bills, and she can't find a rental because her credit tanked. Randall gave her a job at the paper because he felt sorry for her. At least, that's what he said."

"Paying five dollars an hour isn't feeling sorry. It's taking advantage."

"He insists he was paying her minimum wage. Not that it's a whole lot better."

"Did you want to give her a job on the farm?" she asked, imagining the young woman with the high heels and tight dress trying to fix a fence or plow a field.

"That was my first thought. There's sure as heck plenty of work to do. But I wanted to run it by you first. She didn't exactly look like the farmhand type, and I don't want to add another project to your docket without asking first."

"I doubt she'd appreciate being thought of as a project,"

she responded, thinking through the list of things she needed to get done before planting season was in full swing. "The kids and I are going to build a chicken coop."

"We are?!" Moisey asked excitedly. "That's better than knitting hats. Isn't it better, Milo and Maddox?"

"We'll be knitting the hats, too," she clarified. "But the chicken coop is going to replace the one that's standing. I figure we can start with thirty hens and a rooster. Eventually, the farm should produce enough organic eggs to sell to the local market. For right now, we'll just concentrate on raising some chicks who will produce eggs for the family. If Harley wants a job, she can help with that. We'll move from there to expanding the pig pen. I'd like to add another hog, maybe get a few pigmy goats."

"We're not going to eat them, are we?" Heavenly asked. "Because I'll starve before I do that."

"I was thinking more along the lines of a petting zoo. Each of you will choose a pet to hand raise and we'll let kids who visit the farm feed and interact with them."

"Why would people visit the farm?" Twila said. "There's nothing on it but weeds and dead cornstalks."

"Right now, that's all there is on it. But this fall, there'll be a pumpkin patch and a corn maze. Apples to pick. Maybe bonfires every weekend with homemade cider for sale."

"That's what Sunday always talked about," Heavenly said wistfully. "Early in the morning, when it was still dark, and I couldn't sleep, she'd come out on the porch with me, and she'd tell me all about what our farm was going to be like one day. *Our* farm. She always said that. Like I belonged there, and the land belonged to me."

"You do, and it does," Porter said.

"Until when? One of you decides you're tired of me?"

"Family isn't something you get tired of," he replied,

his answer too quick and too blithe and said with too little thought.

Clementine could hear that.

Heavenly must have, too. Heard it. Felt it. Responded to it in the way any teen in her position would.

She lifted her chin, her eyes flashing, the baby clutched so tightly to her skinny frame, they might have been one person.

"Right. We'll see if you're still saying that in the fall when the apples and cider and pumpkins are here, but Sunday still isn't. Then you'll be looking for a quick way to off-load a couple of us, and I'll be the first to go. Because I'm not young and I'm not cute and I don't fit in. Come on, dweebs," she said, heading toward the cafeteria. "Let's go find Rosie so we can get out of here."

To Clementine's surprise, the siblings fell into step behind her, marching toward the cafeteria like they were going to the gallows—somberly, silently. No joking or bickering or out-and-out fighting. They looked like what they were—a bunch of heartbroken kids who had no idea what the future was going to bring, no idea who'd be taking care of them in a month or a year, and no certainty at all that they'd be able to stay in the home they'd been told would be theirs forever.

"They need their mother," Porter said. "And I'm a piss-poor replacement for her."

"You're not a replacement. You're their uncle," she said.

"I am the person who is supposed to be providing all the things she did."

"You are the person who is supposed to be loving them. I don't think there are any rules to how that should go."

"It's not about rules. It's about know-how. When it comes to loving kids, I don't have any."

"It's not complicated, Porter. You just give of your time and your energy and your compassion.""

"And, I still won't be their mother. She knows them better than anyone. She's spent time with them. She understands their personalities and their idosyncrasies."

"And, she might not ever be able to return to them. You need to stop looking at this like it's a temporary situation and start acting like those kids are your responsibility forever."

"I prefer to keep hoping for her full recovery," he muttered.

"We're all hoping that, but *you're their uncle*. You're not just some guy who's here because he's obligated. You're here because you love them, because you want them to be okay, because when push comes to shove, you'd give up weeks or months or years to make sure they are. And, even if you don't feel that way now, you're going to pretend like you do, because that's what they deserve, it's what they need, and giving them less will never be all right."

The words spilled out in waves and then faded into silence.

She wasn't sorry she'd said them.

She'd watched the Bradshaw men walk in and out of Sunday's farmhouse, acting like outsiders, tiptoeing around the kids like they weren't family. If Maddox and Milo were acting out, if Heavenly was planning for the moment when she'd be kicked to the curb, if Moisey was daydreaming about healing powers and little Twila was climbing out windows and sitting on the dock staring at the river, it wasn't because they were troubled kids; it was because they were untethered, cut free from the family bond that they'd been assured would hold them tightly for always.

"You understand that I barely know them, right?" Porter said gruffly.

"You understand that family isn't blood, right? That those kids are yours as much as they were Matt's, as much as they are Sunday's? That you are part of them and they're part of you and that the farm is the thing that's going to tie you together until your hearts know the truth?"

"I have a life in LA, Clementine."

"You have a family here, and they need at least one person who isn't going to act like they're throwaways and second thoughts," she responded. "Come on. Let's make sure they're with Rosie and Peg, and not wreaking havoc on the cafeteria staff."

She turned away, because she'd said too much. Because this wasn't her family, those weren't her kids, the farm wasn't her problem.

But, if they were, if it was, she'd give everything to make it work. Every hour, every minute, every bit of money and effort and love, because that's what family did.

Always.

She might have grown up in an unconventional home. She might have struggled in her marriage. She might have failed at a lot of things, but she knew that.

It was a shame that the Bradshaw men didn't seem to.

Two in the morning wasn't the best time to be awake, but Porter was. Awake and pacing the farmhouse kitchen, listening to the quiet patter of rain on the tin roof.

The kids were all in bed.

He knew. He'd checked every room three times.

He'd checked on Heavenly more, because he couldn't forget what she'd said at the hospital, or the way she'd said it—as if she were expendable in a way no one should ever be.

I'm not young and I'm not cute and I don't fit in.

He should have told her she was all those things and more. He should have said that no one was getting tossed to the side or forgotten, that they'd stick together, make things work. No matter what happened with Sunday.

He should have said a lot of things, but he'd stayed mute, watching as she walked away, all the other kids following along behind her. Every one of them probably wondering if Heavenly were right—if, one by one, they'd be off-loaded to some other place, some other family.

God, he'd made a mess of things, walking into these kids' lives like he was going to walk out again.

But that's what he'd planned.

He could be honest enough with himself to admit it, and to admit that Clementine had been right. The kids deserved more. They needed more. They needed consistency and security. They needed to know who they'd see every morning when they woke up.

This situation—the in and out and back and forth, uncles coming and going—wasn't healthy for any kid, but especially not for kids who'd suffered trauma and loss. No wonder there'd been so much acting out.

Hell, he was surprised there hadn't been more.

He rubbed the back of his neck, uncomfortable with the direction of his thoughts, unwilling to follow them all the way to their logical conclusion, but unable to stop himself.

Someone had to stand in the gap that Matt had left.

Not for a day or a week or, even, months. Not even until Sunday recovered. Forever. Going to ball games and school meetings and recitals. Taking pictures before proms and cheering at graduations. Fishing. Hiking. Camping. Biking. Dating police.

Someone had to be there doing those things day in and day out until the kids were grown, and even then, it couldn't end. Eventually, there'd be wrinkle-faced babies, teddy bears, birthday parties. Illness. Divorce.

"Damnit, Matt," he muttered. "Did you think about that when you decided you needed to father six children?"

Probably not.

Matthias had never been big on foresight. He'd made decisions quickly, and if he'd regretted them, he'd never let on. He was a good-old-boy, the kind of guy everyone liked. Easy going, charming, helpful. He'd have given the shirt off his back to anyone who needed it. Hundreds of people had attended his funeral and told stories about the favors he'd done for them. Money lent, and food purchased, and cars fixed. He'd been well-loved and admired by the community, but his farm was failing, his bills hadn't been paid, his wife had obviously been struggling to keep things going.

Had Sunday been happy? Had she been content, secure, confident that her family and her farm were going to be okay?

And, why in the hell was he just now wondering that?

Why hadn't he asked when he'd visited six months ago? Why had he noticed the broken fence posts and scraggly grass and overgrown fields and not bothered asking what was going on, why the once beautiful farm was being neglected?

Heavenly had talked about the dreams Sunday had for the place, but based on the financial mess Matt had left, it would have been impossible to make them come true. There hadn't been money for chickens or coops or feed. There'd been nothing in the budget for fixing fences, plowing fields, or planting crops. A working farm was expensive to run, and Matthias had seemed clueless about that.

He'd bought a sports car, for God's sake.

And he'd died in it.

The loan papers freshly signed, more debt added to what had already been accrued. If he'd lived, he'd have lost the farm in less than two years.

Sunday had to have known that.

Unlike Matt, she understood what it took to make a place like this successful. Her family had run the farm for generations. As a teenager, she'd worked with her parents to plant and harvest and to keep things running. She'd been their only child, born late in their lives. It would have been easy for them to spoil her, to give her everything and demand nothing, but they'd taught her work-ethic and business savvy, and Porter couldn't help wondering why she'd buried that under the rug and let Matt take over.

It must have been heartbreaking to watch everything her family had worked for and toiled over slip away. But she'd done it, pouring herself into her kids, burying her head in the sand and pretending things were fine.

Just like his mother had.

The thought slipped in and settled deep, his mind going to a dark place. One where the brother he'd loved was a tyrant behind closed doors.

"Damnit, Matt," he repeated, grabbing his coat from the closet and walking outside. He needed fresh air and a clear head, because he was starting to think about his brother's failures, think about the way he could turn them into successes. He was starting to imagine himself sticking around, being there all day every day for the kids that Matt had left behind.

For his family.

That's what Clementine had been trying to say.

Their uncle.

Not just a guy stepping in until someone else could do it.

He scowled, pulling up his hood and walking into the cold rain. It fell in soft sheets, pattering on the grass and the hard earth. He had no destination, just the strange feeling that this was right—walking in the darkness and the rain.

He followed the curve of the driveway, following it to

the country road that meandered through yellow fields and dense forests. To the right, the river cut across the landscape. To the left, lights glowed from the windows of the rancher.

He knew what he shouldn't do.

He shouldn't turn left.

He did, walking as if he had all the time in the world, as if the rain weren't falling and he wasn't getting soaked, his mind circling back to Sunday and Matt and their marriage.

Had it been a good one?

He'd assumed so, because he'd assumed that Matt would never be like their father.

What if he'd been wrong?

What if the slow decline of the farm had been about control or punishment? What if Matt had been purposely destroying something Sunday loved?

What if a dozen things that didn't matter any longer?

Matt was gone.

Sunday was so badly injured she might never recover.

Whatever had been between them was over, but he still wanted to know.

He told himself that was why he was walking to the rancher, why he let the glowing light in the living room window convince him that Clementine was awake.

He told himself that, and knew he was lying.

He'd come because he wanted to see her.

She drew him in the way no woman ever had, her quick wit and sharp mind and soft lips. She was everything he'd have wanted if he'd been looking for forever. Everything he'd have wanted if he'd been looking at all.

He hadn't been. He wasn't.

He knocked on the door anyway, waiting for the soft slide of the bolt and the quiet click of the lock. He heard both, and then the door opened, and she was standing there, hair pulled into a tight bun, body covered by a thick gray sweater and black leggings.

She didn't look any more surprised to see him than he was to be there.

"Porter," she said, "is everything okay?"

"I couldn't sleep, and your light was on."

She nodded as if that explained everything. "I couldn't sleep, either. Too hyped up from all the excitement tonight, I guess. Come on in. Want some coffee?" she asked, already moving toward the kitchen.

"You don't have any, remember?"

"Damn. You're right." She dropped onto a stool that sat next to what looked like an old-fashioned spinning wheel. "I planned to go to the store, but ended up in the hospital instead."

"You're still feeling okay?"

"Right as rain, but I did locate my inhaler, and the hospital sent me home with my own EpiPen. I'm supposed to go to an allergist sooner rather than later because the asthma attack was so bad."

"Supposed to?"

"In case you haven't noticed," she said, lifting tufts of gray and white fiber from the basket at her feet, "I'm a little busy."

"Your health comes before the farm, Clementine."

"My health is fine. It's your house that has the problem. Too much dust." She pressed her bare foot against the pedal and pulled the fibers through her fingers, working a thin thread onto the wheel.

"That looks—"

"Tedious?"

"Relaxing."

"It is."

"Did you learn from your father?"

"From one of his wives. She was actually Scottish, believe it or not, and had learned the skill from her grandmother."

"How many wives did your dad have?"

"Three? Four? He also had girlfriends. Lovers. Mistresses."

"Was that hard on you?"

"It was all I ever knew, so no. I just accepted it."

"But didn't want it for yourself?" he guessed.

"No. I figured I'd get married once and stay married forever. That wasn't in the cards, so now I'm content to stay single and spend my evening spinning wool and binge-watching Netflix."

"You don't have a television or a computer in here," he pointed out.

"Okay. So I'm not into Netflix, but you've got to admit, it sounded good." She glanced up from the fibers and smiled. "Now that we've got that out of the way, how about you tell me why you're here."

"What do you know about Sunday and Matt's relation-ship?" he asked, deciding a straightforward approach was the best one.

"Why are you asking?"

"Because my brother was running this farm into the ground, and I want to know why."

"That's a question only he can answer."

"And that's a cop-out if I ever heard one."

"Maybe, but it's also the truth." She lifted her foot from the pedal and dropped the fiber back into the basket. "You know, I think I'll see if I have coffee in the freezer. Sometimes I keep a bag there."

She stood languidly, as if she had all the time in the world, as if she weren't planning to run from the room and from his questions.

"Whatever you have to say, it can't hurt Matt. He's gone."

"I'm not worried about hurting him. I'm worried about hurting you," she said.

"What's that supposed to mean?"

"Just that sometimes it's better to remember who we thought someone was rather than who they turned out to be."

She moved then, and did what he'd known she would. Hurried into the kitchen.

He should have left it like that—him waiting in the living room while she made a show of searching the freezer for coffee she probably didn't want.

But he couldn't.

It wasn't the way he operated.

He wanted facts and truth and reality. Not sweet little stories that made him feel better.

He stood and followed her, stepping into the kitchen and waiting for her to acknowledge him.

Chapter Seven

She hoped if she ignored him long enough, he'd get the hint and go away.

It wasn't that she didn't want him around.

Having him there was a lot better than lying in bed, staring at the ceiling, imagining she smelled cologne and cigarettes.

But this was Porter she was dealing with. Not Sim.

He'd probably stand in the kitchen for the rest of his life, waiting for her to turn and face him.

She sighed, shifting the contents of the freezer around one more time.

No coffee, but then, she'd already known that.

"Eventually," Porter said, "you're going to have to turn around and face me."

"Actually, there are other possibilities. I could face this direction until you leave—"

"I'm not planning to leave."

"Or I could walk out the back door."

"But you won't."

"No," she said, finally turning around and meeting his eyes. "I won't, but I'm not going to talk about Matt and Sunday, either."

"I can think of a lot of reasons why not. None of them are pleasant."

"He wasn't abusive, if that's what you're thinking," she said.

"It was one of the things I wondered."

"What were the others?" she asked, curious despite herself.

"If he was trying to hurt her by destroying something she loved."

"In my mind, that would be the same as abuse."

"So, he wasn't abusive, he didn't want to hurt her. What does that leave, Clementine?" he asked as he crossed the room, stopped just inches from where she stood.

"I told you, I'm not going to talk about it." Because the things that Sunday had told her were private, shared in moments of stress and heartache, spoken in the darkest hours of the night when it had just been the two of them wandering the farm sleepless.

Clementine because of bills and Sim and a dozen regrets.

Sunday because Matt had been finding excitement away from the house and the kids she loved so much. Late nights at bars far enough away from town that no one but Sunday knew, business trips that were mostly pleasure. A midlife crisis in his late twenties, and Sunday had been terrified she'd lost him for good.

But that was her story to tell. Not Clementine's, and tarnishing Matt's image without a really good reason for it wasn't something she planned to do.

"He was my brother. I have a right to know."

"He was your brother. Maybe you should have asked before he died," she responded, the words sharper and colder than she'd intended.

"I'm sorry. That didn't come out the way I meant it," she offered hurriedly.

"What way did you mean it?" he responded, his expression

hard, his eyes deep pewter. Not a hint of blue in them. "Because from where I'm standing, it sounded like a pretty harsh recrimination of my relationship with Matt."

"No recrimination or judgment. I have no idea what your relationship was like, and even if I did, I'd have no right to speak about it."

"He bought a Corvette," he said, ignoring her comment, his expression still hard and cold. "Did you know that?"

"Yes," she replied, her mouth cottony, her pulse racing, because he didn't look like the man she knew, the guy who smiled easily and spoke warmly.

He looked like a bodyguard or a hit man.

A valuable ally or a dangerous foe.

He looked like a stranger capable of anything, and he looked like someone she might want to get to know.

Her inability to see the truth of who he was terrified her. She'd already been fooled before, tricked by a man who'd pretended to be what she'd wanted. She'd spent ten years pretending with him while he'd lied and cheated and spent money they didn't have on things they didn't need.

She never wanted to live that way again, faking happiness for the sake of broken vows and dead dreams.

She backed up, her hips banging into the counter, her heart thumping painfully. If she ever fell again, it would be for someone like Porter.

Like him?

It would *be* him.

And she couldn't risk that. Not when she was starting over, beginning again, wiping the slate clean and reinventing herself. She didn't have ten more years to lose on another dead-end relationship.

She sidled toward the back door, because being outside in the rain seemed a whole lot safer than being alone in the house with a guy whose kiss could melt the ice around her heart.

She'd walk outside, meander through the newly plowed fields, inhale the scent of freshly turned earth, remind herself of how good it felt to be home. Even if home meant being alone.

It was a good plan. A great one.

But Porter's face changed, the coldness seeping away, his eyes tracking her hand as she reached for the doorknob.

"I'm sorry," he said quietly.

"For what?"

"Scaring you."

"You didn't," she responded. "I scared myself."

"Into running out into the rain?" he asked, his lips curving in a half smile.

She couldn't resist his smile.

She couldn't resist him, and she stayed where she was instead of going outside. Which was a mistake. She knew. One she would probably regret.

"I wasn't running," she pointed out.

"You were thinking about it," he said, moving into her space but giving her plenty of room to step away.

She didn't.

Another mistake, because he set his hands on her waist, his fingers splayed against her back, and she forgot why she was afraid, forgot what she should be afraid of.

Not this—the thrumming desire that raced through her blood, the easy way her body fit against his.

"I was," she admitted, her voice husky with longing, her hands finding their way to his forearms and sliding up to his shoulders. "But I suddenly can't remember why."

"You said you scared yourself," he murmured, his lips touching her forehead, her cheek, the corner of her mouth. "I'm still curious to know how."

"It was nothing important."

"When it comes to you, everything is important to me."

"Did you practice that line, Porter? Because it's probably one of the most perfect things anyone has ever said to me."

"A person doesn't have to practice speaking the truth. Now, how about you tell me about the not-so-important thing that almost scared you out into the rain?" His hands slid up her back and then down, his palms settling at the hollow of her spine.

"I don't want to be hurt again," she said honestly, looking into his eyes and knowing he was going to break her heart.

How could he not?

He had a job in LA and six kids to care for here.

She had a wonderful life waiting for her in Seattle. One she'd given up before and wasn't going to give up again.

They were star-crossed lovers. Destined to meet and then say good-bye. There could be no other ending to the story. At least, not one that she could see.

"Why are you assuming that you will be?" he asked.

"Not assuming. Imagining. Thinking about how it would feel to spend ten years with you and then find out that all the dreams we built together were a lie."

"Was that what happened with Sim?" he asked, his expression unreadable, his eyes the dusky shade of the river at twilight. "You were building dreams and he was pretending to?"

"Something like that."

"He isn't every man. You know that, right?"

"He's the man I chose. What does that say about me?"

"That you want what most people do. To be accepted and valued and to have your faith in others justified." His words were like the rhythmic echo of the tribal drum, summoning her to that place called home.

And she went, because how could she not?

He was the deep fertile soil and the crackling wood, the warm summer breeze and the first winter snow. She could taste them all in his kiss, feel them in his hands as they trailed up her spine, tangled in her hair.

A million moments like this would never be enough.

A million dreams could never compare to being in his arms.

And she was terrified that he'd break her heart and shatter her soul while he was doing it, afraid of what would happen when they finally said good-bye.

"You're crying," he murmured against her lips, and she could taste the briny tears she hadn't realized were falling, the bitter remnants of dreams that would never come true.

"Saying hello is always easy," she said, pulling away because she'd been a fool before, and she never wanted to be one again. "It's saying good-bye that leaves the scars."

"Who says we have to say good-bye?"

"Me. You. Our lives. We're on different trajectories, walking totally different paths. Let's not pretend that we don't see how the story is going to end," she said, turning away and grabbing the teapot because she needed to do something with her hands.

Something besides pulling him back into her arms.

"You're the storyteller, Clementine," he responded, his tone gruff, eyes flashing with something that looked a lot like anger. "Maybe you should explain how this one goes."

"Girl winds up in a small town with a hell of a lot of dead dreams. Girl meets boy. It's the wrong place and the wrong time. The end." She filled the pot with water, set it on the stove, her hand shaking, her nose suddenly filled with the noxious scent of cigarettes and cologne.

"Or, maybe all the dead dreams are just a bridge to better ones. Maybe the place and the time are exactly what they're supposed to be for hellos to happen without good-byes.

But we'll never know how it really goes, will we? Because you've already spoken that sad-ass story to your heart. Your head isn't going to believe in anything else."

"Porter, you know I'm right. You have a job in LA and six kids who are counting on you. I have a life that isn't here."

"What I know is that those are excuses for letting your fear decide your fate. And that's something only a coward would do. I need to get back to the house. See you around, Clementine." He walked to the back door and yanked it open.

"What the hell?!" he growled, because Sim was there. On the stoop. A cigarette dangling from his lips, a key in his hand, his eyes wide with shock.

"Clementine! What are you doing here?"

"It's my place. Where else would I be?"

"I heard you were staying at the hospital tonight," he mumbled, the cigarette falling to the ground.

"So you thought you'd visit me *here*?" she asked.

"You know, now that you mention it, it probably wasn't one of my better ideas. I'll come back another time," he replied, jumping off the stoop and racing away.

"Stay here and call the sheriff," Porter commanded, and then he was gone, too, sprinting into the gray-black night.

It wasn't going to be a fair footrace.

Sim was in about as good a shape as the old, fat tabby she'd had as a kid, and Porter was . . .

She watched as he sprinted after her ex, his legs and arms muscular, his pace quick and easy.

He was a prime example of fit masculinity.

"Don't hurt him!" she yelled. "It would suck to go to jail for someone who smells like cheap cologne!"

Porter wasn't planning to hurt Sim, but the idiot seemed to be determined to hurt himself. He ran pell-mell down a steep hill, tumbling into a muddy culvert that was probably filled with rocks.

"Slow down, man!" Porter called, not because he couldn't catch the guy, but because he didn't want him to break his neck before the sheriff arrived.

"Leave me alone!" Sim replied as he jumped up and kept going. He sounded like a whiny kid on a school playground—the bully who'd finally picked the wrong student to mess with.

"That would be a hell of a lot easier if you'd do Clementine the same favor," he replied, jumping over the culvert Sim had fallen into and following him up the other side.

There was a grassy field at the top, a barbed-wire fence a hundred yards straight ahead. Sim was running toward it. Porter could hear him puffing like a steam engine from twenty yards back.

"You should probably stop before you have a heart attack," he called, but Sim kept going full-throttle. Or as close as he could get to it while limping and panting.

Gentle spring rain was still falling, the ground muddy and slick. Sim slipped, slid, and then fell. He was up about a second later, limping toward the fence and a sporty little car that was parked on the other side of it.

"I hope you don't think you're going to jump over the fence," Porter called, because a guy who couldn't run a tenth of a mile wasn't going to hurtle over a five-foot fence with ease.

Sim growled.

At least, Porter thought he did.

Then he backed up a step, gathered himself up, and ran straight for the glistening metal barbs.

Maybe he thought he'd soar over it.

Whatever he thought, it didn't happen.

Instead of soaring, he flopped, landing on barbs that

caught in his clothes and held him dangling a foot above the ground.

"Help!" he screamed. "Help me!"

"I'll probably have to cut the fence to get you down," Porter responded, pulling his utility knife out and approaching the struggling man.

"The fence or me?" Sim asked, his legs on one side of the barbed-wire, his head on the other. He looked like an understuffed scarecrow, tossed by the gentlest wind. "Because she's not worth going to jail for murder over."

"Who?"

"Clementine. She's boring. Unimpressive. Uninspiring."

"And smart enough to divorce your lazy ass," Clementine said, stepping up beside Porter. "The sheriff will be here any minute, Porter. Let's go back to the house and wait for him there."

"What about me?" Sim asked, not even trying to free himself.

"The sheriff can get you down," she responded.

"You're not serious, Clementine," Sim said. "You wouldn't leave me hanging here."

"You mean like you left me hanging with thousands of dollars of debts and an empty bank account? Sure, I would." She started walking away, her rain-soaked sweater clinging to her gorgeous curves, her skin shimmering with falling rain.

She looked like a goddess, and she tasted like sunshine.

Raindrops.

Fresh air.

Joy.

Porter knew that.

Just like he knew he could love her.

Hell, he probably already did, but he wasn't going to fight for something she didn't want to give. He wasn't going to manipulate her feelings, he wasn't going to be the kind of guy who forced his way into a woman's heart and broke it.

He frowned, turning away from her, from all the things he saw when he looked into her eyes.

"Clementine!" Sim yelled. "I made a mistake. I was an idiot. I'm sorry."

"I don't think she's listening," he said, testing the weight of the wire fencing. It was thick and sturdy, pulled tight along the vertical posts. He wasn't going to be able to cut through it.

He walked to the closest wood post, shaking it to see if he could easily push it down.

"Ow!" Sim screamed. "I'm being impaled in the heart!"

"If only the world could be so lucky," Clementine said, walking back across the field, a wire cutter in her hands.

"You don't mean that," Sim said. "We loved each other for ten years. You wouldn't want anything to happen to me."

"I loved you for ten years. You loved yourself." She lifted the wire cutters, setting the mouth right near Sim's dangling head. "And I really couldn't care less if something happened to you."

"Baby, please. You don't understand. I did all of this for you."

"Did what for me? Steal my money? Run off with another woman? Get yourself hung up in the chicken yard fence?"

"The money was ours. I didn't steal it. I took it with me when I left town. To protect it, because the economy here stinks."

"To spend it on your twenty-three-year-old lover. Yeah. You're right. I can see how that could be construed as a selfless act of love toward me."

Porter laughed.

Sim didn't seem as amused. "You've misunderstood this whole situation. That's why I came back. To explain things."

"What things?"

"I didn't run off with anyone. I went to Thailand to make some investments. Great investments, and they're going to pay off big. I just need a little more cash." Sim was talking fast, his eyes on the sharp edge of the wire cutter that was very, *very* close to his face.

"I'm fresh out of cash and patience," Clementine said. "So, how about you tell me exactly why you were on my back stoop tonight?"

"You have the ring. I thought it was only fair that it be returned to me," Sim responded, obviously not realizing how precarious his situation was.

Porter could have told him to shut up while he was ahead, but he didn't want to ruin the show.

"What ring?" Clementine asked, as if she didn't know.

"The engagement ring. It's worth tens of thousands of dollars, and really, it belongs to me. To my family anyway. I tried to retrieve it before I went to Thailand, but my name isn't on the safe deposit box. I was really hurt by that, Clementine. Deeply wounded that you didn't trust me."

"I think her decision was well-founded, considering that you went to the bank to try to steal the ring," Porter said.

"Steal?! It's my ring. My family's ring, so I should have had access to it. I planned to sell it and give Clementine half what I got for it. I swear."

"Your word means nothing."

"Clementine! How can you say such a thing?"

"Experience. You swore you'd love me forever. You swore that we'd always have each other's backs. You didn't follow through on either of those things."

"I do love you. I will always love you."

"Stop!" Clementine snapped. "I don't want to hear it,

and as far as the ring goes, you gave it to me. You told me it wasn't nearly good enough for a woman of my beauty, but it was all you had. You hoped that I would keep it forever, and that every time I looked at it, I'd remember that it paled in comparison to your love for me."

"Geez," Porter said.

"I know," Clementine sighed.

"I still love you. With all my heart. And the ring still symbolizes those things. I just need to borrow it for a while. I'll return it. After I secure our future."

"Your future, you mean. We're not married anymore."

"That breaks my heart every minute of every day."

"God," Clementine responded. "I can't believe I married you."

"There's no need to be harsh. If you don't want me around, I'll leave. After I get the ring. I'm sure you'll agree that it should be returned to my mother's collection."

"I do, but since your mother didn't want it returned, I'm going to keep it."

"My mother? What does she have to do with it?"

"I called her after the divorce was finalized and offered to return it. She said she'd rather I keep it. I guess she has a son who likes to pilfer her best pieces of jewelry and pawn them."

"She only has one son."

"I know."

"And I've never pawned anything of hers."

"That's not the story she told me."

"She's senile, and you're being unreasonable. I hate to do it, but if you force my hand, I'll have to get a lawyer," Sim threatened, apparently not realizing that he was still hanging upside down from a barbed-wire fence.

Porter leaned his elbow on the fence post, watching as the wire cutters inched closer to Sim's ear.

"Go ahead," Clementine responded. "I wouldn't mind facing you in court. Maybe the judge will force you to repay the money you stole from me."

"Now, hold on! I'm no thief. That money was ours, and I used it to build our future. I already told you that. As for the ring, I just want to use it as collateral to get a loan so that I can capitalize on our investment."

"*Our* investment? The only investment I've made recently is the time I put into this fence. I thought it would keep the vermin out of the chicken yard. Obviously, I was wrong. It's about as useless as a lying, cheating jackass hanging from barbed wire." She snapped the cutters closed. The wires sagged; Sim tumbled to the ground.

"Get off this property," she continued. "And don't come back. If you do, I'll make sure your heart is impaled with something a hell of a lot sharper than barbed wire."

She flipped the cutters up to her shoulder, holding them like a long-range rifle as she walked away. Hips swaying, stride confident, strong and feminine and sexy as hell. Beautiful in every possible way a person should be, and if she hadn't been so scared, so worried about being hurt, Porter would have followed her home and kissed every inch of her gorgeous skin.

"I'm still stuck," Sim moaned, trying to unhook his coat from the barbs.

"Because you're an idiot," Porter responded, yanking him up by the coat collar, pulling the barbs away, and giving him a none-too-gentle shove toward the house and the flashing lights of the sheriff's approaching vehicle.

Chapter Eight

Sim was gone.

For good and forever.

Thanks to the sheriff's promise to arrest him for trespassing *and* harassment if he ever set foot in Benevolence again, Sim had boarded a plane and gone home ten days ago.

Home to his mother.

Clementine should have been amused by that, but all she felt was tired. She'd been working the fields in the morning, building the chicken coop with Harley and the kids in the afternoon, spinning wool and knitting baby hats in the evening.

She'd kept her days and nights busy, because she'd wanted to keep her mind occupied, her thoughts from drifting to places they shouldn't.

Like to Porter.

To his sweet words and tender kisses, to the feel of his hands trailing along her spine.

She shivered, pulling her sweater a little closer and telling herself it was the chill in the air and not the longing in her heart that was giving her goose bumps.

"Goose walking over your grave, Clementine?" Moisey

asked, looking up from the baby hat she was trying to knit. It was a mess of dropped and off-sized stitches, the yarn fuzzy from being worked and reworked as Moisey tried to correct her mistakes.

"That's a weird thing to say," Milo grumbled, setting his fifth hat on the table and picking up another skein of yarn. Yellow with sparkly threads of white woven through it. He had a knack for knitting, each one of his projects beautifully finished, but he seemed embarrassed by the talent, and Clementine tried not to make a big deal about it.

She tried not to make a big deal about anything with the kids. They'd seemed more restful lately, more synched with the tempo of farm life and with each other. Physical labor had been good for all of them. Setting posts and laying foundations and doing all the work Clementine had learned to do when she was Moisey's age had burned off a lot of their energy and eased some of their anxiety. From what Rosie said, they got ready for school in the morning without complaint, did their homework, and hadn't been in trouble at school in a week.

Porter was probably happy about that.

Clementine didn't know. She hadn't seen him since Sim had been carted away. Okay. She *had* seen him. But only at a distance and only for a few seconds. Sometimes, he'd wave. Sometimes, she'd smile. But they didn't talk. Not like they had before.

"Why is it weird?" Moisey asked, scowling at the knotted yarn at the end of her knitting needles.

"Because Clementine is alive. She doesn't have a grave," he responded, taking the needles and hat from her hands and quickly setting them right. "There. Now go a little slower, because the only reason you're messing up is because you're trying to rush."

"I'm rushing because you already did five, and I haven't

even done one. And Maddox did two. And Heavenly did four. And Twila did three. And Clementine did, like, seventeen. And I'm just sitting here like a slug with a bunch of tangled yarn."

"It's not a race, dweeb," Heavenly said, setting a finished hat on the coffee table and lifting Oya from the floor beside her. "And your hats are always the prettiest colors, so why do you care if you make the most?"

"Do you really think they are?" Moisey asked, eyeing the royal blue alpaca yarn she'd chosen.

"The prettiest colors? Yeah. I do. You have an eye for stuff like that. Me? I'd rather just make them all black."

"I think that would be a little sad," Twila said, finishing a pastel green hat and setting it down. "I also think we need to go home. Rosie said we should be back before dark, and the sun's already setting."

"You're right," Moisey agreed, jumping up and rushing to the front window. "The sun is almost down. If we don't hurry, we're going to get in trouble."

"By who?" Twila asked, collecting all the finished hats and carefully laying them in a cardboard box. "Uncle Porter isn't here. Rosie never gets mad."

"Your uncle isn't around?" Clementine asked, surprised and a little unsettled. They might not be talking, but she'd gotten used to seeing him on the farm. He'd fixed the dock and cleaned out the boathouse, sawing and hammering late into the evenings. He'd built a small corral for pony rides and fixed the irrigation system that ran water to the fields.

She'd been impressed by the work he was getting done, but she hadn't told him that.

She'd been afraid to break the silence, and even more afraid of how easy it would be to step into his arms again.

"He left." Twila closed the box and carried it to the door.

"So he's gone?"

"I'm pretty sure that's what she just said," Heavenly muttered. "But don't worry. Sullivan and Rumer came back this morning. They're at her grandmother's getting all her stuff so she can move into the farmhouse with us. And Rosie's moving in, too, because the uncles don't think Rumer should have to do all the cooking, cleaning, and child-care stuff herself. Now that she's family, she says she doesn't want to get paid."

"Rosie's staying on?" Clementine wondered how Sunday would feel knowing that the farmhouse was filling up with strangers. She'd probably love it. She'd been a wonderful hostess and a warmhearted friend.

"Unfortunately," Heavenly griped.

"Why unfortunately?"

"Because, if you ask me, the place is getting too crowded."

"If you ask me," Moisey said, bouncing to the door and throwing it open, "the more the merrier."

"If you ask *me,* there are too many girls," Maddox added. "We need more men."

"We need Mom," Moisey corrected. "And since Rumer and Sullivan are back, maybe we can go see her tomorrow. I can't wait! I finally figured out why my powers haven't been working."

"Powers?" Clementine asked, following them to the door, her mind still on Porter's sudden departure. They hadn't been talking, but he could have at least said good-bye.

"The ones I used to wake you up. They didn't work on Mom, but I know why." She held up her finger, showing a purplish scar. "See? The cut is healed."

"You're not planning on cutting yourself again, I hope."

"No. That would be stupid. I realized the power came from the Band-Aid."

"It did?"

"Of course. Everyone knows that pink ones have magical properties. I tried to get it out of the trash can once I remembered that, but Rosie was appalled. She said trash stays in the trash can forever. I looked for pink Band-Aids in our medicine cabinets, but we only have the tan kind."

"Do you want me to buy you some?" Milo offered.

"No!" Clementine said, remembering his quest to buy her a pencil and how that had ended. "What I mean is, I'll pick some up for her."

"You will?" Moisey's face lit up, her impish smile showing off dimples in both cheeks.

"Sure. I have to run to the feed store tomorrow to order the chicks. I can go to the pharmacy on my way."

"Tomorrow? But what if we visit Mom before you get back?"

"You'll be at school tomorrow," she reminded her.

"Tomorrow is Saturday," Twila said with a sigh. "We all have to stay home."

"See?" Moisey added. "I have to have the Band-Aids tonight. If we go in the morning, and I don't have them, I might miss the very last opportunity to ever wake Mom up."

"Why do you say that, sweetie?" Clementine asked, surprised by the comment. She'd been to see Sunday three days ago. She hadn't improved. She still wasn't completely conscious, but she wasn't any worse than she'd been, either. Had something changed?

"She's lost in the shadow world of dreams, Clementine," Moisey said solemnly. "It's a dangerous place for mortals to be."

"Honey, that's just a myth. Your mom has a brain injury. She's having a hard time waking up from it."

"That's what adults think. I know better. I thought you

did, too. Never mind about the Band-Aids. I'll figure it out myself." She ran outside, sprinting across the gravel drive-way and heading toward home.

"Man, you sure made a mess of that," Heavenly said, following her sister out the door.

Minutes later the house was silent, the old grandfather clock ticking happily in the kitchen.

Clementine wasn't happy.

She was worried. Moisey had a big imagination and a propensity for getting into trouble. She wanted pink Band-Aids by morning, and she'd probably be willing to sneak out of the house and walk to town to get them.

If Porter was around . . .

But, of course, he wasn't.

He'd left town without a word. No explanation. No good-bye.

Not that she deserved one.

She'd made her feelings clear. She'd told him exactly where they were headed. Nowhere together.

He'd called her a coward.

And she guessed she was one, but she'd learned some-thing important after Sim left. She learned that giving someone half your heart made it easy when they walked away.

That's what she'd done with Sim—offered part of who she was. She'd given him love and affection and an un-fathomable amount of grace, but she'd held back pieces of her heart.

He hadn't noticed.

Or, he hadn't cared.

He'd certainly never asked her about the things she'd learned as a kid, the stories she carried with her, the life she'd lived in Wyoming. He'd never wanted to know how many wives her father had or how she'd felt about them. And he sure as hell had never wanted to watch her spin fibers into threads.

Porter had.

He'd wanted everything. Every story. Every memory. Every piece of who she was. He would never have been satisfied with less. She'd known that. Somewhere deep in her soul she'd felt it, recognized it, heard it as clearly as the beat of that tribal drum calling her home.

"For God's sake, Clementine! Get over it!" she growled, irritated with herself, because this was what she'd wanted. No connections. No complications. No soft-spoken, hardmuscled man asking her questions. Just her. Alone. Working on the farm until it was time to return to Seattle.

To return *home*.

Because that's what she'd be doing. Not just going to someplace where she'd stay for a while. She'd be going to a place where she'd stay forever, teaching and lecturing and telling stories.

And she was going to love it, damnit.

She was!

She grabbed her cell phone and called Rosie, asking her to keep a close eye on Moisey and letting her know that she'd drop the pink Band-Aids off as soon as she could find them.

She hadn't planned to go to town. Despite all the work she'd been doing on the farm, all the good she was accomplishing, people still watched her suspiciously when she went out in public. She might be helping the Bradshaws, but she was still the woman who hadn't turned in baby Miracle's mother, the one whose husband had fled town before he could be questioned by the police. She was a stranger and an enigma, and the town would probably be happy when she was gone.

She'd be happy, too.

Except that when she dreamed, she dreamed of the fertile fields and the distant mountains. She dreamed of plants sprouting from rich earth and rain falling on lush crops. She dreamed of apple blossoms and children's laughter and hundreds of things that she'd never have in Seattle.

She put on her coat, hooked her purse over her shoulder, and walked outside, a soft spring breeze tickling the hair at her nape. The air was still edged with winter, but she could feel a hint of warmth in it, smell the sweet aroma of new growth.

All around her, the farm was coming to life. Fields plowed and ready to plant. Chicken coop gleaming white in the setting sun. Barn cleaned out. Stalls fixed. Local suppliers contacted about chicks and feed. She could imagine the place in the fall: teeming with life and overflowing with energy.

"But you won't be here. And that's okay," she reminded herself, climbing into the Pontiac and pulling away from the rancher. "Because you're doing this for Sunday and her kids."

She drove along the quiet country road, meaning to turn toward town. Instead, she headed away from it, the evening growing darker as she wound her way through thick forests and onto a long stretch of highway. Sunday's rehab facility was a few miles south of Spokane, the pretty brick building sitting smack-dab in the middle of acres of green lawn. When Sunday was ready, she'd be wheeled through the gardens and inhale the fragrant aroma of lilac and honeysuckle.

For now, she was confined to her room on the second floor, bay windows on the west wall looking out onto the garden. People visited and brought flowers and cards and pretty little knickknacks. The decor was cheerful, the staff kind. It was a private room. Spacious. Probably expensive. Clementine hadn't asked. She knew there'd been an insurance payout for Matt's death and that more money was coming in for Sunday's care. The drunk driver who'd caused the accident had been driving a commercial truck, carrying produce to a local store.

He'd crossed the center line at seventy miles an hour.

He and Matt had both died instantly.

Sunday's survival had been a miracle.

Every day that passed when she didn't return to her children made it seem a little less like one.

Clementine checked in with the receptionist, slapped a name tag onto her chest, and took the stairs to the second floor. The corridor was quiet, most visitors gone for the day. Even with beautiful paintings and warm wood floors, there was sadness to the place. Sure, there were people there who were rehabilitating from injuries and were going home, but there were others, like Sunday, who, maybe, never would.

She didn't knock on Sunday's door, just walked in, expecting to see the hospital bed, the two empty chairs, the cards and knickknacks and flowers. The window looking out onto a landscape that Sunday never seemed to see, a hint of fading sunlight in the distant clouds.

She wasn't expecting to see Porter, but he was there, sitting in a chair with a book in his hand.

"Porter," she said. "What are you doing here?"

"The same thing you are. Visiting Sunday," he said, setting the book on the table and standing. "I like to read to her when I'm here. *Little Women*, because it's her favorite."

"It is?"

"Yeah. She told me that once when I was visiting. She was reading to Twila, and this was the book. Her favorite, and she said she wanted to share it with the people she loved the most." He touched the cover. "That seems like a lifetime ago, but it was probably less than a year. I was on one of my quick visits. In and out in two days flat."

"You've stayed a lot longer this time. I know Sunday appreciates that."

"If she knows, I'm sure she does. If she doesn't, I don't care. You were right when you said that I'm the kids' uncle. Not some temporary fill-in who's only hanging around until someone else comes along."

"I probably shouldn't have said that. Your family's business isn't mine."

"It sure as hell is. I've seen what you've been doing with the kids—teaching them things that are making them feel strong and capable and in control. They're happier now than they've been since the accident. I'd say that's mostly because of you. So, yeah, you have a say in what's going on, because you've invested in their lives."

"Just for a while. Just until the end of summer," she reminded him, and herself.

"What you've done for Sunday's kids is going to be with them forever." He was looking into her eyes when he said it, and she was looking into his, and she could hear that pulsing drum again, feel an invisible thread that seemed to pull her toward him.

If she let herself, she could believe that's what had made her turn away from town instead of toward it. She could believe that was what had drawn her to the rehab facility on a day when she hadn't planned to go.

If she let herself, she could believe a lot of things.

But that didn't make them true.

She needed to remember that.

She needed to remember her goals.

Mostly, she needed to remember that she and Porter were both planning to go. One to LA. One to Seattle.

She dragged a chair to the bed and sat, focusing her attention on Sunday.

"She's pale," she said, brushing wisps of hair from Sunday's forehead. She'd had three surgeries on her brain, and her hair had been shaved twice. It was growing in now, wheat-colored and fine.

"I thought so, too, but the nurse said she's fine."

"I hope she's right. The kids will be heartbroken if she takes a turn for the worse."

"They're heartbroken every time they come and she doesn't know who they are," he replied, rubbing the back of his neck. "God, this is all such a mess."

"The kids said that Rumer and Sullivan are back. That might make things easier."

"They arrived this morning."

"They also said that Rosie is staying on," she added.

"Right. Those kids have big ears and bigger mouths."

"And that you'd left."

"I did." He gestured to an overnight bag that sat on the floor near the window. "I had some things to take care of in LA. Today seemed like as good a day as any to do it."

She nodded, touching Sunday's cheek. "It would also be a good day for you to come back to us, Sunday."

Sunday opened her eyes. Just like she usually did.

"Good for you, hun," Clementine encouraged, smiling into her friend's eyes. She got a blank stare in return, Sunday's once lively gaze hazy and unfocused.

"It's one of her bad days," Porter said. "She hasn't tried to communicate with anyone. The nurse said that's pretty typical of these kinds of brain injuries."

"It's going to take time for her to completely heal."

"So the doctors and nurses keep saying, but the longer

this goes on, the harder it is to believe that she ever will," he admitted. "The kids are feeling that most of all. Aside from Moisey, they've been reluctant to visit."

"Moisey will probably never be reluctant. Currently, she's obsessing on pink bandages, because she's sure if she puts one on her finger, she'll be able to bring Sunday back from whatever dreamworld she's wandering in. She's got quite an imagination."

"And quite a propensity for getting into trouble. I should call my brother and let him know she might be on the prowl tonight."

"I called Rosie. She's going to make sure Moisey doesn't go wandering tonight. I told her I'd go to town, hunt down pink bandages, and drop them by the house later. Somehow I ended up here."

"This is a long way from town."

"Yeah. It is."

"But here you are anyway."

"Here we both are. For a while. When does your plane leave?"

"It left at three this morning. It returned an hour ago."

"You missed it?" she asked, finally glancing his way again, her breath catching, her heart leaping, that thread pulling taut between them.

"It would be a little difficult to be here if I had," he responded.

"But . . . you're not in LA."

"I was. I had a meeting at nine. Another one at two. I hopped on a return flight as soon as it was over."

"But Sullivan is back."

"And?"

"You did your part."

"I guess you didn't hear what I said earlier: I'm not going to be a fill-in until someone else comes along."

"I heard what you said."

"But you didn't understand what I meant. The kids need consistency and stability. Now more than ever. They can't handle saying good-bye every other day of their lives. So, I'm staying."

"Staying?"

"In Benevolence. In the Lee Harris house."

"But you hate that house."

"I hated what it represented, but I'm not going to turn my nose up at something that will give me a chance to be around for Matt's kids."

"You have a job and a life in LA."

"I *had* those things. Now my life is here. My job is going to be making sure my nieces and nephews know I can be counted on. My most important job, anyway. Since I also have to eat, I talked to the sheriff a couple of days ago. He's looking for a part-time deputy. If things work out, it'll be full-time in a year."

"But when Sunday recovers—"

"I'm going to be here. No matter what happens. Because those kids need at least one person who makes sure they know they're not throwaways or afterthoughts," he said, staring straight into her eyes.

Her heart thumped.

Hard.

Because he'd done what she couldn't. What she wouldn't. And he knew it.

"That's another thing I shouldn't have said," she mumbled, her mouth cottony, the words tight.

"Why not? It's the truth. And here's another one: sometimes, a person's got to brave-up. Sometimes, he's got to forget the past and all the shitty things that have happened, and he's got to throw himself into the future. New plans.

New goals. New dreams. Because holding on to what he thought he wanted isn't going to give him what he needs."

"Are you talking about me? Or you?"

"I guess you'll have to decide that." He lifted the overnight bag and crossed the room.

"You're leaving?" she said, because she wanted to ask him to stay, but the words were stuck in her throat, caught somewhere between fear and longing.

"The silent auction is Friday night, and there's still a lot of work to do to prepare for it," he responded, his tone clipped and a little angry.

"How are the ticket sales? Will there be a good turnout?"

"Life is too damn short to waste time talking about things that don't matter."

"It's a benefit for Sunday's kids. Of course it matters," she said, purposefully being obtuse, because that was easier than being honest. Easier than telling him he was braver than she was, more noble, made of the same stuff as ancient heroes and modern champions.

"Tell you what, if you want to know about the auction, call the mayor. Because it's been a long day, and I'm too tired to discuss it. See you around, Clementine."

"Porter," she began, but he left the room, walking away with the quick, brusque stride of a man who had better places to be.

"Damnit," she whispered, dropping back into the chair, her eyes burning with useless tears.

She could have gone after him.

She could still go after him.

So why didn't she?

Because of her job? Because of the past? Because she really was so much of a coward that she wouldn't risk her heart?

"He's right. Life is too short to waste time talking about

things that don't matter." The words were slurred, the voice almost inaudible, but Clementine heard it. At least, she thought she did.

She glanced at the door, expecting to see a patient who'd been walking through the hall and overheard the conversation. Maybe an elderly woman with white hair and a wizened face.

The doorway was empty.

She crossed the room and looked into the corridor.

It was empty, too.

So maybe she'd imagined the voice, or maybe it was a ghostly manifestation of her subconscious mind. Whatever the case, the voice was right. Porter was right.

Which could only mean that she was wrong.

She could either stand around knowing it and not acting on it, or she could run after him. She could speak the things that mattered. She could tell him what was in her heart. She could throw herself into the future and see where it led.

Because her parents hadn't raised her to be a coward.

They hadn't taught her to be afraid. Not of relationships. Not of love. Not even of heartache.

Sim had taught her that, and she didn't want to carry the lesson with her. She wanted to release it into the cool night air and watch it twirl into the evening sky.

"Where are my children?" the voice whispered again, the words like an icy finger sliding up Clementine's spine. Ghostly. Disembodied. Made of cloud and mist and morning fog.

She turned slowly, not sure what she expected to see. The jug-woman—Pukjinskwes—speaking from the shadows, calling for the babies that she'd stolen? A ghostly apparition hovering above the floor?

She scanned the room. Saw herself, tall and pale, reflected in the bedroom mirror. Saw the empty chairs. The abandoned book. The bed.

Sunday. Looking at her.

Really looking.

No haze in her eyes. No vague emptiness in her gaze.

"Sunday?" she said, rushing back across the room, lifting her friend's hand, terrified that she'd imagined the voice, the alertness in Sunday's face.

There was a heartbeat of silence, then another.

Finally, Sunday's lips moved. "Who are you?"

"A friend." She pressed the call button, desperate to summon a nurse, to have someone verify what she was seeing and hearing. Because this was big. It was huge.

Sunday had spoken previously. She'd seemed semi-alert on a few occasions, but she'd never asked for her children. She'd never seemed at all aware of the situation she was in or the life she had lived. She'd never looked into Clementine's eyes and asked who she was.

A nurse walked into the room moving way too calmly and slowly for Clementine's liking.

"Is everything okay in here?" she asked.

"Sunday is waking up," Clementine responded, her gaze fastened on Sunday's pale face, because she was afraid if she looked away, the moment would end.

"She's been awake since she left the hospital," the nurse replied.

"I know, but she's *really* waking up. As in, she's asking questions about who I am and where her children are."

"Really?" The nurse looked doubtful, but she crossed the room, lifting Sunday's wrist and feeling for her pulse.

"How are you, sweetie?" she asked.

Sunday didn't answer. She was still staring into Clementine's face.

"Sunday?" the nurse persisted, and Sunday's gaze shifted. "Where am I?"

The nurse's eyes widened.

"Evergreen Valley Rehabilitation Center," she responded. "Do you know your name?"

"Sunday. Bradshaw."

"How about your age?" the nurse asked, reaching for the bedside phone and pressing several buttons. She was calling the doctor and other nurses, summoning experts, getting as many people to serve as witness to the event as she could.

That made sense. Call people. Let them know. Gather everyone who loved Sunday around the bed, so they could hear her voice and look into her eyes, see a hint of the person she used to be.

Just in case it didn't last.

Just in case she slipped away again.

Clementine yanked her cell phone from her pocket, scrolling through her contacts. All the Bradshaws were listed, and she could have called any one of them, but Porter was closest. He couldn't be more than five minutes away.

She called him, her hands shaking as she held the phone to her ear and waited impatiently for him to answer.

Porter was six miles from the rehab center when his phone rang. He was in just the kind of mood to ignore it.

He'd had a long day of meetings with people who'd been desperate to convince him to stay at his job. He'd been offered concession after concession. Different hours. More pay. More input into who he took on as client. The option to relocate to Benevolence and travel back to LA when he had a job. Flex hours and bonus pay and a hefty check to put in a fund for the kids' college educations.

It had sounded nice.

Better than nice.

It had sounded like something he couldn't have refused a few days ago.

But this wasn't a few days ago, and he wasn't the same guy who'd flown into town thinking about nothing but how quickly he could fly back out of it. He was an uncle with six kids who needed him.

The phone rang again, and he frowned, pulling to the side of the road and checking the caller ID.

Clementine's name and number flashed across the screen, and his heart sank. This had to be bad news.

Sunday had looked as pale as he'd ever seen her, her body so frail, he'd thought a light breeze could have broken her bones. If she died after all these weeks of the kids hoping and praying, if she fell back into a deep coma and didn't come out of it, he didn't know how he'd break the news to them.

911. Pick up! Now! Clementine's text streamed across the screen as the phone continued to ring. She's talking!

His heart jumped, his pulse racing as he connected to the handless phone system.

"What's going on?" he nearly shouted, useless adrenaline pumping through him, the tires squealing as he made a sharp U-turn and sped back toward the rehab center.

"She's awake," Clementine replied breathlessly.

He could hear hope in her voice. Relief. Fear.

"Is she connecting with people? With you?" he asked, because Sunday had been semilucid just enough times for him to stop getting his hopes up when it happened.

"She asked who I was. She asked about the kids. She remembered her name. She's never done any of those things before."

She hadn't, and he felt something feathery and light spring to life inside him. Optimism. Anticipation. Things he'd stopped having after the first few days of hopeful waiting. Things that he'd buried deep when Sunday had been moved to rehab, because it had been too painful to begin every day believing she'd reenter the world and end it knowing that she hadn't.

"Is the doctor there?" he asked.

"A nurse called him. He's on the way. How far are you? Oh God, Porter! What if she slips away again before the kids see her?"

"Call Sullivan," he replied. "Tell him what's going on, but let's try to keep it from the kids until they get to the center. That way if something happens . . ." He couldn't finish. He didn't want to think about how devastating that would be.

"Right. Okay. I'll call. Just hurry back, okay? She needs her family." She disconnected, and he called Flynn, pressing the gas pedal nearly to the floor.

He wanted to be at the rehab center *now*. He wanted to talk to Sunday, assess things, see if bringing the kids to see her was going to be the right thing to do. The last thing he wanted was to hurt them. If she wasn't herself, if she didn't act like their mother, would their hearts break more?

God, this was hard.

Knowing the right thing to do. Not for Sunday. Not for himself. For them.

"Hello?" Flynn answered on the fourth ring, the connection staticky and tenuous.

"Sunday's awake," he responded.

"What? Are you sure?"

"Clementine is with her. I'm almost there."

"I'll be there as soon as I can."

"You might want to wait. If things change, a trip will be a waste of your time."

"If things change, you and Sullivan are going to be dealing with six heartbroken kids. Like I said, I'll be there as soon as I can. Probably early tomorrow morning. I'll rent a car, so no one has to pick me up at the airport. Text news as it happens. I want to be kept in the loop." He disconnected, and Porter turned into the rehab center.

He parked in the first available spot and jumped from the SUV, sprinting into the building and past the receptionist. Up the stairs and onto the second floor. He could hear voices as he ran down the hall. Men. Women. A buzz of excitement, and it was coming from Sunday's room.

He pushed through a crowd that had formed near her door, shoving his way past a couple of nurses. He didn't care if he was being rude. He needed to know that the kids weren't walking into heartbreak and disappointment. He needed to know that Sunday really was awake. He needed to know, damnit, that everything really might be okay.

"Porter," Clementine said, suddenly beside him, her hair tumbling around her face, her eyes wide. "You made it."

She grabbed his hand, pulled him to the bed, stood there beside him with her fingers curved through his.

Sunday was lying exactly the way he'd left her, sheets pulled up to her chin, a blanket over her lower legs. Soft golden hair poking out in dozens of different directions, the scar from her surgery angry-purple and puckered.

But her eyes were open. She was staring at his face, studying it as if she were trying to figure out who he was.

"Hey," he said. "I'm—"

"Porter," she said, her voice as soft as a butterfly's kiss. "Where are the kids? Where's Matt?"

The question was like an arrow to his heart.

He should have known she'd ask. He should have talked to Flynn, come up with a plan for how he would answer.

"Porter?" she said, grabbing his wrist, her hand ice-cold and dry, her grip weak.

"Let's talk when you're feeling better," he suggested,

knowing she had a right to the information, that she needed it, but unable to speak the words that were going to break her heart.

She and Matt had been grade school friends, junior high buddies, and high school sweethearts. They'd married the day she'd turned eighteen. She'd known him for most of her life, loved him for nearly as long. Despite the troubles they'd been facing at the farm, despite whatever had been going on between them, Porter had to believe that still mattered.

"Where are they?" she asked again, sitting up. Shoving the covers away.

"Sunday," a nurse said, putting a hand on her arm and trying to stop her. "Slow down. You're going to hurt yourself."

"Are they dead? Is that why no one will answer my question?" she asked, still staring into Porter's eyes, her face stricken, colorless.

"Call the doctor," the nurse said to no one. "See if he'll order a sedative."

"No," Clementine protested. "You can't knock her out. She just woke up."

"Not knock her out. Calm her down."

"What's the difference if she can't greet her kids when they come to see her?"

"I agree," Porter said, sitting on the edge of the bed, pulling Clementine down beside him. For the first time in longer than he could remember, he didn't know what to do. Tell Sunday the truth? Keep it from her?

"She needs to know," Clementine said quietly, as if she'd read his mind.

"What? Just tell me, okay?" Sunday said, her voice raspy and hot.

"You and Matt were in an accident," he responded, touching the back of her cold hand and looking into her eyes.

"Mr. Bradshaw," the nurse snapped. "You should speak with the doctor first. He'll be here soon."

"Matt didn't survive," he continued, ignoring the warning, because speaking the truth felt right. Because before the accident, Sunday had been one of the strongest women he'd known. When her father had died of a heart attack, she'd planned the funeral and stood by her mother's side. When her mother had died of cancer six months later, Sunday hadn't crumbled. She'd cried, she'd mourned, and she'd continued on.

"What about Moisey?" she asked, her voice breaking, her eyes dry.

"Moisey's fine," Clementine said, reaching out to hold Sunday's other hand. "Still getting into all kinds of mischief. Just like she always has."

"You know her?" Sunday asked, her brow furrowed. "I don't remember you being at the house. I'm sorry."

"You don't have to remember," Clementine reassured her. "I'll remember for you."

"But you've seen Moisey, right? She really is okay?"

"She's great. The boys are great. Twila is awesome. And Heavenly is doing a wonderful job caring for the baby."

"Heavenly?"

"She's your oldest. You adopted her six months ago," Porter reminded her, glad the teenager hadn't been around to realize she was the child who'd been forgotten.

"And the baby?"

"Oya," Clementine said. "She and Heavenly are half-siblings."

"Okay," Sunday said. "I'll try to remember them."

"If you don't, it's okay," the nurse assured her, glaring at Porter reproachfully. "You had a serious head injury. Getting all your memories will take time."

"If I don't, it's not okay. They're my daughters. My soul should remember that, even if my mind doesn't."

"You're tired. Why don't you lie down for a while and close your eyes, rest until the kids arrive?" Clementine stood and tugged Porter to his feet.

"I'm afraid I'll fall asleep and Moisey will visit me in my dreams again," she responded, but she settled back against the pillows, closed her eyes. "Even when I'm sleeping, that little girl knows how to talk my ears off."

"What did she say to you?" Clementine asked, pulling the covers up around her, tucking them in the way she would for a child.

"That I had to come home," she murmured, her eyes closing, her face relaxing.

Porter resisted the urge to shake her shoulder, remind her that she had to stay awake until the kids arrived.

"She had pink fingers," Sunday continued, as if she were trying to hold on to the memory.

"Pink?" Clementine stiffened, her gaze shooting to Porter.

He knew what she was thinking, but there was no way on God's green earth Moisey had somehow really slipped into Sunday's dreams.

"She was talking about pink bandages the last time she was here," he explained. "Sunday must have heard and stored it away in her memories."

"Right. Sure," Clementine said. "That makes sense."

"What else could it be?" he asked, pulling her away from the bed, afraid Sunday would hear and worry.

"It could be that Moisey really found a way into the shadow world of dreams. It could be she really did put her hands on her mother and heal her. It could even be that she really did tell her that she had to come home." She grinned. "You don't believe that."

"It doesn't matter what I believe. All that matters is what happened." She cocked her head to the side and pointed at the door. "I hear the kids. Better brace yourself."

Seconds later, the group marched in. Single file. Quiet. Solemn. Like they'd been during every visit for as long as Sunday had been in rehab.

Sullivan stepped into the room behind them, his hands shoved in his pockets, his gaze on the bed. "How are things going?"

"Better than I'd hoped they would," Porter replied, and Sunday shifted in the bed, lifted her head, saw her children standing awkwardly near the door.

"You're here," she said softly.

And all six kids turned in her direction. Eyes wide. Mouths open.

Twila broke rank first, darting across the room, hands reaching for a hug before she even got to the bed.

"Mommy," she cried. "Mommy!"

The rest of her siblings followed.

Except for Moisey.

She was standing in the doorway, faux diamonds sprinkled in her curly hair, both hands held out, every finger wrapped in bright pink duct tape.

"It worked," she breathed. "It did! You were right, Uncle Sullivan. Duct tape is just as effective as Band-Aids when it comes to healing moms."

Chapter Nine

There were a lot of things that felt like joy.

Rays of sunshine after a storm.

Hints of spring at the end of winter.

Kittens. Puppies. Dandelions. Summer rain on tender shoots.

And children. Wrapped in their mother's arms.

Clementine watched the reunion for just long enough to see that Sunday remembered Heavenly's name and that she hugged her just as tightly as she did the other children. She watched just long enough to know that a white-coated doctor slipped into the room, shooed out most of the rehab staff, and pulled a chair over to the bed. She watched just long enough to notice Porter and Sullivan, heads bent together, speaking quietly to one another. She watched, but this scene?

This feeling of joy?

It was for family.

So she stayed just long enough to see that everything was exactly as it should be, and then she walked into the hall, jogging down the stairs and out into the quiet night.

The moon hadn't risen, but stars were sprinkled across the evening sky, sparkling against the backdrop of the endless universe. In a place like this—a place where light, billions of miles away, could travel to a viewer on a little planet called earth—nothing seemed impossible.

Little girls could wrap their fingers in pink duct tape and channel the healing energy of the Creator. They could wander through the land of dreams to save their mother's lives. Women could wake from comas. Dying farms could be brought back to life.

And people like Clementine?

They could discover that ever-after existed, that love could last forever, and that the thread that bound lives together could never truly unwind.

In a world like this one, dreams could be changed. Paths could be altered. And things that had seemed so necessary could become what didn't matter anymore.

She walked around the side of the building, in no hurry to leave. The rancher was empty, no drama waiting to pounce when she returned. She had her spinning wheel there. Her carded wool. She had boxes of alpaca fleece and skeins of beautifully colored yarn. She had, if she allowed herself to admit it, everything she needed to be happy. Even without a full-time professorship or a cute little house in Seattle, life felt good. Right even.

But that didn't mean she should give up on what she'd worked so hard for. She'd spent years studying. Years taking tests. Years working to establish herself in academia.

She had a chance, finally, to go back to the dreams she'd given up for Sim. Without him in her life, she was free to do what she wanted, to go where she felt led.

She was free.

Just to be herself.

If only she knew what that meant.

She crossed the center's yard, grass tickling her ankles

as she walked and, then, she crouched to run her palms over the sweet-smelling blades.

Years ago, she'd spent every summer evening lying on the ground, staring up at the stars. After her father died and she moved to the city, she'd forgotten the pleasure of lying in silence, of staring up at the infinite expanse of space, of wondering at the extraordinary mystery of life existing right there where she was.

She dropped to the ground, lying on her back just the way she used to. The sky was just as beautiful, the stars just as bright. She didn't feel lonely here. She didn't feel small. She felt like part of something big and bold and wonderful.

"Can I join you?" Porter asked, his voice breaking the silence and interrupting her solitude.

She could have sent him away.

An hour ago, she probably would have.

But there was room beside her, and a deep ache in her soul that yearned for him.

"Sure," she said. "If you don't mind grass-stained clothes."

"What's life without them?" he asked, and she smiled.

"Cleaner?"

He chuckled, stretching out beside her, shoulders touching. Pinkies touching. The sky above and the earth below, and Clementine could think of a dozen stories that began this way.

"It's beautiful, isn't it?" she said.

"You're beautiful," he responded.

"We're looking at the sky, Porter. Not each other."

"I didn't realize there were rules to the game."

"It's not a game. It's a memory."

"That you're trying to relive?"

"That I'm trying to create," she responded.

"So, a new memory?"

"Making new ones is better than holding on to the old, don't you think? Besides"—she reached for his hand, twining her fingers through his—"I want this one to be with you."

"Be careful, Clementine," he said, levering up so that he could look into her face. "One memory with you won't ever be enough."

"Okay." She turned onto her side, trailing her fingers along his jaw.

"What does that mean?"

"Just . . . okay. Let's make more than one."

"You're going back to Seattle, remember?"

"Not yet."

"Soon."

"Does that matter to you?" she asked, studying his face, looking for some hint that they really could last forever.

"Of course it matters. You'll be there. I'll be here."

"It's not that far."

"Only as far as the east is from the west."

"What does that mean?" It was her turn to ask.

"Long distance relationships seldom work."

"So you're telling me that if I go, we can't try?"

"I'm telling you that if you go, it's because there's something better for you there than there is here." He smoothed his hand over her hair, smiling gently into her eyes. His tone, his gaze, his tender touch, falling like fragrant raindrops on her heart.

"It doesn't have to be better to be important," she said, her throat tightening on the words, because she wanted him to understand. If she went to Seattle, she wasn't choosing her old dreams over him. She was choosing both of them. The dream. The relationship. It shouldn't ever have to be one instead of the other.

"No?" He kissed her gently, tenderly, as if she were the

most beautiful jewel in the queen's tiara, the most brilliant star in the night sky. As if everything he'd ever wanted could be found in her.

And, God. She'd never felt like that before. Never felt so completely certain of the look in someone's eyes.

"You're better than Seattle," she murmured against his lips. "Better than teaching. Better than anything I could find in any dream I've ever had. But I can't live with regrets. Not the way I did for so many years. I can't look back and wonder if I compromised me to be with you."

"I would never ask you to do that, Clementine."

"You wouldn't have to ask. It would just happen. Like the sun rising. The rain falling. Like a million other things that are set in motion by one slow spin of the earth."

"Nothing is inevitable," he said.

"What about death and taxes?" she joked. Because this was too much. The sky. The stars. His steady gaze. And she didn't want to make a mistake. Not with him. And not with herself.

He didn't laugh. Didn't speak. He just watched her the way she'd often watched the sun set. Waiting for that moment between day and night, that perfect time when they were almost the same.

"I don't want to disappoint you, Porter," she found herself saying. "I don't want to leave if you really want me to stay."

"Then go," he responded, kissing her again. "Because I want you to be the person who makes you happiest. And I'll be here whenever you come to find me. No matter how long I have to wait."

"Porter," she began again, but he got to his feet and held out his hand, pulling her upright.

"I need to get back inside before Moisey convinces Dr. Anderson that she really does have special powers."

"Is that what she's trying to do?"

"She's trying to drive us all to the edge of sanity. I think she's succeeding."

"You love her," she said, holding his hand as they walked back to the parking lot.

"I love them all. And that's as surprising to me as it probably is to anyone."

"You didn't think you would love them?"

"I didn't think I could. I thought love was a learned behavior. Like manners. Kindness. Self-control. And I didn't have a very good teacher."

"No one needs to be taught to love. We're born doing it. It's hate that gets passed on from one generation to another."

"In that case, I had an excellent coach."

"What was your mother like?" she asked as they reached her car. Because she wanted to know. She wanted to under-stand how someone who'd grown up with fists and hatred could be so capable of love.

"You saw her books. Those are her."

"But . . . what was she like? To you. To your brothers. Did she give lots of hugs? Did she bake special treats? Did she wake you up in the morning by singing songs about the new day?"

"She tiptoed through my life. And she tiptoed through her own. Every gift she gave, she gave in secret, but every dream she had was for her sons. She used to tell us that we were going to grow up and break free and have wonderful lives."

"She was right."

"Yes, she was. It's a shame she didn't live long enough to do the same. Get in your car, Clementine, because I have to go, and I don't want to leave you out here alone."

"I'm not alone. There are a million insects zipping

through the sky, and probably a million bats trying to eat them."

"You know what I mean," he said, taking the car keys from her hand and unlocking the door.

"I know that you worry too much. It's safer here than it is in the city, and it's safer there than swimming in the depth of the ocean without an oxygen tank, so I think I'm going to be just fine."

"You have an interesting way of looking at life."

"I had an excellent coach. Two of them. Maybe you'll get to meet my mother one of these days. She'll probably want to clear your chakra."

"I think having six kids around has already done that."

"Doubtful. Even if it has, my mother will want to work her magic on you."

"There's only one person whose magic I'm interested in," he said, running a finger from the edge of her jaw to the hollow of her throat.

"I've got no magic, Porter. Not like Moisey. I can't put pink tape on my fingers and heal the world."

"Maybe not, but you've helped to heal my family. You pushed us together when it felt like we were falling apart, and I'll never forget that. Or the way it feels to be in your arms."

"That really is the most beautiful thing anyone has ever said to me," she whispered.

He kissed her, his hands slipping beneath her sweater, his fingers trailing along her spine. Everywhere he touched was fire, every caress a kiss by candlelight.

She thought that if she were standing in that perfect moment between night and day, this would be it. He would be it. That dip of light falling into darkness, waiting for the sky to explode with stars.

He stepped back, his eyes blazing, his chest heaving.

And she wanted to reach for him again, pull him back into her arms.

"God, you're beautiful," he muttered, taking a deep, shuddering breath. "And I'd spend forever out here with you, but Sullivan is probably wondering where I've gone. Either that, or he's been overcome by the six hellions we've inherited."

"They're not that bad." She laughed.

"They're worse, but they're still angels compared to me and my brothers at that age. Get in the car. You need to go home before I abandon good intentions and leave my brother to fend for himself."

She smiled, sliding behind the driver's seat and shoving the key in the ignition.

"Drive carefully, Clementine," he said, closing the door.

She waved, pulling through the parking space and out onto the road, thinking about his words. What he'd said about wanting her to be her happiest self.

Did she even know what that was? Who it was?

She didn't think so. She thought that in all those years of dating Sim, of being married to him, she'd lost the barometer that measured joy.

Maybe she could find it again.

Maybe she'd found it.

Because when she was with Porter, all she felt was happiness.

The problem with Porter's life was that he had too much to do. Not just helping the city council get the house ready for the silent auction. Supervising kids. Correcting kids. Buying concert dresses for kids. Going to parent-teacher conferences for kids. Even with the kid-related chores split between four capable adults, it felt like more than anyone could handle.

He didn't know how Sunday had ever managed it.

She sure as hell wouldn't be able to do it now.

Even after her sudden improvement, she was struggling to accomplish simple tasks. Tying shoes. Brushing hair. Walking. Climbing stairs. He'd visited her twice this week, and each time she'd looked more tired and less capable of ever going home.

He'd tried to encourage her, to tell her that she was doing fine, but she was grimly determined to return home. To her, every setback felt like a colossal failure. Every clumsy effort felt like a reminder that she wasn't where she wanted to be.

She needed time.

That's what the doctors, nurses, and rehab specialists were saying, but time wasn't something Sunday wanted to give herself. Every day, she called the house to talk to the kids. Every day, she asked Sullivan and Porter to bring her home. Every day, she pushed herself too hard.

She was doing more harm than good to her already broken and patched-together body. But telling her that was like telling a winter rose that it was trying too hard to bloom.

"Damnit! Life shouldn't be this complicated." He dropped the paint roller into the paint tray and surveyed his work. Butter-yellow paint on smooth walls. Satiny white trim. Beautiful hardwood floors gleaming in chandelier light. The music room was the last room to be renovated. And now they were officially done.

"What's the cursing for? It looks great," Mayor Ann Williams exclaimed, walking in from the dining room. She wore coveralls, high heels, and a smile that most people found contagious. At forty-two, she was the youngest mayor to ever get elected, and the only woman. She seemed to love the job and the town, even though her family hadn't arrived in Benevolence until her senior year of high school.

"It's far from perfect, but thanks."

"You're being modest."

"I'm being honest."

"You're offering an opinion, and that's the last we're going to say on it," she countered, grabbing a pen that she'd tucked behind her ear and checking something off on the clipboarded pages she carried. She'd been working as hard as anyone on the team, but she didn't have a splash of paint on her clothes or a hair out of place.

"One way or another, it's done. And fortunately, everything looks better in firelight," he said, glancing at his watch. Six in the morning. He'd been up most of the night working, but then, so had a dozen other people.

"Right. Fires. We had the chimneys inspected and cleaned, right?" She glanced at the clipboard. "I wouldn't want to burn the place down while we're in the middle of an auction."

"Burning it down might not be such a bad idea."

"I hope that's a joke. This place is on the historic registry. It's also an icon of the town and of the Northwest."

"You might be reaching a little far on how iconic it is. I doubt anyone outside town knows or cares about the Lee Harris house."

"Thomas doubted, too, and he was proven wrong."

He snorted.

"What? It's true. We've got two-hundred and fifty people coming to the auction tonight. Only half of them are from around here. Everyone else is from Seattle or Portland or some other city far away from our quiet little slice of the world."

Something about the words made his mind skip back in

time, made him think about the night he and Clementine had lain in the grass side by side looking up at the stars.

It had been beautiful.

She'd been beautiful, and he'd wanted to pull her close and tell her all the things she needed to hear to make her want to stay.

Instead, he'd told her to go pursue her dreams.

Maybe he was an idiot for it, but he'd wanted her to make her choices and to be happy with them. No pressure from him. No guilt or remorse. She'd left the next day, stopping by the house and telling him that everything she'd wanted to accomplish at the farm was done, Harley was going to take over as farm manager, and she was heading back home. She had planning to do for her classes at the college, an apartment to find. And she had to see if it fit, the life that she'd been imagining. If she could put it on and wear it like a second layer of skin and feel like every part of herself had finally come together.

And he'd understood that.

He had.

She'd kissed him before she'd left and said she'd see him soon. He was pretty sure his heart had broken into about fifty different pieces, but he'd let her go. He hadn't tried to stop her. She'd been married for ten years to a guy who'd cared nothing about her hopes and dreams.

Porter was going to be the opposite of that.

Even if it killed him.

"Hey, earth to Porter. You still with me?" Ann asked, waving the clipboard in front of his face.

"Yeah. Just thinking."

"About how fantastic this place looks and how much money selling it will bring you and your family?"

"I don't think I ever mentioned selling it."

"I'm not just your mayor, I'm also a real estate agent,"

she said, her eyes twinkling with humor. "I'll be very happy to do that for you."

"What? Sell it?"

"Mention a sale. Tonight. At the auction. I'll ask around and see if anyone would be interested in purchasing the house to use as either a home or a destination wedding venue. It cleaned up very nicely, and you and your brothers should be able to get top dollar."

"First, I don't recall mentioning that we're interested in selling."

"You might change your mind. For the right price."

"Second, Benevolence isn't a destination," he continued, without acknowledging her comment.

He, Flynn, and Sullivan had already discussed selling.

They'd already agreed it wasn't the right time.

Yet.

Eventually, they might unload the place to someone who was interested in turn-of-the-century Gothic revival. For now, it was a decent place to get a good night's sleep. Even with all the bad memories associated with it.

"You're mistaken again," Ann said. "We've got the river, the mountains, the chocolate shop. Lots of people would love to come here to get hitched. Or even for a wine-tasting event. A theater night. I can think of a hundred ways this place could draw a crowd."

"Tell you what, how about we just concentrate on tonight and worry about everything else at a much later date?"

"Right. Just putting a bug in your ear. This place has always fascinated me, and I'm thrilled that you and your brothers agreed to open it to the public eye."

"Hopefully, you'll still feel that way when this event is over."

"Oh, I will. I love Sunday. She's a beautiful, warm, and loving mother. She deserves a little nest egg to tide her over while she recovers. How is she doing, by the way? Prep for this has been so hectic, I haven't had time to go visit. I heard she's actually talking and walking? Getting herself around?"

"She's doing better than we could have hoped a week ago."

"But not as well as you'd like?"

"Not as well as *she'd* like. She's pushing herself too hard, and we're afraid she might have a relapse."

"Sunday pushing herself is no surprise. She's been working her butt off at that farm since her folks died, trying to keep it from going under. It probably would have been easier for her to sell it. I mentioned it once, and she thanked me but said the farm was doing just fine."

"It wasn't."

"Yes. I know. It doesn't take an agricultural degree to recognize when fields are fallow and orchards are overgrown. Poor Sunday. She's always been so sure she could change the world, but she couldn't even get a handle on her home."

"What about Matt?" he asked, the same way he'd asked Clementine, and just like she had, Ann stiffened.

"What about him?"

"He lived on the farm, too."

"Right." She walked into the kitchen. Maybe she was hoping he wouldn't follow, but he wanted to know just what his baby brother had been doing in the years before he'd died. He wanted to understand the dynamics of the family he'd left behind.

"Ann, I'm not asking you to fling dirt on my brother's grave. I'm just asking you to tell me what he was doing while Sunday was working her butt off."

"Nothing."

"That's not an answer."

"It sure is," she responded, tucking the pen behind her ear and meeting his eye. "You asked me what your brother was doing. I told you. If you're not satisfied with that, there's nothing I can do about it."

"So you're saying he literally did nothing?" Porter asked, feeling sick at the thought of Sunday taking care of the kids, cooking the meals, and trying to make her farm succeed. Alone. Even while she was married.

"To be fair, he probably thought he *was* working. He did lots of things for other people. He helped fix cars and mow lawns. He painted the Farmington house the year Elmer died. He loved the town, and we loved him."

"But you didn't respect him."

"What gave you that idea?"

"It's hard to think highly of someone who leaves his wife at home to handle all the problems."

"He loved Sunday. He loved his kids. We respected him for that, and for all the things he did to help people who needed it. We all just wondered, though. You know?"

"Wondered what?"

"Why he didn't do the same at home." She shrugged. "Anyway, he's gone, and that's painful enough for you and yours. Why rub salt in the wound? The caterer is going to be here shortly to start prepping. The tents will be delivered a little after that. The planner is taking care of the exterior decor. She'll be setting some things up inside, too, but I thought we'd leave it more authentic and let the period furniture do the talking. Doors open at seven. Everyone in your family has free entry. If anyone else tries to get in without paying, you can play bouncer."

"Why me?"

"You've got the muscle. I'm just the pretty face." She smiled. "I'd better get going. I'm meeting an appraiser at the church. We're going over the itinerary for the sale. See you tonight."

"See you then." He waited until she was gone, then

cleaned up and put away the paint, walking through each room and checking to make sure everything was exactly like it should be. The crew had carried furniture down from the attic, and the old house actually looked like a home. Chairs. Sofas. Tables. Framed paintings hung. Vases on the fireplace mantels. And the old rocking chair that his mother had loved.

He ran his hand over the varnished wood, wondering what her life would have been like if she hadn't married his father. Not as hard, he didn't think. Or as sad.

"What are you thinking about, Uncle Porter?" Twila asked.

Surprised, he swung around, searched the room until he spotted her, sitting on the window seat nearly hidden by thick brocade curtains.

"I think the better question is, *What are you doing here?*"

"Rosie dropped me off."

"Why would she do that?" He crossed the room, pulled back the curtains so he could see all of her, not just a little hint of her face.

"Because I told her you needed my help before school."

"You lied."

"I didn't." She had a book in her hands, and she tucked it into the neat little purse she'd brought with her. "You do need my help."

"I don't recall asking for it."

"Asking for it is often the hardest thing to do. That's why Daddy didn't help around the farm. Mom never wanted to ask. She said he was too tired from all the work he did for everyone else, and she said they all needed the help more." She stood, brushing invisible dust from her thick black tights.

"If you hadn't been hiding behind those curtains, you

wouldn't have heard that conversation." And he was glad that what she'd heard had been appropriate for little ears.

"I wasn't hiding. I was reading."

"Do Rumer and Sullivan know you're here?"

"I might have forgotten to tell them."

"Forgotten?"

"Last night, Rosie said she was going to run to Spokane to get the boys suit jackets for tonight. She said it was totally inappropriate to show up at a black-tie affair in jeans and sweatshirts."

"What does that have to do with you not telling Sullivan and Rumer you were leaving the house? We had this conversation, remember? You're never to go anywhere without an adult knowing."

"Rosie knew."

"Da-ng it! Twila, you know that's not the same thing."

"It seems like it is."

"Not if you told her that you had permission."

"I didn't," she hurried to say. "I heard her talking about it, and she told Uncle Sullivan and Aunt Rumer that she'd leave really early and stop for doughnuts on the way and make a morning of it. If they didn't mind."

"I take it they didn't mind?"

"They never mind things. They said Rosie could leave as early as she wanted and stay out as late as she needed."

"You took advantage of the situation to hitch a ride into town."

"No. I hitched a ride to you. I said you needed my help, and Rosie never asked if I had permission."

"I guess you had a reason for doing this?"

She dropped her gaze, her glossy braid falling down the center of her ramrod-straight back. Her shoes were polished, her dress pressed, every seam falling exactly where it should. But there was something off about her this morning. Something restless and unsettled.

He crouched, brushing too-long bangs away and looking into her eyes. He saw the tears then, sliding down her cheeks.

"Twila? What is it, sport? Why are you crying?"

"Because everybody leaves. Everybody."

"I didn't leave. I just came here for a while. There's a lot of people in the farmhouse. And I didn't want to sleep in the chicken coop. That's all." He tugged her into his arms and was surprised when she didn't push away. Was even more surprised by the hard knot of grief lodged in his throat.

This was what he'd tried explaining to Clementine.

This is what he'd never understood until now.

That love could be so strong for someone who was so new to you. That when a child's heart broke, yours could, too.

"You're going to leave. Heavenly said so. She said adults always do. She said that you just told us you were staying here so that you didn't have to feel bad about going back to LA and abandoning us."

"Heavenly doesn't always know the facts. Next time she tells you something, maybe you should check with an adult before you act on it."

"You didn't say you weren't going back to LA," she whispered so quietly he almost didn't hear. "You didn't say that. And when an adult doesn't say something, it's because he doesn't want to lie."

"I'm not going back to LA," he assured her. "I quit my job there. I moved here. I'm going to be working for the sheriff."

"Why?"

"Because I need a job."

"No. Why did you quit your job and move here?"

"Because you guys need me, and I need you, and we're a lot better together than we are apart. So, I'm staying, and now that you're here, you're going to help me set up for tonight. That way what you told Rosie won't be a lie." He took her hand and was rewarded with a tentative smile.

"Thanks, Uncle Porter."

"Don't thank me until after you see the horrible jobs I'm going to make you do. Scrubbing floors with toothbrushes. Cleaning windows with newspapers. Chasing the rats out with giant brooms."

"Are there really rats?"

"No. Just a lot of old stuff and a few dust bunnies."

And a million memories that were going to have to move aside to make room for new ones.

Chapter Ten

The problem with chasing dreams is that sometimes they let you catch them.

Clementine could hear her father's voice as clearly as if he were sitting in the passenger seat of her overstuffed Pontiac.

She couldn't argue with the adage.

Not when she'd caught the dream she'd been chasing after for five years. The one where she went back to Seattle and picked up where she'd left off. The one where she had everything she'd thought she wanted, a cumulation of all of her dreams.

She'd caught that dream.

She'd held it in her hands for a few days.

She'd lived it and breathed it and told herself that she was thrilled with it.

But the earth in Seattle didn't smell like home.

The gray-blue sky didn't showcase the stars.

And Porter was in Benevolence.

And she was alone.

If that's what catching the dream had brought her, to hell with it. She'd find a new one.

She hummed along with the radio, surprisingly happy

for someone who'd just said good-bye to something she'd spent her entire adult life trying to achieve.

She'd still teach online classes. She'd still be part-time faculty. It would take her a lot longer to pay off her debt and rebuild her savings, but she could sell yarn online and, maybe, sweaters, hats, mittens, and scarves at farmers' markets.

Maybe even at Pleasant Valley Organic Farm.

They'd be selling cider and jam, pickles, fresh produce.

Why not add beautiful hand-knit mittens? Brightly colored hats?

When she'd left the farm, she'd asked Sullivan and Porter to let Harley move into the rancher; she'd suggested that they also put her in charge of the farm. The young woman had learned quickly and was an apt student. She'd been excited to be part of Sunday's vision, but she'd been nervous about doing it alone.

Now she wouldn't have to.

Because the farm was just ahead, fields stretched out beneath the moonlit sky—a patchwork of soils that told the story of what would be planted there. Corn. Alfalfa. Potatoes. Carrots.

She could almost feel the land rejoicing at the harvest.

She pulled down the gravel road that led to the rancher, headlights illuminating the familiar path. How many times had she driven it? Hundreds? More?

When she'd been there with Sim the house had been a cage of her own making, a place where she'd only been trapped because she'd been too afraid to fly.

She could have opened the door at any time.

She could have walked out into the cold, sweet breath of freedom.

Even back then, when she'd been fighting with Sim and fighting for sanity and trying to keep the creditors at bay, she'd loved the land. She'd loved the expansive fields and the distant mountains and the snake-like curve of the river.

She parked where she always had, pulling in behind Harley's beat-up Chevy. She'd called the young woman before she'd left Seattle and explained that she planned to return.

She'd been worried that Harley might be resentful of having a housemate and upset about sharing her caretaker role. Instead, she'd seemed relieved.

"Thank God! I realized three minutes after you left that I couldn't do this alone," had been her exact words.

So they'd be a team, and when Sunday returned, she'd join them, slowly regaining her strength as she worked the land she loved so much.

Clementine climbed out of the Pontiac, popping the trunk and lifting one of the boxes. She hadn't had much stored at her mother's place. Just the few things she'd salvaged after Sim left. Things he hadn't deemed valuable enough to take. Clay pots and vessels made by various Native tribes. A loom that she could teach the kids to weave rugs on.

The thought excited her, and she hurried to the front door, balancing the box on her hip as she struggled to get the key in the lock.

The door opened before she could manage, swinging inward as Harley rushed out, her dark-brown hair soaking wet, shirt damp, eyes huge.

"Oh my gosh, Clementine! Thank God you're here."

"What happened? What's wrong? Did a pipe burst? Which one? In the kitchen? I knew I should have replaced it before I left. Did you shut off the valve?" She set the box on the floor, rushing toward the kitchen.

"No!" Harley nearly shouted. "I was in the shower. The phone rang. It's Sunday. She's missing."

Clementine's heart stopped.

She could swear it did.

Everything inside her going absolutely still and quiet.

"What do you mean, she's missing?" she said calmly, because that was all there was. Calm focus. Complete concentration. There could be no room for panic or for mistakes. Because this couldn't be. It couldn't. Not when everything was finally falling together for the family. Not when the kids were finally starting to believe that everything would be all right.

"The rehab facility called. She's not in her room. They checked everywhere, but they can't find her."

"And they called you?" she asked, telling herself that this had to be wrong. It had to. Because Harley barely knew Sunday, and she wouldn't have been on the emergency contact list.

"They called the home phone. You must have given them the number. I heard it ringing when I was in the shower and listened to the message after. They tried to call everyone else, but no one is answering. The whole family is at that stupid black-tie auction, and they probably have their phones turned off."

"Jesus, let her be okay," Clementine whispered, and it was a prayer. A real one to the divine Creator who had made Father Sun and Sister Moon. Who had breathed onto the earth and set the seasons into motion. Who could feed every bird in the field, and who sure as hell could protect one tiny woman.

She ran to the phone, slamming her finger against the repeat button and replaying the message.

"Hello, this is Linda Bailey. Head night-shift nurse at Evergreen Rehabilitation Center. Your number is listed as an emergency contact for Sunday Bradshaw. I regret to inform you that she was not in her room when we checked on her at nine. We've searched the premises and she hasn't been located. We're reaching out to the local authorities to help with the search. Please call when you receive this message." She rattled off a number that Clementine didn't bother to jot down.

"Did you call her?" Clementine glanced at her watch. Almost nine thirty. Sunday had been missing for at least a half an hour.

"She wouldn't tell me anything because I'm not on the emergency contact list," Harley said, shoving her bare feet into boots and grabbing her keys. "We need to get over there," she said.

"We also need to let her family know what's going on. Did you try to call them?"

"I've left messages on their phones, but I haven't been able to get through."

"Then we'll call the sheriff's office and ask them to send someone to the Lee Harris house." She made the call quickly, using her cell phone, because she wanted to be halfway to the rehab facility by now. Not standing in the rancher, making phone calls.

"Done," she said as she yanked open the car door, tossed her phone into the console, and grabbed the giant dream-catcher she'd placed on the passenger seat, chucking it out onto the gravel.

"I hope that's not a priceless antique," Harley said, jumping into the seat and buckling her belt.

"It's a piece-of-crap I'm-sorry gift my rat bastard ex-husband gave me when he missed my birthday one year. I only brought it because my mother insisted and because I'd have gotten arrested if I'd tossed it out the window while I was driving."

"Your life sounds as complicated as mine."

"It was. I've decided to simplify things."

But, first . . .

First she had to find Sunday.

She drove like a bat out of hell.

Somehow, she didn't get pulled over.

When she pulled into the parking lot of the rehab center, spotlights were everywhere, illuminating pavement and grassy knolls.

She hopped out of the car, not waiting for Harley, just running into the building and up to the reception desk. A nurse was there, standing with several police officers and a K-9 team.

Seeing that—the dog waiting for the command to find the missing—nearly made her knees buckle.

This was real.

It wasn't a mistake.

Sunday was gone.

"What the hell happened?!" she nearly shouted, the calmness she'd felt gone in the face of the cold, hard truth. "How do you lose a patient?"

"This isn't a memory care facility. Our patients are free to come and go as they please," the nurse said without heat.

"How many exits are there?"

"In this part of the facility? Five."

"And no one saw her leave?"

"I'm afraid not. I know this is terrifying for you, but we're doing everything we can to find her."

"I know. I'm sorry. It's just . . . she has kids. They're counting on her coming home."

"Trust me when I say we want the same thing."

"Do you know the exact time she left?"

"As near as we can tell, right after her meal tray was taken away. That was eight thirty. When we checked at nine, she was gone."

"But why?" Harley panted as she skidded to a stop beside Clementine. "Why would she go?"

"Sometimes patients with head injuries act in ways that don't make sense," the K-9 handler said kindly, his eyes shadowed by the brim of his baseball hat. He was about Harley's age. Slim and muscular. His dog was a border collie, its tail thumping with controlled excitement.

"It doesn't make me feel better to think this isn't a well-thought-out plan," Clementine said, and he nodded.

"I understand. But try not to get too worried. Most people we look for are found quickly."

But what if Sunday isn't? she wanted to shout.

What if she isn't found quickly?

What if she's never found at all?

"Was there any sign of her outside?" she asked, directing her question to the nurse.

"No. I'm afraid not."

"Did she have a coat? A purse? Shoes?"

"She took her purse and her shoes. She left her coat behind."

"Sunday, why?" Clementine muttered, wishing her friend was there to ask, because the world was a big place and people disappeared in it all the time.

She walked back outside, bypassing teams of people peering into cars and knocking trunks. Another group was by the dumpster, tossing boxes out onto the ground.

Across the street, a line of people marched shoulder to shoulder, moving across a field and toward the distant tree line, their flashlight beams sweeping across the amber grass.

They'd search the culverts, the dead tree-falls, the forest floor, looking for clues that Sunday had been there.

Maybe she had, but Clementine thought it more likely she'd taken the road. That she'd walked out of the facility, found her bearings, and started walking home.

Wouldn't Clementine have seen her, though?

The route was a straight-shot—highway all the way until they reached the turn for the old country road.

A lone woman walking in the breakdown lane or through the fields? Could she have missed something so conspicuous?

Or had Sunday taken a different route?

Or not walked at all?

Maybe she'd called for a ride. She had friends. She had family. Someone might have been willing to go against doctor's orders and take her back to the farm.

Clementine walked inside again, ignoring the people at the desk, the police officers who were crowding around a security monitor, the curious residents who were peering out from behind their doors.

Sunday hadn't disappeared. Not yet. She was trying to do what most people would—get back where she belonged. Finding her would be as easy as following in her footsteps.

This had started in Sunday's room.

Clementine would begin there, too.

Porter left Sullivan in the parking lot, speaking with a state police officer, and ran up the stairs of the rehab facility, his heart thumping painfully, his stomach knotted with fear. He'd been expecting a lot of interesting things at the silent auction.

A visit from the sheriff hadn't been one of them.

The fact that Sunday was missing seemed almost inconceivable. He'd spoken to her an hour before the silent auction began and told her he and the kids would visit the next morning.

She'd sounded tired, but fine.

Just like she did every day. She'd asked how the kids

were doing. She'd asked about Matt, and he'd had to remind her that Matt was gone. She'd been embarrassed. He'd heard it in her voice, in the way she scrambled to try to explain her lapse in memory.

But that had happened before, too.

Sometimes she forgot things.

Some days she really struggled.

Some days were hard.

This one was threatening to be even worse.

It was bad enough that Sunday had left, but the kids had heard the news from the sheriff. An oversight on Porter's part. He'd been in a hurry and hadn't thought it through. He'd apologized, but the damage had been done.

Moisey had cried. Heavenly had shut down. The boys had immediately begun planning rescue efforts. Twila had remained silent, her dark gaze following his movements as he'd gathered their things and urged them to the van.

Everyone leaves. Everyone, her silence seemed to say.

And, this time, he couldn't tell her that she was wrong.

Because her mother *had* left. She'd walked away from a place that was supposed to help her stay safe. She'd left of her own volition, without a phone call or a note to anyone.

He glanced at his caller ID for the fifth time.

Just to be certain.

Sunday's door was open, and he could see someone sitting on the bed. For one heart-stopping moment, he thought it was her.

And, then, in another, he realized it was Clementine.

He didn't speak. Neither did she.

It seemed more natural to walk into her arms, to run his hand down the curly length of her hair, to kiss the tender spot behind her ear.

"You got here fast," he said.

"I was already home," she responded, the words hanging

in the air between them, simple and sweet and powerful. "Harley and I drove here together."

"And you and I ended up in Sunday's room while everyone else combs the outdoors, looking for her. Did you find anything?"

"Nothing that wants to tell me where she's gone."

"She's gone home," he said, and she nodded.

"I think so, too, but if she walked, it would take hours, and none of us saw her on the road."

"Maybe she was trying to stay out of sight?"

"Sunday isn't that kind of person. She wasn't sneaking. She was just trying to go back home. I was thinking maybe she got a ride." She touched the phone. "So many people love her. Someone might have been willing to drive her away before the doctor said she was ready."

"Most of them were at the silent auction, and she doesn't have her cell phone here. It would have probably been difficult for her to remember numbers."

"A cab then?" she suggested.

It made as much sense as anything. "The sheriff should be able to get a phone log from the front desk. That will tell us if she made a call, and to who."

"It's already done," Sheriff Kane Rainier said, stepping into the room. Like Porter and Clementine, he must have felt it was the right place to begin.

"*Did* she call a cab?" Clementine asked.

"She called Benevolence Baptist Church first. Then she called a cab," he responded. "The cab company confirmed that they sent a car out here. We're trying to get hold of the driver, to try to find out where he dropped her off."

"She has to be at home," Clementine said, pulling out her cell phone. He could have told her not to bother calling. If Sunday had arrived at the farm, they'd already know it.

"Is she?" the sheriff asked Porter.

"No. What time did the cab pick her up?"

"Eight fifty-six. Right out front. I'm surprised none of the staff saw it happen," Rainier responded, his expression unreadable. From what Porter had heard, he was a good cop, a good boss, and a good guy. That would be helpful when he joined the sheriff's department in a few weeks.

"It's a thirty-five minute drive to the farm. She should have made it there by around nine thirty. She wasn't there when Rosie, Rumer, and the kids arrived."

"I don't think she was there when I arrived, either. But I'm not sure. I went to the rancher. Harley and I left from there at around nine thirty," Clementine added, shoving her phone away again.

"No luck?" he asked.

"She isn't there."

"Sheriff?" A young uniformed officer appeared in the doorway, his uniform pressed, his shoes polished. He looked bright as a new penny and nervous as hell. "I have the cab driver who gave Ms. Bradshaw the lift." He gestured to the man who stood beside him. "This is Calvin Woodward."

"Mr. Woodward," the sheriff said, offering his hand. "I appreciate you coming by to speak with us. This is Porter Bradshaw, the missing woman's brother-in-law, and Clementine Warren, her friend."

"Nice to meet you all. Just so we're clear, I didn't come out of the goodness of my heart. Dispatch didn't give me a choice," he responded, but he looked more curious than annoyed. "Did something happen to my fare? She seemed a little shaky when I picked her up. Made me worry."

"But not enough to call the police?" Rainier asked.

"She told me she'd been in a car accident. I could see the scars, so I didn't doubt the story." He shrugged. "She also said she'd lost her husband, and I know how that kind of grief feels. I lost my Vikki three years ago."

"I'm sorry for your loss, Mr. Woodward," Clementine said quietly. "It's hard to lose someone you love."

"Yeah. It is. So, what's going on with your little friend? Was she supposed to stay here?"

"The doctors would have preferred it," the sheriff said, steering the conversation back. "But that's not our concern. Our concern is that she hasn't been seen since she stepped into your taxi."

"Whoa!" the guy held up his hands. "I give people rides. I don't make them disappear."

"Do you remember where you dropped her off?"

"Sure I do. Pleasant Valley Organic Farm. She said she owned it. Nice little property. Cute old farmhouse. Looked like a better place to recover from trauma than this. I don't blame her for wanting to be there."

"What time was that?" Porter asked, impatient to retrace the path Sunday had taken, to figure out the exact moment when she'd dropped off the grid.

"Maybe nine fifty."

"It took you an hour to get there?"

"Just about. She wanted me to drive past a little Baptist church first, before we went to the farm."

"She and Matt got married there," Porter said.

"That's what she told me," the driver said. "She said they were both babies. Eighteen years old."

"They were."

"She still looks like a baby, if you ask me. I'd have thought she was a kid if she hadn't shown me her ID."

"Her ID?" the sheriff asked, jotting something in a note-book he'd pulled from his pocket.

"She didn't have any cash on her, and she couldn't find her credit cards, so she asked if she could write a check. Normally, I don't allow it. Too much hassle if they bounce, but she seemed like a nice girl who'd had a bad break, so

I said it was fine. Still got the check right here." He pulled it out of his shirt pocket and held it up.

"All right, Mr. Woodward. I appreciate you taking the time to speak with us. Here's my contact information. If you remember anything that you think might be important, give me a call." The sheriff handed him a business card.

"Will do. Now, if you don't mind, I'd like to get back to work. Standing around is costing me money."

"Sure." The sheriff nodded, watching as he walked away.

"What do you think?" Porter asked.

"About Woodward? That he's telling the truth. About Sunday? That she did what we all expected. She went home."

"And now she's gone," Clementine added, pulling out her phone again. "I'm going to ask Rumer to check the barn and the ranch house. Maybe Sunday needed some time to think and went somewhere to be alone."

"Ask her to check the boathouse, too. The dock. Maybe the riverbank." Because, there were dozens of places on the farm where a tired woman could be alone and dozens more where she could get hurt. "And tell her we're on the way home. If Sunday isn't there when we arrive, we'll call in some reinforcements. I want to make a thorough search of the property."

"No problem, *boss*," Clementine said, offering a smile to take any sting out of the words.

But, of course, he *was* being bossy, making demands and expecting everyone to fall into line the way they did when he was working. Time mattered then, and it mattered now. Minutes could be the difference between life and death.

Still, this was Clementine. Not one of his associates.

"Sorry," he said as she finished texting Rumer. "I'm used to issuing orders at breakneck speed."

"No need to apologize," she replied. "The sooner we find Sunday, the happier we'll all be."

"I think she's somewhere on the farm. I hope she is," he replied, taking her hand and hurrying her from the room. "Because the kids need their mother."

"I think we all need Sunday. She's the common thread that's drawn us together. She's what we've all been working toward. Her health and happiness. Her reunion with the kids. She's been the goal all along, really. The reason we're all working so hard. We need her to be okay, because that will be the happy ending we all desperately want."

"Has anyone ever told you that you have a way with words?" he asked as he opened the stairwell door.

"A few people have, but it means more coming from you," she replied.

He could have said a lot to that.

He could have read a lot into it.

But they were racing down the stairs, and the opportunity was lost. Or maybe it hadn't really been there at all.

Sunday was their focus. Their goal.

Everything else would have to wait until after they found her.

"I think I need to work out more," Clementine panted as they finally reached the first-floor landing. "I can't keep up with you."

"I've got longer legs," he replied, taking her arm as they exited the stairwell and moved through the throng of people who still crowded the lobby.

"And more cardiovascular fitness. Also, apparently more proficiency at getting people to move out of your way. You approach, and the crowd parts," she said.

"It parts because I plow through. I don't waste time with niceties when someone could be in danger."

"Do you really think Sunday will be at the farm?" she asked.

"Like I said, I hope she is."

"And if she's not?"

"She won't be far from her children. Sunday is motivated by them. She always has been. Wherever they are, she will be."

"You're wrong," she said as they reached her Pontiac. Harley was already there, leaning against the trunk, typing something into her phone. Clementine unlocked the doors, and Harley slid into the passenger seat, closing the door quickly and going back to whatever she'd been doing.

"How so?" he asked, because he'd known Sunday for a long time, and when he looked at her, what he saw was a mother. First. Most. Always.

"She's not motivated by the kids. She's motivated by love. For them or for Matt or for others."

"How is that different than what I said?" he asked as she slid into the car and started the engine.

"She's not just a mom, Porter. She's a wife. A lover. A friend."

"I'm not discounting that."

"Sure you are. You're looking at one surface of a multi-faceted stone and believing that you see the whole thing."

"Will seeing all of it help us find her?"

"I don't know. But it sure as hell is fairer to her. I'll meet you back at the house. Maybe by the time we get there, she will be, too."

She took off, Harley in the seat beside her, boxes of stuff piled up behind them. Her life, fitting in a medium-sized car. If he only looked at that, he might think he knew her, but she was like she'd described Sunday—cut and polished and shimmering from every angle.

And, if Clementine were lost, he'd know where to find her. Under a pristine twilight sky sprinkled with stars. Beside a spinning wheel, soft fibers in her hands. Pounding nails in wood and setting posts in the ground and telling stories of magical things.

Of course, if Clementine were ever lost, she'd find herself, and then she'd build a bonfire to help guide all the people she loved back home.

Chapter Eleven

Sunday wasn't at the house.

She wasn't in the barn or the rancher or the boathouse.

A dozen men and women dressed in their finest clothes helped with the search, all of them willingly leaving their hundred-dollar meals to put on waders and wander through the property. K-9 teams had been called in. Police. Even divers from the local fire department. Searching the fields and the outbuildings and the water.

They'd come up empty.

Their faces reflected their disappointment and concern as they sat in the farmhouse living room, sipping coffee and discussing a new plan.

"Why is everyone here?" Moisey asked, walking into the room wearing a floor-length princess gown and a tiara. Bedtime had been hours ago. She must have slipped past the watchful eye of Rosie, who'd stationed herself on a chair at the top of the stairs, terrified that one of the children would go looking for Sunday and be lost, too.

"You're supposed to be in bed, sport," Porter said, pulling her onto his lap.

God, he looked good.

Black tux. White shirt. Bow tie. Everything about him

hard and masculine and tough. Except his eyes when he looked at his niece. They were soft with love, his fingers gentle as he tucked ringlets of curls behind her ears.

He must have felt Clementine's gaze, because he turned his head, met her eyes.

Her heart leaped in response, and she wanted to reach for him, pull him into her arms and tell him everything was going to be okay. Only she didn't know if it would. She didn't know how this tale would end. Happy or sad, tragic or triumphant. She only knew how she wanted it to go. Sunday. Home with her family.

"Uncle Porter," Moisey said, putting her hands on either side of his face and forcing him to look at her. "You didn't answer my question."

"Because you're supposed to be sleeping."

"I can't sleep, because Rosie is snoring, and I have something important on my mind."

"What's that?"

"There's been a thief in the house."

"Moisey," he said tiredly. "How about we don't play one of your games tonight."

"It's not a game, Uncle Porter. A thief was here. He took Mom's ring."

Porter tensed.

Everyone in the room seemed to do the same—a collective stiffening of spines and tightening of muscles.

"What ring?"

"Her wedding ring. Remember, they had to cut it off her finger after the accident? Remember that?" she asked earnestly, her hands still on his face. Dark skin against tan. Smooth palms against rough jaw. Every bit of them so clearly connected, so clearly family, it took Clementine's breath away.

"I remember," he said.

"And you put it in the little dish on her dresser so we could fix it when she got better?"

"Right. But no one would take the ring, Moisey. It's broken, and it's not worth much."

"It's worth a whole lot of love and it's filled with a whole bunch of dreams. If you put it under your pillow at night, you'll see the person you're going to love forever," she said, nearly whispering.

"Is there a reason why you know this?" he asked.

"Mommy told me. She said that's why people wear wedding rings, because when they're sleeping at night, and their heads are on their hands . . ." She demonstrated, like the true little storyteller she was, her curls bouncing as she tilted her head to the side and rested it on her cupped hands. "They see the person they will love forever, and they remember all the reasons why that love will last and last. So, every night, that's what I do. Only I put the ring under my pillow. Not on my hand. Because it's broken."

"And who do you see, sport?" he asked, his voice so gentle, his expression so soft, Clementine's heart ached.

"Mommy and Daddy. The uncles. Rumer and Clementine. But tonight the ring is gone, and I can't see anything but the tears in my eyes."

"Ahhh, poor little thing," one of the searchers said, standing up and walking across the room, her floor-length taffeta gown rustling as she moved. "We'll find the ring, honey. I'm sure it's just dropped on the floor or rolled behind the dresser. We'll find your mother, too. When she called the church today—"

"She called the church *tonight*," Porter corrected, setting Moisey on her feet and standing up. "The sheriff said she left a message asking for a return phone call."

"She called today, too. I should know. I've been working in that office for fifteen years. Just me, mind you. To do it all. File things. Make the church bulletin. Order flowers. Answer the phone."

"And you talked to Sunday today?" Sullivan prodded, standing just like his brother had. A little shorter and a lot less muscular, he still managed to move with the same easy grace as Porter.

"I did. Poor dear. She couldn't remember the name of the church or our number. She barely recognized my name. She said she'd called three places trying to find the pastor who buried poor Matt. I was happy to tell her that Pastor Mike had, and I told her what a fine job he'd done. It was sad, really. She didn't even know where he'd been buried. I had to tell her that you'd chosen a plot in her family cemetery. Right near her folks, and I had to explain where that was. She made me repeat it three or four times and give her directions for how to get there."

Clementine's pulse leaped, and she jumped to her feet. "Maybe she's there."

"Oh, now, why would she go there at this time of night?" the woman asked. "It's hard enough to find in the day. A person could get lost trying to get there when it's dark."

"She'd go there because Daddy is there," Moisey said matter-of-factly. "And she hasn't talked to him in a long time. Maybe she wanted to talk. Do you think she did, Uncle Porter? Do you think she's lying on his grave talking and crying like they do in the movies?"

"I think her being there is the best idea we've had tonight, kiddo," he responded, grabbing Clementine's hand and dragging her to the door.

Moisey was running along behind, her princess skirt swishing against the floor, her tiara just a little askew.

"Stay here, Moisey," he said as he opened the door and let cold night air sweep in.

"But I want to come and see if Mommy is there weeping all over Daddy's grave."

"Hush," the church secretary said. "That's enough of that kind of talk. Let's go upstairs and get you tucked into bed."

That might have been what happened.

Moisey might have allowed herself to be led upstairs and tucked into bed.

Clementine had no idea; she was running full-out, Porter clutching her hand, his palm rasping against hers.

"We'll have to take the truck," he said, yanking open the SUV's door.

"Should we all go?" Sullivan asked, running behind them, Rumer at his side. "Or do you think that will upset her? If she's there, I mean."

"I think less is more in this case," Porter replied, and Clementine silently agreed. "She was really embarrassed earlier today because she'd forgotten that Matt was dead. She's going to be more embarrassed if she went to his grave and couldn't find her way back. The fewer people who are witness to that, the better."

"Agreed. What should we do with the search crew? Have them stick around just in case? Or send them on their way?" Sullivan asked, sliding his arm around his wife's waist. They were a matched pair. Easy smiles and bright faces and eyes filled with love for one another. Both looked pensive now, though. Concerned.

Hopeful.

Which was exactly how Clementine felt.

Hopeful and worried and terrified that they were all wrong and that Sunday wasn't at Matt's grave.

Porter glanced at his watch. "I think the best thing to do is send them back to the auction. It's probably going to be another couple of hours before it's over, and they should try to enjoy what's left of the night. If we don't find Sunday . . ."

He shook his head. "If she's not at Matt's grave, we'll have to come up with a new plan and some new ideas. Every other place on the farm has been checked."

"I'll tell them that we'll keep them updated and let them know once she's been found," Sullivan said. "I'll give Flynn a call, too. He's trying to get a flight back. This is the second time in a few days that he's flown in for an emergency. It's a shame he can't pack up his life as easily as we've packed ours."

Porter nodded, but he didn't seem to hear. He'd opened Clementine's door and was urging her into the truck.

She snapped her seat belt as he rounded the vehicle, braced her hand against the dashboard as he turned off the driveway, drove through a grassy field and up a shrub-dotted hill.

"Where are we going?" she asked, her teeth knocking together as they rolled over a sapling tree.

"To the river. There's an old bridge about a quarter mile up. It's not easy to find, but it's a hell of a lot quicker than going the long way to Sunday's family plot."

"I didn't know she had one."

"It's on the other side of the river. She owns a thousand acres there. Her family used to have a small dairy farm, and that's where they grazed the cattle."

"She never mentioned that."

He shrugged. "The land has been wild for at least fifty years. She might have thought it would take more money than she had to cultivate it again."

"She wouldn't have to cultivate it," she said, leaning forward as the Spokane River came into view. Sluggish water flowing across huge boulders, marsh grass poking up from muddy soil. "All we'd need to do was plow and toss grass seed. Maybe irrigate."

"Sounds like cultivating to me. It also sounds like money."

"But imagine how it would be, sitting on the farmhouse porch, looking across the river and seeing cattle grazing in lush green fields."

"I can imagine a lot of things through your eyes, Clementine. But right now, all I want to see is Sunday, sitting near Matt's grave." He parked the SUV and got out.

Which seemed odd, because, as far as she could see, there was no bridge.

She climbed out anyway, walking to the front of the vehicle and standing beside him, looking at the flowing river and the blue-black night. "Are we supposed to be seeing a bridge?"

"It's here. We just have to walk around that curve in the bank." He gestured. "There's a narrow section that was easy to build over. They used to run the cattle from one side of the farm to the other over it."

He led the way, and she finally saw it.

"Holy crap," she breathed, eyeing the footbridge that stretched three feet above the flowing water. It had been sturdy once. She could see that. Now, it looked precarious. Several boards missing, water splashing through the openings. "I hope to God none of the kids know about this."

"They don't, but it would probably be a good idea to have it fixed before they discover it. Come on." He walked toward it with confidence.

She wasn't so sure.

"Maybe we should take the long way," she said, hesitating near the first crossbar.

Porter had already stepped onto the bridge, and he glanced back, his expression hidden in shadows. "It's a thirty-minute drive, and if Sunday is at the cemetery, I don't want to leave her there any longer."

"Maybe she's not there."

"She is."

"How do you know?"

"It feels right."

That surprised a laugh out of her.

"What?" he said, holding out his hand, daring her to step onto the bridge with him.

"You seem like a logical, practical, and organized person. Very left-brain. It's surprising to hear you say that you know something based on the way it feels."

"Maybe you and Moisey are rubbing off on me. Now, come on. I might be working a hunch, but I would never take chances with your life. I've crossed this thing a dozen times since my brother's funeral, and if it can hold my weight, it can hold yours."

She took his hand, stepped onto the first crossbar. It was as firm as he'd said.

"Okay. We're going to do this," she muttered.

"Giving yourself a pep talk?"

"Positive mojo. I'm speaking the truth I want to see."

He chuckled, walking in front of her as naturally as if he were walking on a flat stretch of well-padded earth.

She moved more slowly, picking her way from one sturdy board to another, her heartbeat matching the *thump-thump-thump* of the water lapping at the wood.

She didn't realize she'd reached the end until he grabbed her waist, lifting her up and setting her feet on solid ground. She'd have knelt and kissed Mother Earth if she weren't afraid of her shaky legs giving way.

He cupped her jaw, his fingers brushing her ear, his thumb resting at the corner of her mouth.

"See? Piece of cake," he said, dropping a quick kiss on her lips.

And, if they hadn't been on a mission, if they hadn't been searching for Sunday, she'd have thrown herself into his arms and demanded a whole hell of a lot more.

She cleared her throat, stepping away. "Where's the cemetery?"

"This way. On a hill where the family chapel used to be."

"They had a chapel?"

"They settled here before the town existed. There were no churches. Back then, it was the natural order of business to thank God, so they built a place to do it."

"I don't get it," she murmured, following him along the bank of the river and then up a narrow path through thick grass. "Sunday shared a lot of the history of the farm with me, but she never said a word about any of this."

"Maybe it meant too much to her. To know that her family had cleared this land and made it prosper might have been a challenging thing."

"Why? Because she didn't think she could do the same?"

"I don't know, Clementine. I wish I did. I wish I'd spent more time getting to know her and less time believing I did."

They reached the top of the hill, and she could see the fields that had once been—dotted with scrawny pine trees and tangles of field grass and weeds, stretching to the horizon, abandoned and unused.

But the moon was high and kissing the abandoned field with yellow-white light, and she could sense the hands that had once toiled here, imagine the strength of the men and women who had tamed it. She inhaled the loamy earth and the cool spring night, her eyes burning with the beauty of it.

God, she'd missed this.

So much.

The connection to the land, to the men and women who'd walked the earth before her. To the story that was all humanity—toil and heartache and joy and triumph. Life and death and all the small and wonderful moments in between.

"The cemetery is this way," Porter said, taking her hand

and leading her toward a hill that arched up toward the moonlit sky. They walked side by side, through the grass and up the gently sloped ground, and finally she saw a narrow, paved road that meandered through the overgrown field.

They stepped onto it and turned left.

And like a magical kingdom in a fairy tale, the cemetery appeared. A hundred yards away. Wrought iron gate open, rows of headstones gleaming in moonlight. Unlike the field, it was well-tended, a few large trees interspersed between stones that shone white-gray against the dark grass.

"It's beautiful," she breathed as they approached.

"You may be the first person to ever say so."

"What? Cemeteries can't be beautiful?"

"It's not the cemetery. It's what it represents."

"Death is simply life transitioning into another realm."

"Your mother?"

"How'd you guess?"

"It sounds like something a person who clears chakras might say." He walked through the gate and led her along a path paved with smooth river rocks. It meandered between headstones and past a statue of a crying angel, curved around a tree and . . .

Sunday was there, lying on her side beside a marble headstone, her hands beneath her cheek. Eyes open. Face pale.

She didn't move as they approached. Just watched them come, her eyes black orbs in her colorless face. She could have been a statue, a monument to grief. She was that still, that silent.

"Sunday?" Porter said, shrugging out of his jacket and laying it over her. "Are you okay?"

"Just a little . . . lost," she said, her voice raspy.

Clementine thought she might have been referring to

more than just not being able to find her way home. She might have meant that she was unanchored and uncertain and not sure how to find her way back to the person she'd once been.

"I understand," she said quietly, brushing a few dry leaves from Sunday's hair and urging her to sit up. "Sometimes, it's really hard to find your way home. We'll help you, though. Won't we, Porter?"

"Of course. We've been worried sick about you, Sunday. The whole town has been," he responded.

"I'll text Sullivan and let him know we've found her," Clementine said, pulling out her phone as Porter helped Sunday to her feet.

"I'm sorry. I didn't mean to worry anyone. I thought I'd just . . . come for a few minutes and then go back to the house," Sunday murmured. "But I got here, and then I couldn't get back. I kept following the bank of the river, but I swear someone covered the bridge with an invisibility cloak. I finally just came back here. I thought I'd sleep, and when the sun came up, I'd be able to find the bridge and get back home."

"It's a cold place to sleep," Clementine said, putting an arm around Sunday's shoulders. "Especially for someone who's still recovering from serious injuries."

"I really didn't have much of a choice. I walked to the street, but it's just a country road. Not a house or person in sight. I figured it was better to stay here than risk getting really lost. My memory is too shaky to be depended on."

"It would have been better if you'd stayed at the rehab center," Porter said gently. "I could have busted you out for a few hours and brought you here, if you really wanted to come."

"I needed to do this alone."

"I would have given you time by yourself. I know how important that is when you're grieving."

"Maybe you do," she said. "But you don't know what it's like to wake up every morning wondering if something is a dream or a memory," Sunday said. "You don't know what it's like to forget that you've lost someone and then remember again. You don't know what it's like to feel like a part of your life never really happened. Like you fell asleep and woke up a hundred years later. And everything had changed."

"No. You're right. I don't," Porter agreed. "But none of that is unusual for your situation. The doctor said—"

"Stop." Sunday shook her head. "I don't want to know what he said. And I've probably heard it a hundred times before, anyway. I know I have a traumatic brain injury. I know that causes glitches. I know it all, okay? But that doesn't make me feel better when I wake up in the morning and have to try to remember who he was. Sometimes, I can't even remember his face." She opened her hand, the broken wedding ring in her palm.

And Clementine wondered if she'd been resting her head on it, trying to dream of the one she'd love forever.

She shivered, running her hand over Sunday's silky hair, feeling the soft bump of the scars on her scalp.

"It's going to get better," she told her.

"Says the woman whose name I can never remember," Sunday said, half laughing, half sobbing the words.

"It's Clementine, and we only knew each other for a couple years, so I'm not insulted that you forget. I promise, if I ever lose my memory, your name will go right along with it."

"I may not remember your name," Sunday said, leaning her head against Clementine's shoulder, "but I remember your jokes and your laughter. We could have been sisters, in another lifetime."

"Maybe we were. Come on. It's chilly, and you need to get home. Do you think you can walk back?"

"Do I have a choice?"

"Porter's got enough muscle for ten people. He can carry you if your legs hurt."

"Hurt? Hurt is when you stub your toe on the corner of the wall. This is more like battery acid dripping straight into my veins. But I'll walk, because that's the only way I'm going to get better."

"Or hurt yourself more," Porter chided, sliding his arm around her waist. "You have rods in both your femurs, Sunday. Your left foot was crushed. It's okay to work slowly toward improving function."

"You know what I remember?" she said, ignoring his comment and limping along like a wizened old woman.

"What?" Clementine asked, stepping into place on the other side of her, hooking her arm around her just like Porter had.

His arm was beneath hers, his fingers brushing her hip as they walked.

And for God's sake! Poor Sunday was limping along, and all Clementine could do was think about his arm, his hand, the way his lips had felt against hers.

"I remember seeing the truck."

The words were a splash of ice water in the face.

Every thought about Porter fled, and her hand tightened on Sunday's waist.

"It was a quarter of a mile away, and I saw it swerve toward the side of the road and almost clip a tree. I wanted to turn off until it passed. I don't know if I said that to Matt. I don't even remember him being there. I just know I saw the truck swerve, and I was so scared."

"Sunday," she began, not sure what she wanted to say, but Porter nudged her, and she knew she had to stay silent, let Sunday speak her truth.

"And then it was in our lane. This bright bright light, and I thought I'd died. I thought I'd left all the kids on their own, and the pain of thinking about that was so horrible, I just . . . I guess I just slipped away for a while."

This was the memory she had to carry? Not memories of fun times with Matt or days spent with Heavenly. Just the horrible, wretched moment of despair.

God! If Clementine had the power to take it away, she would. If she could wrap her fingers in pink tape and raise her hands to heaven, if she could have that tiny bit of faith that made things happen, that is what she'd do—she'd take away the memory of the accident and she'd replace it with memories of love.

"I think I might have stayed away forever, but Moisey . . ." She shook her head. "She just kept popping into the gray emptiness of my brain, waving her pink fingers in my face and telling me to come home." She laughed. "At least I had some amusing dreams while I was out of it."

"Yeah. Right. Dreams," Clementine repeated, but Porter nudged her again, so she pressed her lips together and stayed silent for the rest of the walk back to the truck.

It took a half hour to make the ten-minute walk back to the truck. A half hour of feeling the tension in Sunday's body as she braced for every painful step.

He'd wanted to carry her, but he had to respect the boundaries she'd set. This was her trauma and her recovery, and he couldn't dictate how it went.

No matter how much he wanted to.

By the time they reached the truck, Sunday was shaking

with fatigue and pain, and he was shaking with the effort to *not* take control of the situation. He helped her into the backseat, pulling a blanket from his emergency kit and covering her with it. "We'll be back soon."

"Home? Or rehab?" she asked, her eyes closed, her lips so pale they blended with her skin.

"I want to say rehab, but you worked too damn hard to get here for me to force you to go back. We can hire a team to come to the house to help with your physical therapy and recovery. As long as the kids will leave you alone enough to let you heal."

"Thanks, Porter," she said without opening her eyes.

He shut the door, turned away, found himself in Clementine's arms.

"You did good," she whispered, her lips brushing his ear, heat shooting through his blood.

"I didn't do a damn thing," he growled, but his hands were gentle as he slid them up her back, pulled her so close there was no space between them. Just the warmth of their bodies flowing together.

"And that was the most difficult thing of all. Like I said, you did good." She kissed his chin and stepped away before he could capture her lips. "We'd better get her home. That's the best place for her."

He nodded, opening her door and waiting as she climbed in—long arms and legs and curvy body, beautiful words and selfless actions and all dozen things he hadn't known he was missing until he'd found them.

He shoved the key into the ignition, starting the truck and turning the heat on high before heading back to the farmhouse.

Only it wasn't just that any longer.

It was that place on the globe, that pinpoint location where hearts beat for the same purpose, where lives collided and meshed and interlocked. Where love became a thing that was as real as the silent breath of a new morning. A place he'd never understood and that he'd never expected to be. But there he was. Stretching himself to fill the spot that Matt had left, and finding it was his place called home.

He pulled up in front of the house, the windows dark, the yard silent. The search party had left. Gone home or gone back to the silent auction. It was just past one, and the farm had the quiet, restful vibe of a hard day's work completed.

"She's asleep," Clementine whispered, and he glanced into the back.

Sunday lay stretched across the bucket seats, eyes closed, breathing even, her hand tucked beneath her cheek.

Was she still holding the broken ring?

Was she seeing Matt in her dreams?

He hoped, for her sake, that she was. That somehow the power of wanting something enough would make it happen.

"You get the doors," he whispered back. "I'll carry her in."

Clementine nodded, running up the stairs to the front door. She had a key. Just like Rosie. Just like Rumer had even before she'd become family. This was a house where doors swung open wide for anyone who wanted to enter. He could feel that in every corner, every comfortable room.

And it was what he wanted for the Lee Harris house.

To replace all the dark shadows with light.

He lifted Sunday gently, careful not to jostle her too much. Her body had been knit back together by careful surgeons and by time, but it would take years before she was herself again.

If she ever was.

Clementine held the door open as he walked through, and they crept through the dark living room and up the stairs to the room where Matt and Sunday had once slept together.

"I hope she's okay when she wakes in here," Clementine whispered.

"I was thinking the same," he responded. "Should we put her in another bed?"

"There isn't one. With Rosie here, the place is filled to capacity. This is going to have to be okay." She pulled back a heavy quilt and motioned for him to set Sunday down. "Let's just pull off her shoes and cover her up. Anything else, and she might wake."

He nodded.

They worked well as a team, hand brushing hand as they tugged off Sunday's shoes, bodies sliding past one another as they pulled sheets over her fragile frame, eyes locked as they plumped pillows, pulled up the quilt, and moved away.

Clementine was the other thing he hadn't expected.

The gift he hadn't asked for.

A sweet melody drifting into the silences. Laughter drowning out the sounds of even the harshest storm.

"You didn't tell me why you came back," he said as they walked down the stairs.

"For the same reasons you did. It felt right."

"How long are you planning to stay?"

"For as long as they need me."

"Just them?" he asked, tugging her close.

"You don't need me, Porter," she said. "You just like having me around."

"I'm not Sim," he said, and she stiffened.

"I know that."

"Do you?"

"Most of the time."

"I'm not flattered."

"And I'm just being honest. I have baggage. Ten years

of being treated like a personal assistant by the love of your life will do that to a person."

"Is that what Sim was?" he asked, his hands sliding into her hair, tilting her head so she'd look into his eyes. "The love of your life?"

"That's what I wanted him to be."

"I'm sorry, then."

"For what?"

"For the fact that he turned out to be a huge pile of pig slop on a hot summer day."

"Pig slop on a hot summer day?"

"I was going to say horse shit, but there are a bunch of big-eared kids in the house."

"Shhhh!" She laughed, and he caught the sound with his lips, tasting the brightness of her joy.

"Why don't you come back to the house with me, Clementine?" he murmured against her lips. "We can make a bid on that year's worth of chocolate and dance the last set of the night together."

"Everyone is probably gone by now."

"They're closing down the bands at two. We still have time."

"It's probably not a good idea."

"Why not?"

"I'm trying to think of a reason," she responded. "Because I still want to protect my heart."

"Protecting your heart feels like a noble thing. Until you realize you've missed out on something wonderful because of it."

"I don't want to miss out on you, Porter. I just want to take things slow. I want to go on dates and dance in the moonlight and walk in the orchards before dawn."

"Did you take things slow with Sim?"

"Do we have to keep discussing him?"

"You're the one with the baggage," he reminded her, and she smiled.

"You're quick, Porter. I like that."

"I'm also persistent. *Did* you take things slow?"

"No. He swept me off my feet, and then—"

"Dumped you on your ass?"

"You've read my story," she said.

"Not all the way to the end."

"Spoiler alert," she replied. "He empties our bank accounts and leaves me for a college student."

"That's not the end of the story, sweetheart. It's only the beginning." He touched the hollow of her throat, feeling the quick, soft thrum of her heart there. And, then, he kissed her. The way he'd wanted to the moment he'd seen her in Sunday's room at the rehab center. The way he planned to every day for as long as she'd allow it.

Upstairs, a door opened, creaking softly on its hinges. Bare feet padded on the floor, fabric swishing as someone walked through the hall.

"Moisey," Clementine mouthed.

He nodded, motioning for her to follow him up the stairs.

They reached the landing just as Moisey disappeared into Sunday's room, a long blanket trailing along behind her.

"Should we get her?" Clementine whispered in his ear.

"Maybe—"

Another door opened, and Clementine jumped back, dragging Porter with her. Her forearm slammed across his chest, pressing him up against the wall. As if they were two spies in enemy territory about to be discovered.

He scanned the landing, saw the twins slipping out of their room, blankets tied around their necks like capes. They moved more quietly than Moisey, scurrying nearly silently into Sunday's room.

"What? Are they having a party in there?" he muttered.

"Shhh. Here comes Twila."

And, sure enough, she was coming. Stepping out of the room she shared with Moisey and running for her mother's doorway, a pile of what looked like folded blankets in her arms.

"That should be it," he said, because Oya was still in a crib, and there was no way Heavenly would want to sneak into Sunday's room.

Only, apparently, she did.

Her door creaked open the same way Moisey's had—with a soft groan, and then she was gliding across the landing, Oya on her hip, a pillow under her arm.

She walked into Sunday's room, and there were no hushed voices, no under-the-breath bickering. There was nothing but the house settling into quiet again, the siblings apparently settling with it.

"What do you think they're doing in there?" Clementine asked.

"I don't know. Maybe we could check."

"Or leave them alone? They're being quiet. That's a good thing."

"Or a really bad one. Come on." He took her hand, and they crept across the landing. Just like all six of the kids had done.

Chapter Twelve

Clementine wasn't sure what she'd see when she looked into the room. Maybe the kids standing around the bed, watching their mother as if she might disappear if they turned away.

What she wasn't expecting to see was a sleepover in progress, blankets and pillows and kids on the floor, Sunday still resting peacefully.

Clementine counted heads from the doorway. Milo and Maddox near the foot of the bed. Twila to its left. Moisey beside her. Only Heavenly wasn't on the floor. She was laying Oya on the bed near their mother, putting her close to Sunday's arm.

Somehow, in her sleep Sunday sensed it.

She reached out, curving her arm around the baby and pulling her close. Heavenly turned away, and probably would have left the room or slept on the floor, but Sunday's voice drifted into the darkness.

"It's a king-sized bed," she said. "There's room for all of you."

And like sea wraiths rising from the ocean floor, four pajama-clad bodies rose from the ground, crawled onto the bed, and found their spots.

"You, too," Sunday said, holding her hand out to Heavenly.

To Clementine's surprise, the teen sank to the bed, curling her body toward Oya and Sunday.

There was a little wiggling, a little twisting, the rustle of clothes, and then, the steady, deep breathing of sleep.

"Come on," Porter whispered. "Before they realize we're out here and all hell breaks loose."

She turned away, following him down the stairs and out the front door.

"They missed her," she said.

"She obviously missed them, too. Not many parents would want all six of their kids sleeping in their bed."

She smiled, walking to her car and unlocking the door. "I guess I'd better go back to the rancher. Tomorrow will probably be a long day."

"How about I come over and help out for a while? What are you and Harley planning to work on?"

"I'm thinking of going across the river and taking a better look at the property there. I'd like to see if it's still suitable for cattle."

"You're not thinking we should have a dairy farm, I hope. Because that sounds like a hell of a lot more work than any of us has time for."

"I'm not thinking that we should have anything but a very successful organic farm. But there's no harm in doing a little research."

"All right. I'll go with you," he said, and she smiled, because she'd thought he would.

Porter was like that: steady and reliable, one of the few men she'd ever known who could always be counted on.

"While we're there, I want to take a look around the cemetery. If the chapel's foundation is still there, we can get the kids to help rebuild it. I'm sure there are photos some-where of what it looked like."

"You think the kids can help you rebuild a chapel?" he asked.

"They helped with the coop." And they'd done a great job. The structure was sturdy, the facade attractive. If she were a chicken, *she'd* want to live there. In a few days, the baby chicks would be delivered, and she'd show the kids how to set up warming lights and feeding stations. She'd show them how to keep the coop clean and take care of any babies that were being henpecked by their peers. And then the kids would be on their own, because that was the best way to teach them. Let them try and fail and succeed and grow.

"That was a rectangular structure, Clementine. It's a pretty simple thing."

"And the chapel is a pretty simple thing, too, because it's not about building something great. It's about building bonds. Plus, it will be a cool attraction, if we do expand the farm."

"If you're thinking about having visitors over on that side of the river, we may have to fix the bridge sooner rather than later."

"We?"

"You didn't think I was going to sit around twiddling my thumbs in the mansion, while you worked your butt off on the farm, did you?"

"I thought you'd be busy with your new job."

"It's part-time for now, remember? I'll still have plenty of time to spend with you and the kids."

"I thought we were talking about the farm."

"We were. Now, we're talking about us. I don't know about you, but I find the subject a lot more interesting." He dropped a kiss on her forehead and climbed into his truck. "I'd better head back. Things should be wrapping up soon, and I have a feeling there's going to be a lot of cleanup to do. If you change your mind about that last dance, you know where to find me."

He closed the door and drove away, and she stood where she was for a moment, just watching him go.

He was a low-pressure salesman. The kind who knew the value of his product. He hadn't pressed her to go to his place, and she liked that about him.

She liked him and all the things he represented: family, love, home. She liked his approach to life—the passion and commitment he had to the things that were important to him.

Mostly, she just liked spending time with him, watching the way he interacted with others, the way he moved through the world. All those things were their own words and phrases and paragraphs, creating the story that was Porter.

It was a story she thought she would never be bored with. One so filled with scenes, she thought she could read it for the rest of her life without ever having to say *the end*.

That scared her.

And it intrigued her. Because she'd never felt that way before. Not with anyone. And she wasn't sure if that made it more real or less so.

She drove back to the rancher, classical music playing on the radio, all the leftover bits and pieces of her life with Sim sitting in boxes behind her. She wouldn't unpack tonight. She had all the time in the world to settle in.

She climbed out of the car, snagging her suitcase from the backseat. Harley was sitting on the front porch, a cigarette dangling from her lips, the end glowing amber in the darkness.

"You're finally back," she said, flicking an ember onto the ground and rubbing it out with her foot. "How's Sunday?"

"Tougher than most people probably give her credit for."

"Aren't we all?"

"Women, you mean?"

"Nah! Human beings in general. We're born into this crazy-ass world, and then we have to somehow find a way to survive it. All of us who do are a bunch of freakin' warriors."

"I like that."

"Yeah. I'm a regular philosopher."

"A sleepless one. What are you doing still awake?"

"Metaphorically chasing my tail."

"Anything I can do to help?"

"Some things you just have to figure out yourself." She dropped the cigarette and crushed it out. "So, what are you doing here?"

"I live here now, remember?"

"Sure, but it seems to me there's a lot more exciting stuff going on in town right now than there is on this front porch."

"You mean the silent auction?"

"What else?"

"Sim stole every dime I had. I don't have money to bid on anything."

"Who said anything about bidding?"

"Why else would I be there?"

"Gee. I don't know. Maybe to spend time with Porter?"

"Are we that obvious?"

"Do you not want to be?"

"I don't care either way."

"Which means things are going pretty well between the two of you, and you're not embarrassed to have your names affiliated with one another."

"That's one way to think about it."

"Right. So why are you here?"

"I think you asked me that before."

"Well, I did aspire to become an investigative reporter. Maybe asking questions is my thing."

"You actually wanted to be a reporter when you were a

kid? I thought maybe you'd just chanced into that job with Randall, because it's a small town and there weren't any other positions available."

"When I was a kid, I wanted to be a pirate. When I was a teen I wanted to be an investigative reporter. I still wanted to be one when I was working for Randall. Of course, when I took the job, I thought it would require a little more than sitting in his office all day waiting for him to hit on me."

"He didn't let you actually write anything?"

"You've met the guy. What do you think?" She raised a thin brow and kicked at the cold embers.

"I think I'm glad that it didn't work out. For me and for this farm. You can work here and pursue your dreams while you're at it."

Harley snorted. "I gave up on dreams a while ago, Clementine. I'm just glad to have a nice place to sleep and a job that pays more than minimum wage."

"Maybe you'll find your dreams again while you're doing that. One way or another, I hope you'll be happy working here."

"Be? I already am. I'm ecstatic. I get to work outside, and I get to avoid men. Two of my favorite pastimes. But we got off the topic again. You were just about to explain why you're here instead of with Porter."

"It's late. We're both going to be busy tomorrow."

"We're talking about tonight, Clementine. And neither of you is so old that you can't stay up and party for a night."

"I know, but I want to take it slow," she admitted. "Last time I rushed into things, I ended up married to the rat-bastard."

"Got it. Even understand it. But Porter isn't a rat or a bastard, and this is one night. Not a lifetime. It's an hour. Or maybe a little more. Spending time together and having fun. It doesn't mean you have to jump into his bed or into his heart or decide immediately that you're going to be together forever. Hell, maybe you'll just be doing it because you're friends, and he makes you smile. And if that is all it is, it'll still be time well spent. I better go inside. Chasing metaphorical tails is exhausting." She stood and walked into the house, and Clementine followed, because she'd already made up her mind. She wasn't going to Porter's. She'd see him tomorrow, and that would be soon enough.

But her spinning wheel was in the corner of the living room. She'd left it there because there'd been no place for it in her mother's apartment. And because it had seemed like spinning belonged to the farm. She hadn't been able to see herself doing it in Seattle or anywhere else for a while.

She touched the old wood of the antique spindle, and she remembered the way Porter had watched her work. She remembered the way he'd looked into her face and made her feel like someone special. Maybe Harley was right. Maybe this didn't have to be about the big statement and the whole shebang. Maybe it could just be about making each other smile.

She dropped her suitcase on the bed and rifled through it, pulling out the closest thing she had to formal wear—a fitted knit sweater that fell to just above her waist, and a matching floor-length skirt. Both were made from the finest alpaca yarn. Hand dyed and carded, spun and knit. She'd spent four months making the outfit for the faculty Christmas party at the college. She and Sim had planned to drive back to Seattle for the evening and spend the night at a nice hotel.

But Sim had hated the outfit when she'd tried it on for him. He'd thought the sliver of skin showing between the waistband of the skirt and the hem of the shirt was distasteful, and she'd ended up attending the party in a simple black sheath dress. She'd shoved the skirt and sweater to the back of the closet and pretended not to care that she'd never worn it.

But she'd cared.

A whole hell of a lot.

She slipped into the outfit and pulled her hair up in a loose bun. Then clipped silver bangles over her sleeves, the hand-crafted bracelets a long-ago gift from her grandfather.

She grabbed her purse and tossed it over her shoulder, then walked to the front door.

"Looks like you changed your mind," Harley said, glancing up from a book she was paging through. "That outfit is hot. Did you make it?"

"Yes."

"You've got mad skills."

"Thanks." She smoothed her hand over the skirt. It clung to her hips, skimmed the line of her legs, and belled out at the floor.

"You're welcome. Now that we've established that you look amazing, you need to go. I'd hate for the clock to strike midnight before you arrive at the ball."

"It's not a ball. It's a silent auction."

"And you're going to miss it if you don't hurry."

She was right, so Clementine left, her skirt brushing the ground as she walked to her car.

The Lee Harris house was still awake and lively when she arrived, cars lining the driveway, the yard illuminated by jars of fairy lights. They looked magical, and she picked one up, smiling at the gossamer-thin lights tangled in the base of it.

"The party planner will have a coronary if she sees you touching that," Porter said, his voice floating from between two tall pine trees. A surprise, and such a pleasant one her heart jumped with happiness.

"Are you hiding from someone?" she asked, setting the jar down and walking toward the sound of his voice. She couldn't see him. Just those tall trees and the house beyond them.

"Trying to fix the lights. They went out, and the planner is—"

"Having a coronary?"

"She wants everything to be perfect. I could have told her that it already was. The food is great. The musicians are phenomenal. The lights are tasteful, and the silent auction looks like it's going to be a raging success." He rustled in the pine needles and branches, and both trees jumped to life, beautiful golden lights twinkling in their boughs.

"Got it!" he said, and then stepped into view. He'd given his jacket to Sunday, but he didn't look any less fantastic without it, his body muscular and trim, his eyes silver in the moonlight as he moved toward her.

"And, now that you're here, everything is even more perfect," he continued, stopping in front of her, tilting her chin so he could look into her eyes and kiss her tenderly.

It was the lightest of caresses and somehow the most profound. She wanted to hold on to it forever, carry it around and remember the way it had felt to stand in the fairy-lit trees with him, looking into his eyes and feeling his lips against hers.

"Is it actually possible for something to be more perfect?" she asked, her voice husky, her hands resting on his shoulders.

"If you're around? Yes," he responded.

"You're full of compliments, Porter. But I don't need them."

"They're not compliments. They're truth. This is the second time you've surprised me today. I didn't expect you to come back to Benevolence. I didn't expect you to show up here tonight. Having you here really does make everything better. Even the perfect things."

"Funny, I didn't expect to make friends when I returned to Pleasant Valley Farm. I didn't think I needed them. Not here, anyway."

"Friends, huh?" he asked, taking her hand and walking her around the side of the building. She could hear the quiet hush of conversation and the gentle refrain of the string quartet. Tents had been set up in the center of the yard and groups of people were sitting in chairs conversing quietly. Other groups were strolling through the garden, following the paths lit by the fairy-light jars.

And his question was hanging between the two of them, daring Clementine to answer honestly.

Friendship, sure.

But with him, so much more.

"The best kinds of relationships are built on friendship," she finally managed to say.

It was a lame answer. Really a nonanswer, but he didn't seem to mind. Maybe because the music was mellow, the lighting just right, and the people only interested in enjoying what was left of the night.

"If that's true, then I guess we're off to a good start," he responded, squeezing her hand and making her feel like even more of a loser for not just saying what she felt—that she wanted so much more than friendship from him.

"Meanwhile, things around here look like they're ending," she forced herself to say, shifting the conversation before she could fail it even more than she already had.

"They are. Everything has been auctioned off, the winners are celebrating, the losers have gone home."

"I don't think anyone who came here tonight went home feeling like a loser. It's stunning. The lights. The tents."

"You." His fingers skimmed across the sliver of flesh that

Sim had been so opposed to, and she suddenly knew her own power again. The strength of rounded curves and smooth flesh and femininity. Of knowing who she was and where she belonged and how she fit into the world.

Where she fit into the world.

Right here. With Porter.

"Porter," she began, wanting to say what she should have the minute she saw him. That she'd come home to him, because there was nowhere else she'd rather be.

"It's okay," he said, as if he'd read her mind. "I already know."

"What?" she asked as his hand skimmed across her skin again, his palm resting on her hip as they walked through the yard.

"That our story is just beginning. But I still need to tell you that I've never known anyone who could make me feel the way you do. As if I've finally found what I've spent my whole life looking for."

"I don't think anyone has ever said more beautiful words to me." And she wanted desperately to be as brave as he was. To be as honest and forthcoming and authentic.

"They're not just words, Clementine. They're my heart. I have something for you. Come inside. I'll get it."

"What is it?"

"Just something I bought at auction."

"Porter, you shouldn't have done that."

"Why not?"

"Because . . ." She could think of plenty of reasons, but none of them mattered when she was walking by his side.

"Exactly. There's no reason why I shouldn't. Friends do these kinds of things for each other all the time. They buy things at auction. They search for missing relatives. They

plow fields and barter skeins of wool yarn for old tires so
they can do the work that needs to be done."

"It was alpaca yarn," she said, her eyes burning and her
throat tight. Not because he'd bought her something, but
because with every word he said, he was giving her a piece
of his heart. "And how did you know about that?"

"Half the town was here tonight. You've bartered with a
lot of them."

"Bartering should be like going to confession. No one
knows what goes on behind closed doors."

He laughed, opening the door and ushering her in. They
walked through the kitchen where the caterers were cleaning and getting ready to leave, and into the music room.

A piano sat in the center of the room, a man dressed in
a tux playing quietly. Long tables filled the room, each one
displaying items that had been up for auction.

"Wow," she said, impressed by the sheer volume of
auction items.

"It really is astounding. We had so many people gifting
items because they love Sunday and her kids that we almost
didn't have the space to display everything. As a matter of
fact, the item I purchased for you isn't down here." He
walked her into the hall, where old photos lined the walls
and high-backed chairs took stately residence in the corners.
"We've got some of the less popular or more delicate offer-
ings up on the second-story landing."

"You got me something no one else wanted?" she asked
with a laugh.

"I got you something that reminded me of you."

"Let me guess: a box of black lamb's wool that looks
like my crazy hair?"

He smiled, reaching for the pins that secured her hair
and pulling them out so that it tumbled down her back.

"Hey!" She swatted his hand away. "Why'd you do that? Do you know how hard it is to tame this mane?"

"No, but I wouldn't mind learning. I love your hair," he said. "It's like you: both wild and tame and fantastically unique."

"You make me sound like a wild mustang fresh off the range and in need of breaking."

He chuckled. "I've never called myself a poet. I don't think anyone else has, either."

"So, is the gift a bridle? A brush, maybe? Or a gift card to get my hair cut?"

"If I tell you, it'll ruin the surprise."

They reached the top of the stairs, and he gestured to dozens of framed pictures and gift cards and certificates hanging there.

"See if you can guess," he said, and he gave her a gentle nudge toward the display.

God, he was nervous.

There'd been hundreds of things he could have chosen. Beautiful things. Expensive ones. There'd been trips and bags and clothes and even a few pair of brand-new shoes. Jewelry. Sparkly, shiny, showy stuff that he'd heard lots of people oohing and ahhhing over.

But nothing had said her name like what he'd chosen. Nothing had reminded him more of the person she was.

He didn't know if she'd see that. He didn't know if she'd understand. He didn't think she'd find it, though, hidden there in plain view. Something only Porter had bid on.

She moved forward, her hips swaying beneath soft knit, her hair spilling down her back. Each time she moved, a tiny flash of porcelain skin danced between her slim-fitting sweater and her curve-hugging skirt.

His hands ached to touch her again, to slide his palms across her silky skin. He fisted his hands to keep from reaching out to her, but his feet refused to stay still.

He walked across the landing, standing next to her as she studied the display.

"There are a lot of choices, Porter. They all look wonderful."

"Even the stuffed fish head?" he asked, pointing to the offending item.

"It will be perfect for someone's house, but if you bought it for me, I may have to hang it on an outhouse door." She moved to the right and stopped in front of his donations. The ones he'd decided last minute to include.

"Porter . . ." She touched the frame, leaning close to study the pages set beneath it. The mother cat. The kittens. Their journey to find the way home. "This is your mom's book!"

"A copy of it. I couldn't make myself auction the original."

"If I'd known it was for sale, I'd have made a bid. I love this story."

"So did Twila. She was here earlier, and I showed it to her. She paid twenty-two dollars of her hard-earned money to buy it."

"She's a doll."

"She is. Now, keep looking, because you still haven't found your gift."

"I don't really think this is fair. I've never been good at games like this. You know the ones. Where you search for words in a hodgepodge of letters or try to find the hidden images in a picture. I like things straightforward and in my face. Not disguised by a bunch of useless details. Besides, you could have chosen anything for me. Half these things probably remind you of me. Rusty shotgun. Frilly apron. Wading boots." She stopped, and he knew she'd seen it. She was staring hard, leaning in, eyeing the thing that no other person had.

"It's this, isn't it?" She lifted the framed photo of the item that had been too big to bring in the house—the green tractor with its giant tires and gleaming chrome sitting in the middle of a field of cut hay.

"Yes. Doug Minton got a new tractor last week and wanted to get rid of this one. I went over this afternoon and . . ."

His voice trailed off, because she was crying, huge tears slipping down her cheeks and splattering onto the glass.

"Clementine, I'm sorry," he said, pulling her into his arms, the tractor between them, the frame poking at his gut, taunting him with the foolishness of his gift.

"I should have bought one of those sparkly rings."

She shook with the force of her tears, her hands still clutching the photo.

"Or a purse. Twila told me to buy a purse, but I thought I knew more than a ten-year-old about what you'd want."

"You do," she murmured against his chest, her tears soaking through his shirt. "This is the best gift I've ever received."

"Then why are you crying?"

"Because . . . it's the best gift I've ever received," she replied, lifting her head and looking into his eyes. "And I can't understand why it took me so long to find you, why I had to spend ten years doing things wrong before I could get them right."

"You didn't do things wrong. Sim did."

"I did, too, because I didn't believe in people like you. I

didn't believe in an easy, beautiful, breathless kind of love. The kind where you can look at thousands of things that anyone could love and buy the thing that only I would choose." She was looking at the photo again, wiping the drops of tears away. "It's that thread that I've felt from the first day I met you, the one that keeps bringing me back to your arms. It's connected us in a way I didn't think was possible, and there's a part of me that is terrified that it's too good to be true. That somewhere out there, the great Creator is holding thread clippers and is about to snap them closed on us."

"It's good that you're so optimistic, about our long-term chances of survival," he said dryly, and she laughed.

"I can't help it. I was raised on stories about star-struck lovers. Terrible things generally happen to all of them."

"I was raised to never be star-struck. So I think we're going to be okay."

"You always know the right thing to say," she said.

"Try to remember that in a few years, when I've said so many stupid things, you're buying me handkerchiefs for Christmas just so you have something you can tie around my mouth to keep me quiet." He took the photo from her hand and hung it back on the wall.

"How did you know, Porter?" she asked. "Out of all those things, how did you choose?"

"When I looked at the photo, it felt like home. And that's how I feel when I'm with you. I've never had that, Clementine. I've never stood in a spot and known that it was my space in the universe. And then you walked into my life, and every time I was with you, I knew where I belonged. That's what that photo reminded me of. When I realized that, I knew the tractor would be the perfect gift for you."

"You were right about the tractor, but feelings change.

Life happens and sometimes the world is so dark, it's hard to find our way," she said.

"Maybe, but friends stick together. Even in the darkness. Even in the toughest times. If everything else changes, that will be the same." He kissed her then, with all the passion that she deserved, with all the love that he felt, and when he broke away, her cheeks were pink, her lips rosy, and she was smiling.

"You know what I was thinking?" she asked.

"Does it have anything to do with plowing fields at some god-awful hour of the morning, because I bought you a new toy and you can't wait to play with it?"

"No," she said, then shook her head and laughed. "Actually, I *was* thinking about that. But the other thing is more important."

"Okay, I'll bite. What were you thinking?"

"That I can still hear piano music, that the fairy lights are still out in the garden, and that there is nothing I'd rather be doing than dancing in the moonlight with you. I love you, Porter. I may be afraid to be hurt again, but I'm not going to be afraid to try."

"I love you, too," he said, kissing her one more time, because she was everything he hadn't known he needed, and he wouldn't ever let her forget just how much she meant to him.

"Come on. Let's go," she said with a smile. "Before the sun comes up and the kids are awake, and one of them decides they need to come to town to find us."

"It could happen," he said. "It *has* happened."

She laughed, taking his hand and leading him across the landing.

It felt right to walk down the stairs beside her. It felt good to step out into the early morning air, to cross the yard and walk into the garden where the first sweet buds of spring were nestled in tender green leaves.

And, when he took her in his arms, when he swayed with her beneath the silvery moon and the glittering stars, when he looked into her eyes and kissed her lips, it felt like finally coming home.

Epilogue

The heat was getting to her. She'd admit that, but Clementine had never been a quitter, and she wasn't going to start now. She'd sent the kids home an hour ago, right around the time the sun had reached its brutal zenith. It hung there now, lazy in the clear blue sky, blazing down on her as she pounded another nail into the last shingle.

The very last one.

She slammed the hammer down again, sweat beading her brow, her brain fuzzy from too much sun and heat. But she was done. They were done. Finally.

God! It was hot. Putrid. Horrible. But she was sitting on the roof of the little chapel she and the kids had built, and she could see the fields stretching out around her, the cemetery below, the river spilling languidly across the landscape.

And it was all more beautiful than she'd imagined it would be. Sunday would love it.

If Clementine could convince her to come out and take a look. Mostly, Sunday spent her time inside, sitting in the easy chair by the front living room window, staring out into the yard.

Watching the world pass by.

Maybe this would free her from whatever held her there. A nearly exact replica of the chapel her family had built over a hundred years ago. Clementine had found photos at the town historical society, and she'd worked with a local architect to make sure she got things right.

But she and the kids and the Bradshaw men had done most of the work, building up over the old foundation and recreating a beautiful little building that Clementine hoped Sunday would be pleased with.

If she could ever get Sunday out of the house.

Clementine frowned, wiping sweat from her eyes and grabbing the hammer, heat seeping through her cotton T-shirt, the sun baking her exposed arms. She needed to climb down the ladder and grab a water bottle from the cooler she and the kids had carted across the bridge that morning. Then she'd go home.

Maybe Porter would be there. Finished with a meeting he'd had with local merchants who wanted to sell products at the country store that would soon be opening on the farm.

That was another thing Clementine had hoped would pull Sunday out of her lethargy.

Thus far, she'd only shown mild interest in the project.

"Tomorrow is another day, though," Clementine murmured to the pristine sky and blazing sun.

She crawled to the ladder, lowering herself over the edge of the roof. A little dizzy. A little light-headed. Obviously overheated, but she couldn't stay there forever, fifteen feet above the ground, hands on the roof, feet on the ladder.

She stepped down, blood *whoosh*ing in her ears, took

another step down and wondered if the ladder was moving or if she were.

"This is not good," she mumbled, her mouth cottony, her mind fuzzy.

"That just now occurred to you?" Porter said, his voice so unexpected she nearly lost her grip on the ladder. "The kids said you sent them home an hour ago. Didn't it occur to you that if it was too hot for them, it was too hot for you?"

"It occurred to me that I wanted to finish this project before the cows came home."

"We aren't getting cows this year." His hand settled on her hips, and he guided her down the next few steps.

Thank God.

She wasn't sure she could have made it on her own.

"Figure of speech," she replied, finally reaching the ground and turning toward him.

The world turned with her.

Actually, it spun. Quickly. Blues and yellows and bright greens, all the colors of midsummer flying across her field of vision.

She grabbed Porter's arms, holding on because she was afraid if she didn't, she'd fall over.

"I do know a figure of speech when I hear one," Porter said, frowning as he stared into her face. "I just thought you might need a reminder that there's no rush on any of this. Creating a successful working farm takes years. As you keep reminding me."

"This isn't about the farm."

"No?" He kept his hand on her waist and guided her to a shady spot beneath an old spruce. "Sit."

She did, because her legs felt weak, and because he was heading for the cooler, grabbing a water bottle out and carrying it back to her.

"Of course not. The chapel really isn't part of the working

farm. It's just part of its history. This"—she waved at the building—"is about Sunday. She's just . . . not herself. I was hoping this might cheer her up a little."

"That's a nice thought, Clementine, but you dying of heat stroke wouldn't be anything but devastating to all of us." He opened the bottle and handed it to her. Then grabbed another one, wet his hands with it and ran them along her nape.

She shivered, closing her eyes as she took several large gulps of water. It tasted like a little piece of heaven, and having Porter so close felt like it.

"You okay?" he asked, and she nodded.

"Just enjoying the moment."

He chuckled, kissing the spot where his hands had been. "How about next time, when we enjoy a moment, it doesn't come right after you nearly die?"

"I wasn't near death. I was just overheated."

"You almost fell off that ladder."

She wasn't going to argue. Not when she was so happy, so content to be sitting there with him, the finally finished chapel just a few feet away.

"I can't believe it's done," she said.

"It looks fantastic, Clementine. You did good."

She smiled, opening her eyes and looking into his face. "I didn't do anything. Just bossed around five kids and asked you and your brothers to do the heavy lifting."

"You did way more work than any of us," he said seriously, turning her hand so he could run his finger over the calluses on her palm. "So, like I said, you did good."

Her smile broadened, and she leaned in for a quick kiss that turned into a longer one. One that stole her breath and made her feel dizzy all over again.

"Wow," she murmured, shifting away, looking into his gorgeous eyes.

"I agree," he responded, his lips following the column of her neck and blazing a trail to the hollow of her throat.

And, God! It felt good.

He felt good.

The sound of a car engine broke the afternoon quiet and drifted through the haze of longing that had stolen every thought from her head.

She pulled away, breathless and wanting nothing more than to throw herself in his arms again.

"Someone's coming," she managed to say.

He nodded, his gaze hot, his hands resting on her waist. "The kids told us the chapel was nearly complete. They were begging us to come out and see it. They've been shouting about it for an hour. Sullivan and Flynn are driving everyone over here. I hope you don't mind."

"Mind? This is a family thing, Porter. It's for everyone. Do you think Sunday is coming, too?"

"Yes. My brothers and I agreed that a little fresh air would do her good, so we've enlisted the kids and managed to talk her into coming." He pulled Clementine to her feet, held her hand as they walked to the chapel. The wooden door was open, the interior shadowy and cool-looking.

"I hope she likes it."

"She'll love it," he said as two vehicles drove into view. An old Chevy passenger van and an SUV. "And so will everyone else."

Clementine planned to tell him that she wished she had his confidence, but the trucks were there, kids and adults climbing out. All of it noise and chaos and bickering and laughter.

Except for Sunday. She limped along next to Heavenly, leaning on her daughter as if she didn't have the strength to hold her own weight.

Somehow, they made it to the chapel door.

Sunday stopped there, running her hand over a wooden door that was exactly like the one that had been on the original building. "It's beautiful, Clementine. I can't believe you did this for our family."

"Mostly, I did it for you, Sunday," she said, taking her friend's hand and helping her across the threshold.

It was much cooler inside, no glass in the windows to block air circulation. Just wood floors, high ceiling, and sparse furniture. Clementine had found several old wooden pews in a salvage lot and a local artist had donated a beautiful cross that now hung at the front of the chapel.

"I had to guess at the interior," she said, filling the silence that had fallen over the group as they'd entered the building.

It felt sacred. The ground. The space. The air.

Even the children could feel it, their bodies still, their mouths shut. Somehow, in the silence, Clementine thought she could hear the hushed whisper of long-ago prayers.

"I think God must like this place," Moisey whispered. "I can feel Him here."

She grabbed Sunday's hand. "Come on, Mommy. Let's sit and listen for a while."

"Listen to what, sweetheart?" Rumer asked, following them to the front pew, hovering a little too close as Sunday took a seat. Clementine wanted to remind her that they'd all agreed to try to give Sunday some space, but she didn't want to embarrass either woman, and she didn't want to ruin the calm and peaceful mood that seemed to have enveloped everyone.

"To all the people who prayed here and worshiped here and married here. I bet there were hundreds of them who stood right here on this very spot. And now people can be here again." Moisey sighed, leaning her head against Sunday's shoulder. "Wouldn't that be lovely, Mommy?"

"What?" Sunday said, motioning for the other children to sit beside her. She might be struggling, but her love for them was as obvious as it had ever been.

"A wedding here in the chapel. We could do that one day, right? Have a wedding here?" Moisey asked.

"We'd need a couple who wanted to get married on a farm, but yes. We could have a wedding here."

"A couple who wanted to get married on a farm, huh?" Harley said, standing near the door and looking oddly uncomfortable.

"Come sit with us, Harley," Twila said, patting the pew.

"I don't know, kid. I haven't been in a church in a while."

"God doesn't care," Twila announced. "Come on."

"Right. Okay. Sure." Harley stepped into the chapel, glancing up as if she were afraid the ceiling might fall on her head. "So, since I'm in here, I'd like to point out that I can think of a couple who'd probably love to get married on the farm."

"Really?" Sunday asked, and for the first time since the accident, she looked excited by something. "Who?"

"Yes. Who?" Heavenly asked, her gaze darting from her mother to Porter, and then, finally, settling on Clementine.

"Why are you looking at me?" Clementine asked, but suddenly her mouth was dry, and her heart was pounding, because it wasn't just Heavenly looking. It was everyone.

"Probably because I've been telling them about the plans I've been making for when this place was finished," Porter responded, his hands on Clementine's waist as he turned her so they were face to face.

And suddenly, they weren't in a chapel filled with family and friends. They were in a space meant for just the two of them. And she was looking into his eyes, seeing the man who had become so much a part of her life, she couldn't imagine a day without him in it.

"What plans?" she asked, and he smiled. The kind of gentle, sweet smile that always made her pulse leap.

"For a wedding. After a proposal." He reached into his pocket, pulling out an old velvet box, dull with age and faded from many years of handling.

And beautiful.

So very beautiful.

Just like the chapel and all the people who filled it. Like the sacred air and the sweet trill of a songbird outside the window. Just like the words Porter was speaking about friendship and love and forever. About tractors and children and plans that he only ever wanted to make with her.

"That's it, Clementine," he murmured, kissing her gently. "Everything I have in my heart. Every word I can possibly say, and it still doesn't seem like enough. You mean everything to me, and if I spend every day of the rest of my life with you, and then find you again in eternity, I'll still want our story to continue. I love you, Clementine. Will you marry me?" He opened the box, revealing a flower-shaped ring. The center a sapphire. The petals diamonds. All of them old. The gold band scuffed just like the velvet box.

At least, she thought it was scuffed. Her eyes were too filled with tears to see much.

"Yes," she said, and she thought she heard Moisey squeal and Sunday shush her.

"I found this in an antique shop, and it made me think of you. Unique and beautiful," Porter said, slipping the ring on her finger, kissing her knuckles and then her lips. "If you don't like it, we can find something else."

"Like it? I love it," she whispered. "But I love you more. I can't wait to be your wife."

"In that case, how does autumn sound?" he asked.

"Autumn?"

"You can't mean this autumn," Harley said. "That'll hardly give you time to prepare."

"It's plenty of time," Clementine corrected, seeing it all in her head and knowing it would be just the right time and just the right place with just the right man. "The crops will be in. The weather will be beautiful. The foliage will be stunning."

"And we'll be starting our lives together," Porter said.

"I can't think of anything better than that," she replied.

And he kissed her again, right there in the chapel surrounded by the people they cared about most. While the kids squealed, and the women sighed, and the songbird continued to trill its wordless melody.

Please turn the page
for an exciting sneak peek of
Shirlee McCoy's

HOME AT LAST,

coming soon wherever print and eBooks are sold!

She was out of breath by the time she made it down the stairs. Panting and sweating like she'd run a marathon when all she'd done was descend fifteen steps.

Fifteen!

Her legs were shaking, her heart thumping, either from the effort or from the nightmare. Sunday Bradshaw didn't know which, and it didn't really matter. She'd made it down the stairs, and now she'd do what she'd done dozens of times in the past couple of months—walk into the living room, sit in the easy chair. No light. No television. No sounds except the sleeping house settling around her. Just herself, her thoughts, and the fading memories of the nightmare that had chased her from her room.

She crept through the hall, her feet sliding along smooth hardwood. There was a throw rug in the living room, a coffee table, a couch, a love seat, and an easy chair. They were all shadows in the darkness as she stepped across the threshold.

Someone had left the curtains open, and she almost closed them before she sat, but she felt wobbly, and she was afraid to push things too far. Not because she was afraid to fall. Because she didn't want anyone to hear and come running.

Some things a person had to do herself.

This was one of those things, and lately there had been very few challenges she needed to meet. If she was hungry, someone made her food. If she was tired, someone encouraged her to nap, helped her to her room, found the comfortable sweatpants and tank top she slept in. When the floor needed cleaning someone else did it. Same for dishes and the laundry. Like magic, everything in the house was tended to. She was driven to doctor appointments, physical therapy, counseling. She was brought to church when she had the energy to attend. Which was almost never.

Her days consisted of appointments and of sitting in the old rocking chair in the parlor, blanket over her legs, book in her lap, noises drifting in from the yard as the children played or helped with the farm. Sometimes friends stopped by to say hello. They smiled cheerfully and shared stories about the past. More often than not, Sunday pretended she remembered the event or the person. More often than not, she didn't.

It took energy to play the part and put on the act. Every visit exhausted her. Every *day* exhausted her.

Nights were different.

At night, she was alone.

There were no people asking questions, no unmet needs or concerned gazes. No invitations to go outside or go for a ride or watch one of the children turn cartwheels in the yard.

There was no need to pretend. No need to try.

No need to feel guilty.

There was nothing but herself and her thoughts.

That was how she preferred it. Which was probably wrong and unhealthy, but it was the truth. A truth she hadn't dared speak to anyone. Not even the therapist her brothers-in-law had insisted she start seeing.

She had six children, for God's sake. They were depending on her to get her act together, to pull herself out of the strange world she'd fallen into.

And all she wanted was to be left alone.

She shook the thought away, focusing on crossing the room without bumping into anything. She didn't want to wake Rosie. The live-in nanny had a room right at the top of the stairs. She slept soundly, but that didn't mean she wouldn't hear a thump and come running.

The easy chair stood in the far corner of the room, turned to face the fireplace on the opposite wall. She lowered herself into it, the two large windows letting in just enough light to turn darkness to hazy gray.

Tonight, the moon was full.

She knew because of Moisey.

Just like she knew that tomorrow would be sunny and hot, and that Uncle Sullivan was going to take the kids to town for ice cream.

It should have been Matthias doing that, but he was gone, and Sunday's brothers-in-law had been working hard to fill the spot he'd left.

And the one Sunday should occupy but didn't.

She'd survived the accident that had killed Matthias. She'd come out of a coma that doctors had doubted she'd recover from. She'd returned to the house and to her children, but she was like a ghost drifting through the life she'd once had.

She let other people do what she should and probably could, because the children seemed happy and the farm was thriving, and it was much easier to drift than to join in and take part. It wasn't that she couldn't accept her new reality. It wasn't that she didn't want to be there for her children. She'd lost huge chunks of her memory. She'd forgotten more about the kids—their likes and dislikes, their personalities, their goals and dreams—than she remembered.

She didn't want them to know that.

She didn't want them to understand how deep the divide was between the person she'd been and the person she was.

How many times had she been reminded of what an industrious person she'd been before the accident? How many people had told her that she'd been a fantastic mother, a loving wife, a savvy businesswoman who'd had big dreams for the farm?

So many that she could almost pretend that she remembered who that woman was: Sunday Bradshaw. Admired by the town and by the church and by her friends.

Now, in their eyes, she was the woman who'd survived what should have been a fatal car accident, the young widow, the invalid with six kids. The object of a town's pity. The reason for fund-raisers and silent auctions and meal trains coordinated by the church.

She still hadn't figured out who she was in her own eyes.

She only knew that it was easier to sit in silence thinking about it than it was interacting with all the people who loved her and wanted her to go back to being what she'd once been.

But, of course, she wouldn't.

Traumatic brain injuries changed people. They flipped things around. Turned things off and other things on. Complicated things that should be easy. Like life.

It shouldn't be so hard, and she shouldn't be so tired from the simple act of living it.

She sighed, leaning back in the chair and staring at the fireplace. There were framed photos on the mantel. Maybe a dozen of them. Pictures of the kids, Matthias and Sunday doing ordinary things together. They looked happy.

She refused to cross the room and lift the photos, to study them one by one the way she had when she'd first returned home after the accident, searching for things she'd forgotten.

It had been early spring then.

Now it was summer. Closing in on the end of it. She still didn't have all the memories back.

And, God! She wanted to.

Desperately.

She didn't want to put on a show with the kids. She didn't want to pretend. She didn't want to lie about remembering what it was like to be their mother. But that's what she did. Every day. If they found out the truth, they'd be devastated. She'd poured through their adoption files. She'd tried to memorize the details of their lives before, but like her long-term memory, her short-term memory was faulty. No matter how hard she tried to hold on, the details slipped from her mind and then slipped back again. Randomly. She had no choice about what she remembered or how, so she pretended.

"It's going to be okay," she whispered, the words hanging in the air. If Matthias were around, he'd agree. It was one of his favorite things to say. *It's going to be okay.*

Even that last day, he'd said it.

It's going to be okay. As her heart shattered and her stomach sank and her mind screamed that it wasn't.

She remembered that.

God! She wished she could forget.

She stood, her legs still wobbly, her heart thumping that heavy, strange beat that had been part of her life since she'd woken in a rehab center a few months ago. She should go upstairs and get back in bed, pull the covers around herself and try to fall asleep. The sun would rise soon enough. Another day would begin, and she wanted to think she'd be doing more than sitting in the old rocking chair.

Maybe she'd go outside for a while.

Sit on the porch. Watch the kids turn cartwheels or tend the flowers that had been planted nearby. She'd been on enough tours of the farm to know it had changed for the better. Crops were growing in fields that had been fallow for decades. One of the old barns had been converted to a store that would soon be filled with farm and local produce. There were animals and activities and all the things that she'd been told she'd talked about before the accident.

She didn't remember that.

She only remembered how much her parents and grand-parents had loved the land and the old house. She remembered being a kid, watching as her grandfather tended the fields. She remembered knowing that Pleasant Valley Farm was home.

Only now, it was Pleasant Valley Organic Farm, and it didn't feel like home. It felt like a house she used to live in.

She walked back through the hallway and into the kitchen, determined to do something for herself. One little thing. And, just like she'd done dozens of times, she kept the lights off, reaching for the old kettle and filling it with water.

She set it on the stove, turned on the gas burner, and watched as the blue-white flames shot out. She wouldn't let the kettle boil. She didn't want the noise. She just wanted to know that she could still do this—make a cup of tea the way she had for her mother and grandmother. Grab the chipped white mug from the cupboard and a tea bag from the tin on the counter. Take a little milk from the fridge. A little sugar from the pantry. Somehow, those simple acts made her feel more connected to the past than anything else had.

Cool air drifted through the old windowpanes. It was summer, but nights were already showing hints of fall. There'd been a nip in the air the previous morning. She remembered that, but she couldn't remember what she'd eaten for breakfast. She could remember what Heavenly had eaten—a fistful of sugary cereal. She'd been sashaying down the hall with it when Sunday had spotted her. Shorts an inch too short. Shirt a few inches too tight. Nearly thirteen and dressing in a way Sunday would never have approved before the accident. She was certain of that.

After it . . .

She still didn't approve, but she hadn't said anything. She'd just watched as her daughter continued down the hall. She'd listened as the front door had opened and closed. She'd wondered where Heavenly was going so early in the morning. She hadn't asked anyone.

Which made her feel about as much like a failure as anything could. These were *her* children. Not her brothers-in-laws' or their significant others'. Not Rosie's or the community's. It was her job to make sure they were okay.

And all she seemed to be able to manage was a cup of tea in the wee hours of the morning.

She frowned, turning off the burner and pouring hot water over the tea bag. She set the kettle back in its place, poured a little milk into the mug, spooned in a little sugar. Put everything back where it belonged.

This, at least, was easy.

Making tea.

Sipping it as she stared out into the backyard.

Someone had mowed a few days ago. She'd inhaled the scent of fresh cut grass as it drifted in the parlor window. It had smelled like family and hope, like endless summer days and starry summer nights.

She tried to remember what it was like to walk barefoot

through the grass. She was certain she'd done it. When she was a kid and, probably, as an adult. She couldn't quite grab on to how the blades of grass or the cold earth had felt against her skin.

It didn't matter.

In the grand scheme of what she'd lost, that memory was insignificant. She still resented that she'd lost it. Just like she resented her willingness to be content with the way things were now. With other people doing all the things she once had. Resented it, but seemed unable to change direction, to shift her thinking and her outlook so that she could embrace life again.

A shadow passed in front of the window, blocking the moonlight, and she leaned over the sink, the mug still in her hand, nose so close to the window she could feel cold air on her skin. A man walked parallel to the back porch, his stride long and confident, his shoulders straight, his head up. The angle of his chin, the way he moved, the quick way he pivoted away from the house were familiar.

Not Matthias, her brain shouted, but her heart still jumped the way it did every time a man walked through the front door. She knew he was gone. God knew she did. She'd been to his grave. She remembered the moment she'd seen headlights swerving toward their car. She remembered knowing that they were both going to die and that the children were going to be left alone. She remembered the split second of terror before impact. Of all the cruel things that the accident had brought, that was the cruelest. That she could remember the worst moment of her life so clearly and had forgotten so many of the best.

She shuddered, setting the mug on the counter and spinning toward the door that led to the mudroom. She walked as quickly as her legs would allow. Through the mudroom to the back door. Yanking it open and stepping onto the porch.

She planned to call out to the man, ask what he was doing and who he was. She expected it to be either Sullivan or Porter. Two of Matthias's brothers had moved back to Benevolence. Sullivan and his new wife had moved into the farmhouse while Sunday was in rehab. She had no reason to ask them to leave. Porter lived in town in the house the Bradshaw brothers had grown up in, but he spent plenty of time on the farm.

Of course, this was an odd time for either to be wandering around outside, but maybe, like Sunday, they were having trouble sleeping.

So, yeah. She planned to call out. To ask who he was and what he was doing, but a cool breeze rustled the tender summer grass and carried a whistled melody through the darkness. She spun back in time: standing on the back porch, watching as Matt walked across the yard, listening to his cheerful whistle as he headed toward the fancy sports car he'd purchased on a whim.

"Matt!" she called, as if she were still back in time, and he was still walking away. As if she could stop him from climbing into the car they'd argued over.

Their first major disagreement.

His first big blowup.

The exact moment she'd realized that the life she loved was one he resented.

She sprinted across the porch, the way she should have that night, because if she'd stopped him then, the rest might not have happened. He might be alive, and their lives might be tattered but mendable.

Only, of course, this wasn't the past. This was now. And her body had been broken and put back together again. Her left leg gave out as she hit the first porch step, and she stumbled, her right leg giving out, her body tumbling.

She thought she heard someone call her name, but she landed with a thud that knocked the wind out of her, and all she could do was lie where she was, face to the cold earth, right arm crushed beneath her, the cheerful sound of Matt's whistled melody still dancing around in her head.

She wasn't moving, but she was breathing.

Thank God for that!

Flynn Bradshaw crouched next to his sister-in-law and touched the side of her neck, feeling for the carotid pulse. She hadn't fallen that hard, but her body had been through a lot, and he wasn't sure how much more it could handle. A little accident could be a big one to someone in her physical condition.

She jerked away and scrambled to her knees, face pale in the moonlight, eyes wide.

"I'm fine," she mumbled before he had a chance to ask.

She didn't look fine. She looked as rough as Sullivan had said when he'd called Flynn at the beginning of the week. Dark circles. Sallow complexion. So thin a strong wind might carry her away.

"That was quite a tumble you took," he responded, keeping his hands at his sides even though he wanted to wrap an arm around Sunday's waist and help her to her feet.

"I'm fine," she repeated, meeting his eyes. "You're not Sullivan or Porter."

He wasn't Matt, either, but she'd called Matt's name. He'd heard a lot in that one word. He'd heard longing and sorrow and anger.

Was she angry that Matt had died?

Angry that he'd left the farm in such a mess?

Angry that her life had been turned upside down and would probably never be the same?

"I'm Flynn," he offered, finally taking her arm and helping her to her feet. She felt as fragile as she looked, her arm nothing but bone and sinew beneath a thick flannel shirt. Unbuttoned. He noticed as she pulled free and stepped back. She had a tank top beneath it, the neckline sagging to reveal jutting collarbones. He could see the outline of her rib cage, the narrow bones that crossed her chest.

"Flynn." She tried out his name as if she hadn't heard it before.

"Matt's oldest brother," he reminded her. "I come every weekend to help with the farm."

"I remember," she responded, but he suspected she didn't.

"I'm sorry if I—"

"You didn't." She cut him off.

"You don't even know what I was going to say."

"Whatever it was, you don't need to apologize. I was in the kitchen and saw you. I thought you were Porter or Sullivan."

But she'd called for Matt.

Something he decided not to point out.

"How about we talk about it inside?"

"There's nothing to talk about." She stood in the moonlight, gaze focused on a distant field. Corn, he knew, because he'd helped plant it. He'd also helped design the maze that would be cut through it in a few weeks. He'd purchased an old wagon that the farm would give hayrides in. He'd ordered baskets for people to use when they picked their own apples from the orchards. He'd been able to do it all from Texas, making calls and placing orders and planning things out.

But fall was approaching rapidly, and so was Porter's

wedding. Something that Flynn had been reminded of every day for a month.

It was his turn. He knew it. To return to Benevolence for more than two nights and three days. To step in like his brothers had. To take on more responsibility so that Porter could take on a little less. To fill in so that life could continue for his nieces and nephews in the house they knew, in the home they loved.

He'd sacrifice a lot to give them that, but he sure as hell didn't plan to stay any longer than necessary. The wedding date was set for the first weekend of November. Flynn planned to be back at his ranch in Texas by the first week of December. He had a great ranch manager, fantastic ranch hands; even without his presence the cattle ranch ran like a well-oiled machine. Things went wrong, of course. There were emergencies, but he felt confident in his employees. He could easily stay in Benevolence year-round and the ranch would thrive.

But he wasn't going to.

Unlike his brothers, he had no desire to settle down in Washington.

Besides, with Porter and Sullivan nearby, Sunday and the kids would be fine.

Or, at least, that's what he'd been telling himself.

Now, watching Sunday, he wondered why it had taken him so long to hear what his brothers had been saying. Sunday was up. She was walking.

But she wasn't there.

Not really.

Even now, when she was dragging her feet through thick grass, heading across the yard and toward the cornfield, she seemed focused on some other place and time. Separated, somehow, from the cool breeze and rustling leaves.

He walked with her, stepping onto a well-worn path that

stretched from the yard, through a pasture, and to the first of many planted fields. If wandering around before dawn was a habitual thing for her, he didn't approve. Not that it was his business to monitor her life, and not that it was his job to decide what she should or shouldn't do. She was an adult. She might still be recovering from several serious injuries, but she had the right to make her own decisions.

He still didn't like the idea of her wandering around by herself in the dark. She could trip, fall, hit her head. Reinjure herself.

"Where are we headed?" he asked.

"Nowhere," she responded.

"It's a little chilly to be walking around without a jacket or shoes. How about we go back to the house and you get both?"

"That would defeat the purpose."

"Of?"

"I was trying to remember what it felt like to walk barefoot through the grass. I couldn't, so I'm making a new memory."

"A jacket would still be good." He slipped out of his and dropped it around her shoulders.

She tensed.

He expected her to shrug out of the jacket and hand it back, but she continued walking. Silent. Focused. One step after another. Her stride short and hitched. Her movements tightly controlled, as if she were afraid she might come apart—all the knit-together pieces of herself shattering.

"Do you do this often?" he asked as they reached the edge of the yard and the gate that opened into the ten-acre horse pasture. Beyond that, the cornfield was a lush sea of green-gold stalks.

"Walk outside barefoot? I don't think so."

"Walk outside at night alone," he corrected.

"I'm pretty sure this is my first time since the accident."

"Pretty sure?"

"My memory isn't all that great," she responded, still walking. She made it halfway across the grassy clearing before she stopped. There was nothing there. Just summer growth of alfalfa, eaten down by the three ponies that had been purchased a few weeks ago. Stormy, Sammy, and Cupcake.

Cupcake had been Moisey's choice. The scrawny, spindly-legged old man had been retired from an equestrian farm that gave riding lessons. Flynn had attended the horse auction with his brothers and nieces and nephews. He'd voted against taking on the fifteen-year-old pony. First, it didn't look sound enough for even the lightest rider. Second, it had an attitude.

But Moisey had fallen in love, claiming that she was the only one who would ever be able to see the pony's beauty and value.

She'd probably been right.

No one else had bid on the old man, and they'd loaded him onto a borrowed horse trailer with two beautiful young ponies that would be perfect for young farm visitors to ride.

"You okay?" he asked.

"The cornfield is farther than I remember," Sunday responded, spinning a slow circle, her short hair fluttering in the breeze. "Everything looks great, and the grass feels just like I thought it would."

"So you have your new memory."

"Yes," she agreed.

"But you'll get a better look at the farm in the morning when the sun is up and you can see it more clearly. How about I take you for a ride to the cornfield and show you the plans for the maze?" he offered, because he hadn't just come to take his turn and do his part. He'd come with a goal. One that his brothers had been discussing for weeks. It was nothing to do with Porter's wedding and everything to do with Sunday.

"That might be nice," she said.

He didn't know her well.

He couldn't really claim to know her at all.

The fact was, she and Matt had begun dating a couple of years after Flynn left town. He hadn't returned for a visit until long after they were married. As a matter of fact, he'd met Sunday for the first time the Christmas after she and Matt had adopted Twila. Their first child, and it had seemed like a momentous enough thing for Flynn to return for a couple of days.

He'd been smitten with his only niece, but that hadn't made his visits any more frequent. Once a year for two or three days wasn't enough time to get to know anyone, and what little he did know about Sunday consisted of memories of her carrying little kids, feeding little kids, smiling at Matt. Cooking, cleaning, running errands. Always, it had seemed to him, happy.

The woman who was eyeing him through the darkness was nothing like his memory of her.

So, yeah.

He didn't know her, but he was sure she had no intention of going to the cornfield in the morning.

"If you'd rather not, that's okay," he said, watching her expression change, seeing the way her eyes suddenly shuttered, her lips pressed close together.

"I didn't say I'd rather not," she replied stiffly.

"But you were thinking it."

"Is that your superpower, Flynn? You read minds?" she asked, looking straight into his eyes.

That was like the woman he remembered—direct and to-the-point.

"According to my brothers, my superpower is my ability to ignore the fact that you're struggling."

"I'm not struggling."

"No?"

"No." Her gaze shifted away, and he knew she was lying.

"So, we'll go to the cornfield in the morning. We'll look at the plan for the maze. You can see the wagon, too. The one we'll be giving hayrides in."

"I've seen it. I do, sometimes, leave the house," she said, and she sounded just annoyed enough for him to want to tell her that she had every right to be angry. She'd gotten a raw deal, and there wasn't a person who knew her story who wouldn't say so.

But she was looking at him again, maybe reading the pity in his face.

"Don't," she said.

"What?"

"Tell me that I have a right to be upset. That this"—she waved her hand toward the house—"sucks. That losing my husband and my memories and most of my independence gives me the right to a little self-pity and anger."

"I guess that I'm not the only one who can read minds."

She smiled, the soft curve of her lips so surprising, Flynn found himself studying her face, seeing the woman she'd been hidden beneath the sallow skin and frail body.

"That's not what you were thinking?" she asked, heading back toward the house.

"It wasn't what I was going to say," he responded.

"You're honest. That's a good quality in a human being."

"And you're strong. Another good quality."

"That's a platitude, F . . ." Her voice trailed off, and she frowned.

"Flynn," he offered, and her frown deepened.

"I should have remembered that."

"Why?"

"Because, you told me your name ten minutes ago."

"It's been a little longer than that."

"Not long enough for me to have forgotten. And this isn't the first time we've met. You came for Christmas almost every year."

"You remember that?"

"You're in a lot of the pictures."

He supposed that was her way of saying she didn't remember.

"Even if you weren't, you've been here every weekend for months." She started walking again, stepping through the gate and into the yard, heading around the side of the house.

He wanted to remind her that they should go inside. That it was cold, and she was still recovering, but he'd just said she was strong, and she'd just called it a platitude.

So, he kept his mouth shut and followed.

She stopped at an ancient elm tree. A swing hung from a thick branch, the wooden bench seat cracked with age.

"I remember this," she said quietly, lowering herself onto the seat. Her feet brushed the ground but didn't quite reach it. "It's been here since I was a kid. It was probably here long before I was born. I remember my parents and my grandparents, but I can't remember a name that I've heard dozens of times recently. It's frustrating."

"It's probably more than that."

"Probably." She smiled again, and he caught a quick glimpse of the dimples in her cheeks.

"My brothers are worried about you."

"Is that why you're here?"

"Partially. I'm also here because Porter is getting married, and I thought he and Clementine might want some time to prepare."

"I forgot about that," she murmured, using her toes to push away from the ground. "The wedding is in October?"

"November. After pumpkin picking and apple harvest."

"There's a lot going on at the farm nowadays." She leaned back, her hands gripping frayed rope, his jacket nearly sliding from her shoulders.

"Does that bother you?"

She stopped the swing. "That's an interesting thing to ask."

"Is it?"

"Interesting might not be the right word."

"Then what would the right word be?"

She shrugged. "There isn't one. It's just been a while since anyone has asked me how I felt about what was going on at the farm."

"I'm sorry."

"There's no need to be. Your brothers have been doing what they think is right, and they're doing a great job." She stood, shrugging out of his jacket and handing it to him. "I'll go inside, so you can stop worrying."

She was walking away before he could reply. Moving slowly, and he could have easily walked with her.

He stayed where he was, letting her make her way to the back porch and up the stairs. He watched as she opened the door and stepped inside.

She didn't turn on a light, but he thought she was walking through the mudroom and the kitchen. Out into the hall. Up the stairs. He knew where her room was, and where each of the kids slept. He knew that Sullivan and Rumer shared one of the guest rooms and that the live-in nanny had the other.

The ranch house that stood at the edge of the farm was

occupied by Clementine and Harley, the young woman who helped her manage the farm.

Which left Flynn with two options. He could sleep on the couch or he could stay in the monstrosity of a house he'd grown up in. Porter had fixed the place up. He'd made it seem more like home, but Flynn's memories were enough to keep him away.

He'd take the couch for the next few months.

He'd slept in worse places and for longer amounts of time.

He walked around the side of the house, grabbed his suitcase from the SUV he'd rented. He'd packed light. A reminder that he wasn't planning to stay forever. His brothers had fallen in love and fallen under the small-town spell that Benevolence seemed to weave.

Flynn had no intention of doing the same. But that wasn't a good excuse for spending so little time helping on the farm. He had four nieces and two nephews who'd desperately needed stability after the accident. He'd allowed Sullivan and Porter to provide that while he used the ranch as an excuse to stay away.

Your brothers have been doing what they think is right, and they're doing a great job.

Sunday hadn't meant the words to be an accusation, but they echoed in his head as he unlocked the front door and stepped into the farmhouse—accusing and convicting. He knew the truth. Knew what he could have done and what he'd chosen to do. Not because he didn't care, but because he hadn't thought he could ever be what Matt's kids would need.

He set his suitcase down near an old umbrella stand in the corner of the foyer, stretched a kink from his back, and listened to the silence.

No footsteps. No hint that Sunday was awake.

Somewhere upstairs, someone was moving. Light footfalls. Quick steps. A soft rustle of fabric. No lights turned on. He didn't think it was Sunday. She moved more cautiously.

Probably one of the kids.

If he had to guess, he'd say Moisey. That kid was always finding trouble.

He walked through the foyer, had his foot on the first step and was heading upstairs when a scream shattered the silence. Ear-piercing. Soul-shattering. There was a heart-beat of quiet and then another scream, choked off by sobs that made the hair on Flynn's nape stand on end.

He sprinted upstairs as doors opened and lights turned on and the quiet of the sleeping house turned to chaos.